"DEATH AT ITS BEST IS NEVER PRETTY."

Lt. Mendoza and his men in the Robbery-Homicide Squad have met death often. Now death has come again!

Pretty Lila Wescott—
tied to the bed, tortured, raped, killed.

Old Mrs. Rittenhouse—
bludgeoned in her home

Mike Deasy—
a bullet between the eyes

Elderly Mr. and Mrs. Beebe—
*treated to "Mouse Noh" Rodent Killer
for their Sunday dinner.*

Nurse Joyce Bradley—
dragged into her car and abducted.

Each time, Mendoza discovers death has a different face...and so have the murderers.

Bantam Books by Dell Shannon
Ask your bookseller for the books you have missed

APPEARANCES OF DEATH
FELONY AT RANDOM
STREETS OF DEATH

APPEARANCES OF DEATH

DELL SHANNON

*This low-priced Bantam Book
has been completely reset in a type face
designed for easy reading, and was printed
from new plates. It contains the complete
text of the original hard-cover edition.*
NOT ONE WORD HAS BEEN OMITTED.

APPEARANCES OF DEATH

*A Bantam Book/published by arrangement with
William Morrow and Company, Inc.*

PRINTING HISTORY

*William Morrow edition published October 1977
A Selection of Mystery Guild February 1978
Bantam edition/November 1980*

ISBN 0-553-13953-3

Published simultaneously in the United States and Canada

---

*Bantam Books are published by Bantam Books, Inc. Its trademark, consisting
of the words "Bantam Books" and the portrayal of a bantam, is Registered
in U.S. Patent and Trademark Office and in other countries. Marca Regis-
trada. Bantam Books, Inc., 666 Fifth Avenue, New York, New York 10103.*

PRINTED IN THE UNITED STATES OF AMERICA

0 9 8 7 6 5 4 3 2 1

For Evelyn Cerny
because it was Mendoza who
brought us together

Appearances to the mind are of four kinds. Things are either what they appear to be; or they neither are, nor appear to be; or they are, and do not appear to be; or they are not, and yet appear to be. Rightly to aim in all these cases is the wise man's task.

—EPICTETUS

APPEARANCES
OF DEATH

1

IT WAS A QUARTER PAST MIDNIGHT ON THE LAST SUN-
day in February, and raining steadily. The men on
night watch at Robbery-Homicide, LAPD, were feeling
rather bored; they'd had only three calls since coming
on shift. Expectably there'd been a heist, at a liquor
store on Seventh, and that might tie up to another one:
let the day men sort it out. There'd been a freeway
crash with two dead, and later on Traffic had come
across an apparent felony hit-run on Broadway, a
middle-aged white man with no I.D. on him, so there
hadn't been much to do on that but call the morgue
wagon.

They'd be glad to see the end of watch tonight.

"I wonder," said Piggott through a yawn, "how
Nick is doing with that girl. Funny, his falling for her
all of a sudden."

"Funny his falling at all," said Bob Schenke. "Con-
firmed bachelor like they say."

The third man on night watch, Shogart, didn't offer
any opinion; he was immersed in a western magazine.
Shogart had been a holdover from the old Robbery
office before it got merged with Homicide, and still
vaguely resented the change; he was a good deal older
than any of the other detectives, with retirement coming up next year.

Piggott yawned again and abandoned the subject of
Detective Galeano's love life. The phone buzzed on
Schenke's desk, and he said resignedly, "You might
know, nearly end of shift. Robbery-Homicide, Schenke."

"Traffic's got something for you," said the desk

1

sergeant. "Central Receiving, the parking lot, probable robbery rape."

"Well, a little change from the usual," said Schenke. "Come on, Matt." They collected their raincoats and started downstairs. It had been raining steadily since eight o'clock, and showed no sign of letting up. They took Schenke's car the thirty blocks up to Central Receiving Hospital.

There was a big parking lot on two sides of the building, and as Schenke turned into the nearest one they spotted the flashing roof-light on the black and white at the far end of the lot on the other side; Schenke threaded his way between lines of cars round the back of the hospital and drew up beside the first squad car; a second was parked at an angle nearby. A man in uniform came up, swinging a flashlight; the tall arc-lights all round the parking lot were dimmed by the heavy rain.

"What've you got?" Schenke opened his door. The bulky dripping figure raised the flashlight in a half salute. "Zimmerman?"

"Yes, sir." The patrolman opened the rear door and climbed in, switching off his flash. "We've got the witness in the squad, you'll want to talk to her. But she couldn't give us much to go on with—we've called the husband, he should at least give us a make on the car. She's a Mrs. Nora Brinson, one of the nurses here. We got the call at eleven thirty-two."

"O.K.," said Schenke. He and Piggott got out and ducked into the first squad car's front seat. The second uniformed man, Bill Moss, was in the rear seat with a woman.

"These are the detectives, Mrs. Brinson. Mr. Piggott, Mr. Schenke. If you'll just tell them the story—"

"Again? All over? But what are you *doing*? Why don't you *do* something? I thought you'd do something right away—what *are* you doing? How many times do I have to tell you before—"

"Take it easy, Mrs. Brinson," said Schenke. "Just tell us what happened."

She uttered a sound that was half sob, half snort. The little light from the ceiling bulb showed that she was a round-faced woman in her thirties, dark-haired; she had on a nurse's white uniform under a blue raincoat. "All right, all right! We were coming off shift at eleven, only we were both late——Joyce Bradley and I——I was late because I had to see the superintendent about a patient, but I don't know why she was. It was about a quarter past eleven, she caught up to me at the door and we came into the parking lot together. I was parked farther up, in the last aisle, and she went up to her car with her keys out, and just as I got to mine and was unlocking it, I heard her scream, and I looked back just in time to see this man attacking her——I don't know where he came from, but he hit her and then he shoved her into the car and got in after her and gunned out of the lot——I heard her scream again——"

"Which way?" asked Piggott.

"Onto Sixth, up toward Alvarado—— But that was more than half an hour ago, and you haven't done a thing! Not a thing! And heaven knows what——"

"This Joyce Bradley——a nurse here too?" asked Schenke.

"Yes, yes, yes. I don't know her very well, she's an R.N. in Surgery, I'm in Emergency——I told the other officer——but why aren't you——"

"Can you give us any description of the man?"

"Heavens above, how?" she asked helplessly. "It was raining so hard——I had an umbrella up, and it was just a minute——he was bigger than her, I think lots bigger, dark clothes, a hat——"

"You don't know what her car is?"

"No, it's a sedan but——"

A car came bucketing into the lot from Sixth Street and pulled up behind Schenke's. "This'll be the husband," said Moss.

It was. Moss had called him, getting the number from the hospital desk. Zimmerman got him into the other squad car, and Schenke and Piggott transferred to talk to him in there. Dennis Bradley was a good-looking young fellow, now distraught and frightened and belligerent; they had a time calming him down, but he was keeping his head and listened to reason.

"The car, yes, of course,", he said, "of course you couldn't—It's a Nova two-door, two years old, green. Yes, I know the plate number, I've got it here"— fumbled in his billfold—"I've got a thing about keeping records—it's 210-MQX, a blue and gold plate."

"Thanks very much, sir, we'll get that out right away." Piggott went to relay it in; in thirty seconds there was an A.P.B. out on Joyce Bradley's car. Everything else Bradley told them was unimportant, but they let him ramble a little, listening politely. Joyce was twenty-eight, they had two children, her mother looked after them while she was at work, until he got home; he was in Personnel at Bullock's, they lived in West Hollywood, Norma Place; and nobody had any reason to hurt Joyce, she was a dedicated nurse, didn't believe in mothers with small children working away from home but she liked her job and on this shift it meant she could be with the kids most of the day at least. "One of these Goddamned hopped-up hoods," raged Bradley. "She wouldn't have had more than a few dollars on her, she never—but these Goddamned hopheads running around—what the hell are you doing, aren't you doing anything to find—"

"All we can, Mr. Bradley," said Schenke sadly. It probably wouldn't be enough. Even with that plate number and the car's description out to every squad car in town, it wasn't apt to be spotted immediately on a dark rainy night, before the hood had robbed and possibly raped Joyce Bradley. He might end up killing her. All they could do was hope the car got spotted soon, but it wasn't a good chance—unless he was high enough on something to crash it.

The Traffic men went back on tour. Schenke and Piggott wasted a little time in the hospital, asking questions; there was a remote possibility of some personal motive. The staff on duty in the lobby was just waking up to what had happened, and asked excited questions back. Then, all they could do was hope the

A.P.B. turned up the car. Piggott and Schenke went back to the office and Schenke left a terse report for the day watch. Shogart had already left.

It was still raining on Monday morning when the day men drifted in: the two senior sergeants Hackett and Higgins, Conway, Glasser, Galeano, Landers—it was Palliser's day off. Mendoza had been early for once and was already at his desk, reading a report, looking dapper as always in silver-gray tweed. "Happy birthday," said Hackett, hoisting a hip on a corner of the desk.

Mendoza grunted. "Don't remind me, Arturo. I'm feeling my age these days. So now we're handed an abduction, and I'll give you five to one it turns into a homicide. We've also got a new body—the sergeant downstairs handed me the report as I came in—and it sounds a little offbeat." He passed over Schenke's report on the Bradley woman, and Higgins read it over Hackett's shoulder.

"No takers," he said. "By the time anybody spots her car, she'll be raped or dead, or both. Some damned hophead needing money for a fix, or just doing what comes naturally. It also looks as if that same heister was busy last night—same description, and if we talk about offbeat—a heist man with a stammer, now there's something."

"What's the new body?" asked Hackett disinterestedly.

Mendoza brushed his mustache back and forth absently. "Just by the Traffic report, it sounds a little—mmh, different, shall we say. I think I'll go and look at it." He stood up and yanked down his cuffs. Hackett went with him, to escape the routine for an hour. The workload at Robbery-Homicide this last week was uninteresting: the usual heists, two unidentified bodies, both dead of an overdose, the paperwork on a suicide: murder of a small-time pusher probably by a client, which would probably end up in Pending, no leads on it at all.

They rode down in the elevator with Landers and

Conway, who were heading for R. and I. to see what
the computer might say about about that heister.
"What's the interest in the new body?" repeated Hackett
as they ducked into the Ferrari out of the rain.

"Eso tiene gracia," said Mendoza. "It just sounds
offbeat." He thrust the report at Hackett, switching on
the ignition.

"Adams and Figueroa. In a phone booth—that is a
little funny. Found six oh-five—just about as there was
any light to see, I suppose. Elderly woman, no purse,
no I.D.—oh," said Hackett, "I see. Diamond ring and
wedding ring on her. Otherwise, an ordinary mugging."

"Exactamente," said Mendoza. At the morgue, the
attendant was apologetic, pulling out the drawer.

"She was only brought in a couple of hours ago, and
then we had the bodies from a freeway crash—we
haven't undressed her or tagged anything yet."

The body was surprisingly undamaged; there was
only one dully cyanotic bruise over the left eye. Mendoza touched it lightly with one long forefinger and
said, "Skull fracture." She'd been a nice-looking woman; she didn't look elderly to them, but the Traffic man
was probably young and anybody past middle age
would be elderly to him. She was a medium-sized
woman with a still-trim figure, silver-gray hair, regular
features. Her face had been made up discreetly: traces
left of pinkish lipstick, a touch of rouge, eyebrow
pencil; her complexion was fair, her skin good. Mendoza lifted the right arm: rigor hadn't set in yet and it
flexed at a touch as he turned the hand. "So there you
are, Art," he said interestedly. The diamond ring
wasn't a headlight, but not all that modest either: a
center stone somewhere near a carat, twelve or fifteen
baguette side stones around it, in a yellow gold setting:
and a plain wide gold wedding band. Mendoza tried to
move the first ring and found it was a snug fit: he
tugged at it patiently, working it around, for several
minutes before he got it off the finger.

"So that's the answer," said Hackett. "No mystery.
He slugged her, grabbed her purse, tried to grab her

rings, couldn't get them off, panicked and ran with what he had."

"*Es posible*," said Mendoza, "and then again maybe not. All I will say is, why should he have panicked, when a little more effort would have got them off? No rigor—it was probably after midnight, and even at Figueroa and Adams there wouldn't have been a crowd. A phone booth—she was calling somebody, or about to, when the mugger—mmh, yes. And I'll tell you something else, Art. All right, I'll give you the rings"—he had just discovered that the wedding ring wouldn't come off at all—"but now I look at her, it's even funnier. What the hell was she doing at Figueroa and Adams, after midnight, in the pouring rain?"

"A lot of people live around there," said Hackett. "Some people don't have private phones, Luis."

"Now, really, Arturo, you're supposed to be a trained detective," said Mendoza. He squinted at the diamond ring. "That's a nice stone—not a new ring, but it wouldn't have sold for peanuts even twenty years ago. More to the point, look at her clothes." She'd been laid on the tray unceremoniously, and sometime in the next few hours the attendants would undress her, fold the clothes away neatly tagged. Now her coat was bunched up under the body, her dress pulled up over her knees. Both were still soggily wet all down the left side, dry on the other. "Look at that and deduce something else. It started to rain about eight o'clock. She hadn't walked far in the rain or the coat would be wet all over. And her hair isn't wet. If you tell me she had an umbrella and the mugger took that and left the diamond—well, I know people do queer things, but all the same—and Art, her clothes didn't come from anywhere around Figueroa and Adams. At a guess I'd say Robinson's, or somewhere comparable. Not the most expensive, but good quality, and not very old. She wasn't dressed to slip out to make a phone call—she dressed to go out somewhere. A restaurant, a show." The dress was a black velvet sheath, severely cut with three-quarter sleeves, a high neck: to Mendoza's ex-

pert eye, it cried out for a long necklace, an important
pendant. The coat was heavy black velveteen, long and
full, with an attached hood.

"So that's why her hair didn't get wet," said Hackett
as Mendoza pulled that from beneath the body.

"Not altogether. It'd keep her dry on the dash from
doorway to car, but not much longer." Mendoza lifted
the skirt delicately; she was wearing pantyhose. Her
shoes were tailored black leather pumps, looking new;
the left one was still wet, the right one dry.

"I see what you mean," said Hackett. "She was
inside the booth when he hit her, and she fell with her
left side mostly out the open door. I'll take your word
for the clothes, you know more than I do about that.
So what else do you deduce?"

"*Nada*," said Mendoza. "Or just one thing. Let's
have a hard look for a block or two around that
intersection, for a stalled car. It's the first reason that
comes to mind for a woman like this to be there at
such an hour, alone, in a phone booth. Otherwise, we
wait for her to show up on a missing list somewhere.
This one wasn't alone and friendless. She'd just had
her hair set," he added inconsequently, "and probably
an expensive rinse. She had money enough to take care
of herself—recent manicure, you notice, the ladylike
rose-pink polish—I'd lay you another bet she was wearing another ring on that hand, a necklace, earrings—
no, her ears aren't pierced, he could have snatched
those off with no trouble—and, of course, she had a
handbag. Possibly black velvet, or gold mesh—no, I
don't think so, a trifle too garish for such a discreet
lady. A well-bred lady, Art."

"You've always had an imagination," said Hackett.

"Use your own eyes. Funny," said Mendoza. "Unless we find her stalled car—"

"You can set Traffic looking. In this downpour I'm
not about to tramp six square blocks examining parked
cars."

"Mmh, yes, it would be parked, or Traffic'd have
spotted it by now," agreed Mendoza. "Died on her,

and she coasted up to the curb—streets empty that time of night—and she looked for the nearest phone booth to call for help. I know we tell women to stay in the locked car and wait for a squad to show, but who would, that time of night? Well, we'll see what shows up." He stopped to give the attendant a receipt for the diamond ring, and sat examining it in the car again before switching on the engine.

Down in R. and I. Landers had argued that the computer could give them a lead. Conway said, "You just seize any chance to ogle your bride, is all. What the hell kind of lead is a stammer?"

Landers smiled fondly at Phil, his cute frecklefaced blonde, and said they weren't exactly newlyweds, married six months now, and the stammer was as likely as some leads they'd worked. Phil looked doubtful but went away to see what the computer could offer.

The stammer had only just turned into a lead. The first time the stammer had been mentioned was last month, by the only witness to a heist at a drugstore on Alvarado. "He was a young guy," the pharmacist had said, "kind of thin, he had this wool cap pulled way down, I couldn't say much about his face except he was a white man, but he kind of stuttered. Well, stammered, if that's what I mean. Like when he showed me the gun, he said, now wait, I'll try to say exactly—he said, this is a—a—a s-s-stickup—like that, see? Like he couldn't hardly get it out."

Which said nothing at the time; he might just have been nervous, pulling a heist—maybe a first one. Then last Friday night there'd been a heist at an all-night dairy store on Venice Boulevard, and the two witnesses were excited but both said the same thing: the heister young, thin, and he'd stammered, could hardly get the words out, stickup, hand over the loot. They wondered then, the same boy?—and now, here was last night's heister also stammering, by Piggott's report. This time, another drugstore and only one witness, the owner, who said a young man, thin, wool cap pulled down, and the stammer: he called it a speech impediment. The loot hadn't been spectacular: under thirty bucks on each job.

Phil came back and said, "Afraid we can't help you. The only pedigree including a stammer is a pro burglar named Weaver, and he's been in Folsom since last year."

"Can we be sure about that?" said Conway cynically. "The way they get let out on P.A. after ninety days—"

"Well, I don't think he's your boy anyway," said Phil. "You said, young. Weaver's fifty-four."

"So we go back and talk to the witnesses and try for a better description," said Landers philosophically. "Thanks anyway, lady."

"Chasing around in all this rain," grumbled Conway.

"Don't complain, Rich. Think how happy the farmers are after the long drought. I wonder if anything's turned up on that nurse who got abducted. By Schenke's report, the only thing they had was the make on the car."

"Traffic'll be looking. She's probably already dead," said Conway gloomily.

"Just a little ray of sunshine."

Higgins and Glasser had gone out on a new call, and Galeano was just on his way down to Communications to see if anything had turned up on that nurse—though if her car was spotted they'd hear about it soonest—when Sergeant Lake came in with a fat woman and said, "This is Mrs. Kelty. Detective Galeano. Mrs. Kelty's son is missing and Lieutenant Carey thought she should look at a body."

"A body, oh, my God," she said.

And why couldn't Carey have taken her down to the morgue himself, wondered Galeano. Stay in out of the rain and catch up on paperwork, let somebody else do the legwork. But he didn't really mind; he was amiable as a rule, and these days he was feeling rather fatuously pleased with himself. On the way to the morgue, he let Mrs. Kelty's voice drift in one ear and out the other, thinking about Marta Fleming, that nice girl he'd met in January on that queer homicide. "Hope to God you're wrong, it's not Pat, but he's been in with this wild crowd of boys . . ." He'd surprised himself, really, the settled bachelor at thirty-six; it began when he'd felt sorry for her, and then . . . "All this terrible dope, I don't understand how anybody—but you can't talk to kids, they know it all . . ." Marta so straitlaced, stiffnecked you could say, and all the bad luck she'd had—but he'd got her to go out with him a few times, just quiet places, she didn't think it looked right with her husband dead only a couple of months. But he knew how to make her laugh now, and she seemed a lot more cheerful just the last couple of weeks. They got along fine, liked the same things, and he was seriously starting to think . . . "And without a husband it's been hard to raise an only boy, his father died ten years ago—"

At the morgue she looked at the corpse found three days ago in an alley in Boyle Heights, and let out a shriek, and began sobbing. "That's Pat, that's my boy, oh, my God, to see him like that—only seventeen, it's not fair, oh, my God—was it this terrible dope or what? Oh, my God, if only he hadn't met up with those other boys—"

Galeano soothed her down and got a few names: she couldn't tell him much. It was a familiar story: teenage son running with the anonymous pals, last names never mentioned, uncommunicative about plans; but one thing did emerge, that he'd had a car. It was an old Ford, registered to Mrs. Kelty because he was under age. Galeano explained tactfully about the mandatory autopsy, told her she'd be informed when she could claim the body, asked if she wanted a ride home.

"I'm all right," she said heavily. "It's just, it's not fair—only seventeen, his whole life—I tried hard to raise him right, but it seems there's nothing you can do, they're that age, bound to go their own way. I'll be all right, thank you, Mr. Galeano."

Galeano sent an inquiry up to D.M.V. in Sacramento and got the make on the car, a ten-year-old Ford white over blue, plate number such and such. He put out an A.P.B. on it and came back to the communal detective office to see who was in doing what. Landers and Conway were still out, Policewoman Wanda Larsen alone in the big room typing a report, but a couple of very wet raincoats on the rack by the door bore mute witness to the return of Higgins and Glasser.

"What was the new one?" asked Galeano.

Wanda grimaced. "Robbery assault. He made the mistake of knocking a woman down and grabbing her purse in plain sight of a couple of phone lineman up a pole. They grabbed him and called in. Did I ever think this job was glamorous or even exciting?"

"Just now and then it can be interesting." Galeano sat down to write a follow-up report on Kelty, and he'd just finished it when Higgins and Glasser emerged from an interrogation room down the hall with a sullen-looking man between them. He was about fifty, paunchy and unshaven, in stained ancient pants and turtle-neck sweater. Higgins collected his coat from the rack and marched him out silently; Glasser came over to his desk and rolled a report-form into his typewriter. The paperwork went on forever.

"Who's your friend?"

"One Clarence Huber," said Glasser. "The only thing we know besides that, he's just out of the pen—Illinois state. He had his discharge papers on him, he's been out three months. He wouldn't say what he was in for, or what he's doing out here or even where he's living. We'll ask Illinois. Meanwhile we'll put in nineteen hours of paperwork on it, and the taxpayers can foot his board and lodging in jail till he comes up in court, and it'll get called attempted robbery and he'll get sixty days."

"There's nothing in yet on that nurse," said Galeano. "By the report it was the straightforward thing—you'd have thought she'd have turned up by now."

"Yeah. Which probably says she's got dumped somewhere off the beaten track."

"In the middle of the inner city? Don't say it—freeways," said Galeano. He sighed, lit a cigarette and looked at his watch. He thought he'd call Marta when he went out to lunch, tell her he'd meet her to drive her home. She didn't have a car; she'd moved to another apartment, on Alexandria, but it was a half-hour bus ride from the restaurant where she worked, and there was only one bus an hour. "Where's the boss?"

"No idea," said Glasser.

Mendoza had, as Hackett told him, been too eager to jump the gun. "Wait for it, boy. If you're right, she'll be missed sooner or later and we'll hear who she is."

"Sooner rather than later," said Mendoza. "By her general type, she was leading a regular life, probably a rather strict routine life. If she hasn't a family, she has friends, neighbors to notice comings and goings. It's possible she's already been missed, even this soon. I'd just like to find out." He stopped off at Missing Persons to ask, and of course, as Hackett could have told him, drew blank. Nobody conforming to the description of the lady in the morgue had been reported missing.

"But," said Mendoza, swiveling around in his desk chair and regarding the gray curtain of rain streaming down the window, "possibly not all the precinct calls have got relayed yet." He picked up his new cigarette lighter and Hackett got out of the way, muttering about flamethrowers. The lighter was a full-sized pearl-handled revolver, which belched flame from its muzzle when the trigger was pulled; Mendoza lit his cigarette and picked up the phone.

"No harm in asking," said Hackett. But none of the precincts had had any overnight report about such a lady missing from home. Nor had Glendale, Pasadena, Santa Monica or Beverly Hills.

"Wait for it," said Hackett again. They had Traffic

poking around for the possible car; if it were anywhere near that intersection, it should be spotted soon. "If she was living alone, she wouldn't be missed this early. Give it a couple of days."

Mendoza had the ring out again. "She looked like a nice woman," he said absently. "Of course that's another thing—I wonder if she was wearing gloves? Took them off to dial the phone— *Condenación,* that phone booth—no use to turn out the lab now, I suppose—on the other hand—"

"You've got a tortuous mind," said Hackett.

"So you're always telling me."

Traffic called at eleven-twenty to report that there was no inoperable automobile to be found within four blocks in all directions of Figueroa and Adams. The sergeant who called was polite, but there were overtones in his voice; that must have been a tedious job, checking every parked car in that area.

"So your first bright idea is a dud," said Hackett. "Sitting here wasting time—there are things we could be doing."

"I don't know—we have been busier. And that," said Mendoza, "makes it all the funnier, Art. No car. So she was with somebody, in somebody's car. She had to be. She wasn't dressed for walking around in the rain, and everybody knew it was going to rain before it started, it'd been working up to it all day, and—"

"And the *Times* forecast said no rain expected. Well, that's so, but once we get her identified—"

"I'd just like to know," said Mendoza, sounding dissatisfied. Hackett, eyeing him amusedly, was aware that that was largely the reason Luis Rodolfo Vicente Mendoza was still sitting at a desk here at LAPD headquarters: his eternal " 'satiable curiosity." After twenty-five years of observing human nature in the raw—out of a squad car, down in Vice, here in this office—he was the complete cynic, if he hadn't always been that: no police officer got emotionally involved with cases. And 99 percent of the time, in police work, there were no mysteries and no surprises: only people acting expectably. Occasionally the little mystery came along, and it worried Mendoza: he would gnaw at it, dog with bone, until he worried the truth out somehow.

Today was his forty-sixth birthday, which he seemed to have forgotten; but in the thirteen years Hackett had known him he hadn't changed an iota: the black hair just as sleek and thick, the hairline mustache as precise, the elegantly tailored clothes as fastidious. His grandmother used to say that he'd get up off his deathbed to straighten a picture crooked on the wall; maybe it was that fanatic neatness that worried him about a mystery—anything untidy he had to straighten out.

They started out for lunch together presently, and Sergeant Lake at the switchboard said nothing had come in on that A.P.B. on the nurse's car. "I've had the husband calling in half a dozen times, I told the desk to choke him off but damn it, you can't help feeling sorry for the guy—"

"There are a lot of places both of 'em could be," said Hackett, "the nurse and the car, Jimmy. Yeah, that is so. Where is everybody and what's been going on?"

Lake told them about the attempted street-robbery and the routine on the heister; and the stammerer wasn't the only heister they were hunting, of course. "I haven't laid eyes on Jase all morning—no idea where he is. At least we got one body identified, that teenage kid, probably an O.D."

They went up to Federico's on North Broadway, and ran into Higgins and Glasser and Galeano. The waiter brought coffee, and they all ordered, Hackett as usual sighing over the Diet Special.

Higgins sat back and lit a cigarette. "How's Alison, Luis? Over the morning sickness yet? Mary was saying she should be."

"*Tiene su pizca de gracia,*" said Mendoza darkly. "I suppose you could say it has its funny side, George. Me getting domesticated at all, by a redhaired Scots-Irish girl, funny enough—but at least I thought I was settled down. With the twins, the assorted livestock,

and so forth. Alison"—he sipped coffee and lit a new
cigarette—"is just fine. She says we need a bigger
house, with another offspring due, and more room
around it. Getting grandiose notions, money going to
her head at last. Talking, *Dios*, about ponies for the
twins. She's out wandering around looking at mansions
and attached acreage, and God knows what she's going
to get me into."

Higgins grinned. "All due to your vulgar millions. If
she had to live on a regular cop's budget, she wouldn't
get such ideas."

Mendoza laughed ruefully. "How right you are."
And that " 'satiable curiosity" the reason he was still
at the thankless job, when he needn't be at any.

Jason Grace came up to the table and pulled out a
chair. "Well, and where have you been all day?" asked
Hackett.

"I suppose you could say goofing off," said Grace in
his soft voice, sounding a little subdued. "Coffee and
the steak sandwich, Adam. I got in early and heard
about that nurse—Joyce Bradley. She used to work for
my father—one of his office nurses before he went to
the General."

"Oh?" said Mendoza.

"Um." Grace contemplated his coffee and in absent
imitation brushed his mustache back and forth; his
chocolate-colored face was grave. "Nice woman," he
said. "A good nurse. She came to Dad right after she
graduated, was with him three years, when he was still
in private practice." Grace Senior was now chief of
Gynecology at the General Hospital. "You know what a
a simple mind I've got. When I saw Schenke's report—
well, sure, it looked like the straight violence, abduction for robbery, rape—but it also looks a little funny
that she hasn't already been found. I just thought I'd
go and ask."

"About possible personal motives. You've got a
simple mind," said Mendoza sardonically. "I don't
suppose anything showed?"

"Not so's you could notice," said Grace. "The family's wild. Nice people, husband, parents, two sisters.

All very respectable, upright, hardworking citizens. She graduated from Hollywood High, trained at the General, got her R.N. at twenty-one. She got married while she was still working for Dad, five years back—took time off to have two kids—boy three, girl ten months. No hint of any trouble at home. No hint of anybody with a possible grudge on her. Waste of time. I just thought I'd look," said Grace. "Being thorough."

"It was a thought," agreed Mendoza, "but that one's just what it looks like—robbery and rape, and we'll just hope she turns up alive." If she didn't turn up within twenty-four hours, the FBI would come in, under the supposition that she could have been taken over a state line.

They got back to the office at one-fifteen. The A.P.B. still hadn't turned up the Bradley car; the other one, on the car registered to Bernice Kelty, had panned out. A Traffic unit had just spotted it down on a side street off Exposition Boulevard, had it towed in.

"We haven't had an autopsy report, but that looks like the usual O.D.," said Hackett. "If I labeled things right we should call it suicide. The lab won't turn anything."

But they had to go by the book; they called the lab men to go look at the car, see what might show.

Higgins got on the phone to Illinois, about Clarence Huber. He stayed on the phone awhile; evidently Illinois had something interesting to say. When he put the phone down he was looking thoughtful, and swiveled around in his desk chair to where Glasser was still typing. "Say, Henry. This woman—Mrs. Barrow—she said Huber hit her and grabbed for her purse—but didn't she have a kid with her? A little girl?"

"That's right, kid about six I'd say. Why?"

"Well, this Huber," said Higgins, "was just out from a ten-to-fifteen on child rape, and it was a third count on the same charge. The linemen said it looked to them as if he was trying to force her into a car—there wasn't any registration in it, the lab's on that now. Now, what I heard from Illinois, I'm wondering if he was grabbing for the kid instead of the purse."

"I do wonder too," said Glasser. "The woman was pretty upset. But where's the evidence to say?"

"Nowhere," said Higgins, annoyed. "The most he'll get is sixty days on the robbery charge, and there he is loose again. And not one damned thing we can do about it, damn it."

Landers and Conway were still out somewhere. Traffic called in to report another body and Galeano went out to look at it: another old wino dead in a dirty room on Skid Row, but the paperwork had to be done on it.

At four o'clock Mendoza was on the phone again, checking Missing Persons and all the precincts; nobody reported missing conformed to the lady in the morgue. He was annoyed; he felt she should have been missed by now. There was also that nurse. Wait for it, said Hackett. Mendoza was constitutionally impatient. He went down the hall to the coffee machine, and as he came back Lake was on the phone. "Right away— Reynolds Ford, Western—yeah. Lieutenant! Shooting at a car agency, one dead."

"*¡Condenación!*" said Mendoza. "You'd think the rain would keep people home. All right, who's in?"

Only Hackett and Grace, as it happened; they all went out on it, up Western Avenue. It was a big Ford agency, a crowded used-car lot next to the main showroom, and the Traffic men were still trying to calm down the witnesses. The two salesmen were more excited than the blonde secretary.

"But who'd want to shoot Mr. Morrison? Just walk in and let off a gun, for God's sake—"

"He just walked in off the street, no, I didn't see a car, I thought he was a customer—nobody in all day, I asked what could we do for—and he just—my God, Dick's *dead* in there—"

"But he shot him too—I'd swear he got him, way he ran out—"

They got something more coherent from the girl. "I didn't see him coming in, no, I was in Mr. Morrison's office, I just heard Mr. Albertson say, you know, good afternoon, sir, like to a customer—but he just came walking right in, and when I saw the gun I guess I screamed, I ran out—and all of a sudden there was all this shooting—I don't know how many shots, but Mr. Morrison kept a gun in his desk—"

They didn't give the detectives much in the way of a description: agreed the man was young, fairly tall: but he'd been bundled up in an overcoat, hat pulled over his eyes; they couldn't even say what color the coat was. There'd been a lot of shooting, and the man had come running out of the office and out the door. Nobody had seen a car.

In the office, there was a dead man slumped over the big flat-top desk: a rather handsome man in his forties, dark and thin, conservatively dressed. He hadn't had time to get out of his chair, but he had had time to fight back. Under his right hand on the desk was a .32 Colt revolver. He had taken at least two slugs in the body, probably died instantly.

2

A COUPLE OF QUESTIONS ELICITED A LOT OF INFORMA-
tion thrown at them excitedly, some of it pertinent. The
dead man was Richard Morrison, owner of the agency,
he'd kept the old name when he bought it, he was a
fine boss, a great guy, he was divorced, he had a son
Gordon, nobody would have any reason to want to kill
him, yes, that was his gun. The two salesmen were
Albertson and Jay, the girl Linda Northcott. There
were four mechanics in the garage behind, who hadn't
been out of each other's sight and came up to join the
chorus.

Mendoza used a phone in the showroom to call up
the lab, while Hackett traced down the son. The lab
truck came, and Scarne and Horder shooed everybody
out of the office while they got to work.

The son came. He was a willowy young fellow about
twenty-three, with a wisp of beard and curly long hair.
"But I thought he was in Vegas," he kept saying. "I
thought he left yesterday."

"He was going tomorrow," said Albertson, "that's
why he went to the bank this morning—oh, my Lord,
all that money! Could that be it? That wad of cash—"

"How much money?" asked Mendoza.

"A wad," said Jay, "is all I could say. He liked to
carry a good bit of cash anyway. My God, if that's
what the guy was after—the bank could say how
much, it's the Security Pacific down the block—"

"But he told me he was going over to Vegas," said
Gordon.

There wasn't much more to be made out of any of
them; the lab men had more to offer. "Fairly open and
shut," said Scarne when they let the detectives back

20

into the office. "All we don't know is, was his gun carrying a full load? I take it the Colt was his. It's empty, recently fired. Three slugs went into the wall beside the door, one into the door, and the fifth one smacked into the fender of that big sedan in the showroom. Pity. Number six is nowhere, if there was one."

Hackett looked out the door and asked. Everybody assured him that Morrison had always kept the gun fully loaded. "Sometimes there'll be a lot of money around here, he's had that gun ever since I worked here," said the secretary. But Albertson was practically jumping up and down.

"I heard what he said—a sixth bullet—I'll be damned but Dick must have winged him—I said so, the way he ran out, it was all so fast but I just got a flash, he had one hand up to his shoulder—do you think Dick winged him, by God?"

It looked like a distinct possibility; they couldn't find the sixth slug anywhere. "But that's an interesting little picture you give us, Bill," said Mendoza. "One in the door, one going through the door—mmh, yes." They'd heard then that the bandit, leaving, had rather curiously closed the office door after himself, even in flight. "X appears, Morrison saw the gun and went for his. No time wasted on words, was there? He fired at X, the slug hits the car out there. They go on exchanging shots, and Morrison was still alive, if only just, when X walked out—he got off a last shot and it lodged in the closed door. Queer." It didn't seem likely that X had left any prints, but the lab men were dusting everything just on the chance. There was no wallet on the body. The wagon came to pick that up. Grace was talking to the son in a corner of the showroom as Mendoza and Hackett came out of the office.

"Wide open," said Mendoza. "I get tired of the stupidities, Art. Read Morrison like a book—typical salesman, hail fellow well met, liked to carry the cash, liked going over to Vegas. Somebody noticed the wad of cash, take your choice who or where. And I don't care for the looks of that lout," he added, staring at Gordon. "No regular job, at home in the afternoon?"

"Don't let your prejudices show. Yes, that's more or less what it looks like," agreed Hackett. "See if the lab gives us anything. See if any doctor reports a patient with a gunshot wound."

It was still raining as hard as ever. Mendoza didn't go back to the office, headed up the Hollywood freeway and idly switched on the radio. Let Hackett or Jase get out the initial report; he'd written enough of those before he made rank. "And on the local scene," said the radio suddenly, "there is still no news of Joyce Bradley, the nurse abducted from the parking lot at the Receiving Hospital last night. The only witness, Mrs. Norma Brinson, told police she saw an unidentified man attack and abduct Mrs. Bradley in her own car as they were both coming off duty at the hospital on Sunday night—"

"*Caray,* don't they teach grammar any more?" muttered Mendoza.

"—feared that it may be a kidnapping. However, no ransom note has yet been received, according to police. Now some news about the weather, coming up after this word."

And where the media had got that idea—out of thin air, reflected Mendoza. Just where Joyce Bradley and her car had got to—vanished into limbo. There was also that nice-looking woman in the morgue; woman of some substance, by her clothes: she'd have people to miss her, and why hadn't they? Wait for it—she wasn't twenty-four hours dead.

The rain was steady as he drove through Hollywood, turned up Laurel Canyon, presently turned up the drive of the house on Rayo Grande. The garage door was considerably up; he slid the Ferrari in beside Alison's Facel-Vega and shoved the dashboard button to lower the door. The big yard was empty. Coming in the back door, dripping, he was aware of appetizing smells from the kitchen. Mairí MacTaggart was in the act of removing a pan from the oven, and she straightened to regard him severely. Her silver curls were disarranged and her blue eyes snapping.

"And it isna exactly that I'd say a man should be master in his own house," she informed him as if they'd been in the middle of conversation. "That's easy to say, but with a redhaired McCann female under the same roof, I'd say not all that feasible. But listen to me she won't. I've told her until I'm tired there'll be all the time in the world to think about it, after the baby's here, this is no time to be rushing about over four counties looking at houses, but she's not to be led or driven."

"Are you telling me?" said Mendoza. "You don't suppose she listens to me either, Mairí."

"There's just no sense in it, but that's the Irish for you—get an idea in their heads and it's got to be done the next minute. At any rate," said Mrs. MacTaggart a trifle more cheerfully, "I've got your favorite for dinner, the Roquefort dressing and steak and baked potatoes and asparagus and my scones. The twins are just settled down after their supper."

Mendoza shed his wet coat and hat and proceeded down the hall to the living room. Alison was curled up in his big leather armchair surrounded by clouds of discarded newspapers. Three of the cats—Bast, Sheba and Nefertite—were delightedly playing tunnels through the papers, while El Señor brooded on top of the credenza. The shaggy dog Cedric was dutifully at Alison's feet, and bounced up clumsily to greet master.

"Hello, darling, I didn't hear you come in. You know, unless we want to get into building again, which I don't feel inclined to, it's not going to be so easy to find just the right place. Five bedrooms—"

"You don't feel inclined to shelve the problem until after July and the new offspring?"

"I feel fine now," said Alison, "and I'd like to have it settled and know *where*, even if we don't move right away. I'm being sensible, really, Luis—that place in Hidden Hills would have been too far for you to drive, but La Cañada, Flintridge, somewhere like that—" Suddenly she cast the papers aside and scrambled up.

"Amado, I'd nearly forgotten—happy birthday! Here's your present." She brought out a small gaily wrapped box from her pocket.

Mendoza removed the paper, folding it neatly, and regarded the green velvet ring box with suspicion. "I don't need a new ring. I've got a ring."

"It'll make a nice change from your signet," said Alison. "Your birthday was the farthest thing from my mind, but when I saw the ad, you were writing all those letters to the editor, and it seemed rather appropriate—it's all eighteen-karat and handmade, exclusive design of this jeweler up in Ojai, and I thought—"

Mendoza looked at his present and immediately approved of it highly. Last month he'd got into an altercation in the letters column of the *Herald* with an ACLU member over Thomas Jefferson, the party of the other part seeking to disparage the Founding Father Mendoza had always felt to be somewhat overlooked in importance. "It's called The Jeffersonian," said Alison. "I thought you'd like it." The ring was a heavily handsome affair with a profile of the Founding Father in white gold on a florentined yellow bezel, and white gold scrolls round each side of the shank with engraved quotations from the Declaration in tiny script. "They're all numbered, and that's only the fifth one he's made—You *do* like it," said Alison, pleased.

Mendoza liked it very much and told her so, taking off his signet ring to try it on. "Well, I thought you would," said Alison. "And really, Luis, you can see it's only sensible to start looking for a new place now—the way Mairí carries on, you'd think I was going to call the movers next week, but these things take time—"

"Yes, yes," said Mendoza cravenly. *"Seguramente que sí.* Absolutely."

Cedric barked and bounced to the door as the twins dashed in, having just discovered Mendoza was home. "Daddy, come see my picture, I did it all myself—" "Mine's bigger, Daddy, Terry just draws silly girl's things but I can do a horse—" The twins had matured almost frighteningly in the five months they'd been

attending the private nursery school. They dragged him
back down the hall to admire their art work, and
Alison looked after them fondly, said, "The darlings,"
and sat down again with the Sunday real estate section
of the *Times*.

It was still raining on Tuesday morning. Palliser got
in first and was reading the night-watch report when
Hackett, Higgins and Landers came in together, Glasser and Galeano a minute later. It was Grace's day
off.

"Another heist," said Palliser, handing over the report. "A funny one maybe."

"Not the stammerer?" asked Landers. "He hasn't
got much loot anywhere, of course."

"A pair," said Palliser. "And that's damned funny
about that nurse—I suppose there's an A.P.B. out on
the car, you'd think it'd've been spotted by now."

"I'm offering odds she's dead," said Conway, coming in and taking his raincoat off.

"Yes, and it's over twenty-four hours now, the
Feds'll have to be notified," said Hackett. "Waste of
time, but there it is. Well, what routine have we got
and how do we split it up?"

The Morrison thing had to be followed up; maybe
sometime today or tomorrow they'd get a report on
what the lab had picked up there, the slugs out of the
body. There were all these heist jobs, a couple of
witnesses from last night's due in to make statements,
and still a list of possible suspects on other jobs to look
for and bring in to question; that was always the
commonest job showing up forever to keep them busy
in this office. The Kelty thing wouldn't pose any more
work unless the autopsy showed something different
than they expected; any names they got there, anything
the lab turned in his car, would probably be handed on
to Narco for what it was worth. The hit-run victim
hadn't been identified yet, but he'd looked like a drift-
er. Without much doubt there'd be something else
coming up to make more work.

Mendoza came in and Hackett reminded him about the FBI. "Waste of time," said Mendoza. "Anything in from Missing Persons?"

"The lady'll be missed sometime, Luis. Would you have any hunches about Joyce Bradley?"

"No sé." Mendoza sat down at his desk and laid a hand on the phone. "But the wild ones in the jungle, Art—he could be holding her somewhere. Not a pretty thought. There's no way to go hunting, on that."

"No. New ring," said Hackett. "Very nice, let's see it. Well, trust Alison to find something unusual."

"I'm only hoping," said Mendoza, "she doesn't find something too unusual in the way of a house." He told Lake to get him Missing Persons; Carey told him patiently that no new reports were in. He got an outside line and started calling the precincts. Hackett shook his head at him and went away to help out on the legwork.

Palliser stayed in to talk to the two witnesses on last night's heist. They came in about ten o'clock, Alfred Kurtz and William Cady. They'd have been a little excited last night when Schenke and Piggott talked to them; Palliser started asking questions again.

"I know it sounds funny," said Kurtz. He was the owner of the little liquor store that had been held up, over on Olive; he was a big fat fellow in too youthful sports clothes, gaudy green and yellow. "We said afterwards how funny it was, didn't we, Bill? I mean, a stickup, a guy pull something like that, you naturally think, a young guy—like all these damn fool kids on dope, like that. But it's just how we told the other cops last night, they didn't have any masks or nothing on—"

"Funny isn't the word," said Cady. He was a younger man, the clerk at the store, a smaller man with a surprising bass voice. "Country going to hell all right when the kids *and* the senior citizens take to crime, my God."

"You told Detective Schenke they were both older men," said Palliser. "Anything to add to the descriptions?"

"I guess we covered it. I'm not saying we had a close look," said Kurtz thoughtfully. "They were both all bundled up in coats, kind of night it was. But old men, sure. Real old, I'd say, like seventy something. The taller one, his face was all wrinkled up, he had a big hooked nose—maybe six feet, kind of thin. The other one was fatter, not so tall, but he was old too, I noticed his hands was all bent, crippled, looking like he had arthritis, you know? But it was the other one had the gun, and he seemed spry enough—I wasn't about to argue with that gun, anyways."

"Not nohow," said Cady. "It looked about seven feet long."

That was the other funny thing. "A long gun?" said Palliser. "Rifle, shotgun?"

"I dunno, what's the difference?" said Kurtz. "I don't know much about guns. It was a gun like, you know, guys hunt with."

"It wasn't a shotgun, I don't think," said Cady, "if it's a shotgun that has a double barrel or whatever."

"A rifle," said Palliser. Something offbeat all right, the two oldsters pulling a heist with a gun like that. "Did you see any car?"

"Nope. They come in off the street, we was just about to close, had three customers in the whole night. And after I cleaned out the register for 'em, they went out the same way. We looked, a minute later, but with the rain and all, no sign of 'em. I been over the register this morning, they got a hundred and fourteen bucks. Oh, and the short one took a fifth of Scotch."

"Really?" said Palliser. "Well, do you think you'd recognize a picture?"

"You want us to look at some mug-shots? Sure," said Cady. "Anything to oblige, but I wouldn't be absolutely certain of either of 'em."

"I think I'd know the other guy," said Kurtz. "That big beak of a nose—"

Palliser typed up a statement for them to sign, and took them down to R. and I. where Phil Landers settled them down over a couple of books of mug-shots. "If you spot any, just tell Mrs. Landers, O.K.?"

"Little change from minding the store," said Cady. "Sure."

"Well, my God, I've got to say you read him the right way," said Carl Albertson rather mournfully. He looked from Hackett to Higgins. "I guess people in sales, well, we got to have the gift of gab to start with, I see what you mean. Dick might have opened his mouth to anybody, that's so. About going to Vegas, about the money."

"But you said he usually carried a good deal of cash," said Hackett.

"Not as much as that. I don't know exactly, but I'd say he had a thousand, twelve hundred on him yesterday. Usually, well, he might carry a hundred. But when he was going to Vegas, he'd have more."

"He was a habitual gambler?" asked Higgins.

"No, not really. Not at all, really," said Albertson.

"He was funny," spoke up the other salesman, Lester Jay. "About that, I mean. He didn't like credit cards, said they tempted you to spend more than you should—you paid out cash, you knew it was money. He didn't gamble at all, when he was here. Just now and then he liked to go to Vegas, pick up the new shows, and then he liked a little action. Roulette mostly, I think. He never even broke even, we'd have heard about it."

"Few gamblers do," said Hackett dryly. "He'd got the cash yesterday morning?"

"That's right, he went out about ten-thirty, and when he came back he showed it to us—there wasn't anybody else here. Except Linda, of course. He just took this wad of cash out of his billfold and riffled it through and said, hoped he wouldn't lose the whole pile—kidding, see."

"Did he go out again?"

They both shook their heads. "It was a slow day—I don't know why any of us came in. Monday, and raining—you wouldn't expect many customers," said Albertson. "Dick was working on the books—the office door was open, I didn't even hear him make any phone calls. He went out for lunch about one."

"Where, do you know?"

"Probably the cafe up the block, Jeanie's. He wasn't gone long, and it's the only place right around here except for the bar on the corner and they don't have anything but cold sandwiches. He usually went to Jeanie's if he didn't want a fancy lunch, a drink before—he didn't drink much anyway."

"Well," said Hackett, "thanks very much." They wouldn't hear for a while what the lab had found here. They went out into the rain again and plodded up the block to Jeanie's Cafe, a small bright place with red-checked tablecloths and plaid wallpaper.

They didn't get much there. Besides Jeanie, who was behind the scenes doing the cooking, there was only one vacant-eyed waitress, a gum-chewing, stout girl about nineteen, who said vaguely she thought she knew the man they meant only she'd never heard his name. She didn't remember whether there'd been anybody else in when he was, yesterday. There hadn't been many people in all day, on account of the rain. She hadn't noticed anything when he paid, it was a couple of dollars and he left her a tip.

"Dead end," said Higgins. "But look, Art, he'd owned that agency awhile—people around here would know him, maybe know his habits." This was all business along here; the agency took up an entire block this side, with the showroom, garage, used lot on either side, and across the street was another garage, a motorcycle agency, a hole-in-the-wall store offering used typewriters, the bar on the corner.

"True. Only no way to guess who decided to make a try for that wad, George. And then there's all the bullets."

"I thought of that as soon as I heard about it," said Higgins. "Most heisters don't expect to have to fire the gun at all."

"No. So, all right, he went in—and that was a pretty cool M.O. too, past three people in the showroom—

and Morrison saw the gun and went for his own. Even
so, there was the hell of a lot of shooting in the next
thirty seconds."

"Personal kill?" said Higgins. "Somebody with a
grudge on him, and the cash a bonus?"

"All up in the air," said Hackett, rubbing his jaw.
"He was divorced. Did he have a girl friend? Jealous
rival?"

"We can go and look," said Higgins. The weather
forecast had said, clearing today, but it didn't look like
coming true.

Galeano had gone out looking for the heisters out of
records; this legwork was a holdover from a job two
weeks ago, and it was doubtful they'd get anywhere on
it now, but while there was anywhere to look they went
on looking.

He had three names; one of the men was still on
parole. That one he found, and his boss could give him
an alibi; cross that one off. The second one had
moved, and he spent a while trying to find out where,
with no luck. The third one had just been removed to
the General Hospital with a case of D.T.'s.

"Not my day," said Galeano to himself. But it was
noon, and he had to have lunch somewhere. He drove
out Wilshire to the restaurant where Marta Fleming
worked. There was a table at her station.

She came up half-smiling, and he looked at her
approvingly. He'd once thought of her, like a Saxon
madonna: Marta with her tawny russet hair and grave
eyes; but these days she was smiling more, and you
noticed the cheerfully tiptilted nose and wide mouth
instead.

"You are taking advantage on the office time,
Nick?" She'd never lose her little accent; it was only the
last week he'd got her to call him by name.

"Have to have lunch somewhere," said Galeano.
"You working tonight? I'd better pick you up, it doesn't
look as if it'll stop raining."

"Once I reminded you, we Europeans are used to
rain. It is kind, but I am off at six."

"So am I. I'll pick you up," said Galeano comfortably. "You can bring me the roast beef sandwich. French dressing." He watched her unobtrusively as she moved about the tables. She was taking a secretarial course at night school now; and he was feeling serious enough to hope she'd never have to use it, get a better job. Maybe in a couple of weeks, or say a month—she had some old-fashioned notions about how a girl should behave after losing a husband—he could persuade her to come and meet his mother. He thought his mother would like Marta; for one thing, she was a good Catholic.

He got back to the office at one forty-five and found Wanda and Glasser typing reports, two interrogation rooms occupied, and Sergeant Lake absorbed in a paperback. Mendoza's office was empty. Palliser came in just as the switchboard lit up, and Lake plugged in automatically..

"Do any good?" asked Palliser.

"No such luck. I heard we had another heist."

"A funny one—couple of senior citizens with a long gun. The witnesses just finished looking for mug-shots, didn't make any. Talk about women's work," said Palliser.

"Hey, John—you've got a new one," said Lake. "Break-in and assault." He passed on the scrawled address. Crawford Street. There was a Traffic unit standing by.

They took Palliser's Rambler. That was an address in the middle of a black area: an old residential area, but not slums. Like people of that particular economic status anywhere, some people here kept up their houses, some didn't; there were blocks of old old apartment houses as well as single homes. And like almost any area of any city, it all looked dreary and tired seen through the drizzling rain. The address was a single frame house between two others like it, with a tiny front yard green with lawn, a couple of rose bushes. The black and white was in front, and an ambulance just pulling up. Neighbors were out across the street, on the porch next door, down the block, staring up here.

"What's the word?" Palliser asked the Traffic man.

"A Mrs. Ellen Rittenhouse—widow, lives here alone according to the woman next door. Evidently attacked by somebody who broke in. She managed to knock the phone off the hook, call for help, but by the time they traced it down and sent us out she was unconscious. No way of telling if they got anything."

Palliser and Galeano went in behind the ambulance attendants. The woman was in the little square living room, a stout old lady in a neat printed cotton dress, huddled beside an overturned table, the phone dangling off the hook. A gray felt slipper had fallen from one foot; she was breathing heavily, and there was a deep gash on her left temple. She wouldn't be telling them anything for a while, but the blood was still wet; it had happened recently. There was no sign of a weapon.

They looked around, and Palliser used the radio in the squad to call up the lab truck. They might pick up some latents; it was worth a try. They went next door to see if the neighbors had heard or seen anything.

"She isn't dead, is she?" the woman on the porch called anxiously as they came up. She was a thin middle-aged woman, very black, with steel-rimmed glasses. "I got such a start, policeman come knocking on the door, and when he told—that's just awful, poor Mis' Rittenhouse, such a nice woman—"

"No, she's not dead, but it doesn't look too good, Mrs.—"

"Buckler," she said automatically. "Sweet Jesus, think of somebody break in like that—harmless old soul like her—"

"Did you see anybody around, in the backyard or out here, the last hour or so?"

"No, sir, I surely didn't. These days a person don't know what can happen, I keep all the doors locked day 'n' night, and I know Mis' Rittenhouse does too, livin' alone like she does. I haven't seen anybody all day, since my husband left for work. Oh, I see Tommy Widgeon out in the backyard next door about an hour back, but I didn't think nothing of that, he takes care of Mis' Rittenhouse's yard for her, cuts the grass and so on, he's a real nice boy."

"Widgeon? You know where he lives, Mrs. Buckler?"

"Why, surely, the house on the other side. Mis' Widgeon's a real nice woman too, she'll be awful sorry hear about this. But they couldn't tell you nothing, she'll be at work and I s'pose Tommy's back at school now. Sweet Jesus, to think of somebody doin' that to that poor soul—"

The lab truck came, and Marx started looking around, dusting the place. Palliser and Galeano left him to it and went back to the office to start the paperwork on this one.

When Hackett came into Mendoza's office at four o'clock, he found Mendoza brooding over a pile of clothes on the desk. He started to tell him what he and Higgins had thought about, on Morrison.

"It could have been a private kill. We thought we'd look around on that angle, but so far it hasn't panned out. We saw the son again—it seems he's a student of the drama, full-time course at the Pasadena Playhouse."

"I knew there was some reason I didn't like him," said Mendoza.

"Prejudices. He tells us Morrison's been divorced for fifteen years—she was a lush, since dead. Morrison sometimes dated women, nobody regular and the son says definitely nothing serious. He gave us names—a legal secretary, hostess at a swank restaurant, a couple more like that. We talked to two of them—George is still out looking for another one. They say, nothing serious, he was a nice guy, quite the gentleman, just innocent merriment. They also said he liked to spend money when he did go out, nothing but the best."

"Así, así," said Mendoza. He stabbed out his cigarette, got out a jewelers' loupe from the top drawer and squinted at the diamond ring through it.

"We went through his apartment," said Hackett. "The son had a key. I gather he was doing right well with that agency, if mostly on paper. Pad on Rosewood in West Hollywood—I'd say about three hundred per. A very nice setup—good stereo, big color TV, closet full of good clothes, and however careless he was about money, he was a finicky housekeeper. Like you. All very neat and tidy."

"Maybe he had a daily maid."

"I think they're mostly extinct. We asked the manager. He didn't."

"Mmh," said Mendoza. "Son doesn't live with him?"

"No." Hunting the son yesterday, they'd had only a phone number from Morrison's address book. "Shares an apartment in Eagle Rock with some other students."

"No job?"

"We asked. Papa was paying the freight—proud of having a son ambitious to make a mark in art. That's not a cheap fly-by-night theater college, Luis."

"I'm aware. *¡Allá va!*" said Mendoza suddenly. He'd been turning the ring at this angle and that, bent close to the desk lamp. "I thought there was something—damn it, now I've lost it again. *¡Por Dios!*— there we are—ah—isn't that pretty? And what an engraving job—*Olga from Harry June 1942*." He put the loupe down and then picked it up again.

"In the ring? That tells you a lot. Somebody will miss her eventually," said Hackett.

"But I wouldn't have said," said Mendoza meditatively, "that that ring was that old." He screwed the loupe in his eye again. "It's eighteen-karat. The setting looks more modern. Thirty-five years. I thought it might be an old mine cut, it in which case the first guess would be a family stone reset, but it isn't—it's a full brilliant cut. At least we can deduce one thing. She didn't wear it all the time, or that engraving would have been worn down."

"This is nitpicking," said Hackett patiently. "A waste of time. Sooner or later somebody will come to the morgue and say, it's Mary—"

"Olga."

"All right. And then we'll know all about her, and why she was trying to make a phone call at Figueroa and Adams after midnight on Sunday. I don't suppose there's an autopsy report yet."

"No. Damn it, it's thirty-six hours—more. Well, that tells us she was probably living alone," said Mendoza.

"Not necessarily. I can imagine circumstances—oh, I thought she was still in San Francisco, or, we had a little spat and I thought she went to a hotel."

"Cold water, Arturo." Mendoza put down the ring and looked at the pile of clothes. "Just as I said— quality but not exclusive, good brand names but no way to trace who bought them. She had good taste, and sufficient money. She'd kept her figure—five-three, about a hundred and twenty, size twelve. She didn't have to wear a girdle." He held up a pair of white lace panties, a white lace brassiere, contemplating them through the smoke of a new cigarette, and added the pantyhose. "But here, Art, we have something more unusual." He picked up one of the shoes. "Paradise Kittens. About thirty bucks. Size four A."

"So?" said Hackett.

"So she had an unusually small foot for her size and weight."

"Is that what you call a clue? How many jokes are there about women buying shoes too tight?"

"You're behind the times—I'm surprised your wife hasn't let you in on that. They don't very often, now. Too many of them going around in pants, loafers—and manufacturers making stylish-looking low-heeled shoes, like these. Let's see, Alison's five four and wears a six and a half—I'd say Olga had unusually small feet, all right."

"This is silly," said Hackett. "Sometime we'll hear all about her."

Mendoza sighed and put down the shoe. "So what do you think about Morrison?"

"We'll never prove anything either way, unless Ballistics can make the gun and we're lucky enough to find it. Pay your money and take your choice. Somebody who knew his habits with money, knew he'd have that wad of cash on him, and just barged in after it. Or Gordon."

"Yes," said Mendoza. "Oh, yes."

"As against both, I'd say anybody who knew him would also know he had that gun, and that he always said at least that he wouldn't hesitate to use it. But there is the possibility—"

"*Yo caigo en ello.*" Mendoza laughed. "Gordon wouldn't do the job personally—egg on one of his pals? And maybe he—or somebody else—didn't think Morrison would be so quick on the draw."

"Yeah—and if Morrison did wing him, it wasn't anywhere important or we'd likely have heard by now." Even that wasn't certain; there were crooked doctors to be found, too.

"Lieutenant—" Lake came in looking excited. "The Bradley car just turned up—sheriff's boy just called in. It's way out past Whittier—Turnbull Canyon Road, in the wilds."

"*¡Vaya por Dios!*" said Mendoza. "*¿Para qué es esto?* No sign of the girl?"

"Not yet, but what they say, it's wild country, brush and trees. They've called up some help—she could be around somewhere."

"So, *¡vamos!*" said Mendoza, on his feet. Hackett followed him out and they picked up Landers just coming in.

Mendoza used the siren on the Ferrari all the way out there, through Monterey Park, El Monte, La Puente, Pico Rivera, large sections of the county, Whittier; after a few false starts they found the tail end of Beverly Boulevard out here in the boondocks, and all of a sudden it turned into Turnbull Canyon Road. That was the end of Whittier; out here was nothing but a two-lane blacktop road with thick brush either side down a steep drop, rolling hills in the distance.

About half a mile up they came on three sheriff's cars, and the other one sitting parked on the shoulder, headed up the canyon. Joyce Bradley's car all right,

the green Nova, right plate number. It looked undamaged.

They piled out in a hurry. "Well, here it finally is,"
said the sheriff's deputy waiting for them. "Not an area
we patrol just so often, nothing up here much—neckers
like it. But I turned up here, no reason, awhile ago,
and there it is. But it's about all there is, just the car.
And, of course, some blood."

They went to look. The Nova might look innocent,
clean, sitting there; it wasn't. "Doors were all shut,"
said the deputy. "Unlocked. But as you can see—"

Joyce Bradley's handbag was in the front seat, a
plain workaday bag of tan cowhide, its flap gaping
open. "No billfold," said the deputy. "We didn't poke
around much, knew you'd want your lab on it." There
was also an eloquently large stain of dried blood,
splashed across the inside of the passenger's door and
that side of the front seat.

"The doors were both latched?" asked Mendoza.

"Yep. There are five men hunting all around out
there, both sides, in case she was left in it and tried
to—"

Mendoza leaned against the Ferrari and lit a cigarette. "I'm the last man to be a defeatist, but I think
you can call them off."

"What?"

"Well, use a little elementary logic," said Mendoza
gently. "However you read it, for ninety-nine percent
sure that's Joyce Bradley's blood, a respectable
amount of it, whether she was shot or stabbed or
whatever. So X left the car here. If he left her in it,
and she was still alive and thinking enough to try to get
away, find help, she wouldn't have carefully latched the
door behind her once she was out of the car. Very
likely she wouldn't have had the strength. And there's
no trace of blood on the ground, either side."

"My God," said the deputy, "we never thought of
that one. I guess you're right."

"Just to be on the safe side, go on looking. But I
don't think we'll find her," said Mendoza.

They looked, and they didn't. They called in and got the lab to tow the car back in to the police garage: wait to see if anything useful turned up in it, besides the blood. But the odds were a lot better now that Joyce Bradley was dead—somewhere, somehow, of the senseless violence.

And they could all think of the similar cases—abduction, assault, or just simple disappearance—where the victims had never been found at all, or turned up as a few bones years later.

"This kind can be a bastard to work," offered the deputy.

They agreed. Mendoza drove them back downtown, using the siren to save time; it was seven-eighteen. They met the night watch coming on, and passed on the news.

3

IT WAS PIGGOTT'S NIGHT OFF, A FACT WHICH SCHENKE regretted rather violently. He missed Nick Galeano, who'd been a fixture on night watch a couple of years; he had the feeling that Nick would go for another tour of it except for that girl he'd got mixed up with. He rather preferred night watch himself, somewhat shorter hours and usually not so much legwork; but when Piggott was off he was alone with Shogart, who had got increasingly sourer and more taciturn the last couple of months. Shogart, the holdover from the old Robbery office, was a lot older than the other men, marking time to retirement next year. The prospect of seven hours in his exclusive, silent, grouchy company wasn't a pleasant one.

In self-defense Schenke had brought a paperback book along; he wasn't a great one for pleasure reading, but Piggott had passed this one on, assuring him he'd find it interesting—a book by somebody named Carr. Shogart as grumpy as usual, Schenke started to read it, yawning and largely uninterested, his mind wandering to that nurse—funny, finding the car out there like that.

He hoped they might have a busy night, something to do, but they didn't get a call until eight-forty, a heist at a movie house on Broadway. Schenke went out on it alone. The ticket seller, a voluptuous blonde named Sandra Spicer, was being soothed by the manager. "Fainted dead away," she told Schenke complacently. "I never did such a thing before. But seeing that gun—I never was so scared—I didn't think people held up theaters, for gosh sakes! Only my second night on the job, I never expected anything like this, for gosh sakes." The manager said it was the first time they'd ever been held up and he'd been there eleven years.

"Could you tell me anything about him?" asked Schenke. "What he looked like, his clothes, the gun?"

"For gosh sakes," said Sandra, "it was dark, nearly, only the light in the booth. I dunno what he had on—he was kind of young, I guess, and not awful tall."

"Young?"

"Yeah, I guess—his voice sounded like that. Sort of—" She hesitated and finally said, "Like he wasn't sure of himself."

Schenke repeated that blankly. "How do you mean, Miss Spicer?"

"Well, he sort of stuttered. He held up the gun and I knew what he was going to say, for gosh sakes, I was petrified. But he couldn't seem to *say* it—you know—it's a holdup, give me the money. But he finally did, and I did, and he ran off down the street and I yelled for Mr. Barker."

"You didn't see him get into a car?" She shook her head; and she didn't, she added, know anything about guns.

"He wouldn't have got much," said the manager. "We'd only been open a couple of hours, and it's been slow." The rain was slackening off, but everything was still very wet and as usual in Southern California with the cessation of rain it was turning very cold. And here was their stammering heister again, very probably, and nowhere to look for leads. Nobody so far had even guessed at what gun he had. Schenke was annoyed.

He went back to the office to write up the report, and Shogart didn't even ask him what the call was. Schenke got himself some coffee, finished the report and picked up the book again, but he couldn't get interested in it and was almost pleased when the desk buzzed him again. It was ten thirty-five.

"It's a homicide call," said the desk. "Traffic unit there now." The address was Scott Avenue, and Schenke had to look it up in the County Guide hastily: the complex of old streets around the Echo Park area.

"Come on, E.M.," he said. "Do a little work for a change." Shogart grunted but came along, silently, in Schenke's car.

It was an old apartment building on a corner, four stories, about sixteen units; one of the uniformed men was waiting on the street for them. "What have you got?" asked Schenke.

"Oh, a Goddamned mess," said the uniformed man. In the faint overhead glare of the sodium streetlight his face looked green; he was very young, maybe not long on the job. "Some damned nut—I hope you get this one. God, what a mess. It's the left front, second floor."

"O.K." They climbed thinly carpeted stairs, and on the landing met the second uniformed man and a little crowd of curious neighbors bunched down the hall, hanging over the banisters above.

"If you'd just keep back, please, let the officers through—"

It was a typical place for the area: probably more space than in newer apartments, and the building seemed well maintained: this living room had been painted recently. It was a long narrow room, with a glimpse into a kitchen with a dinette-area at the front end, an open door into a bedroom. Modernistic Danish walnut couch and chairs, burnt orange: bookshelves across the end wall, crowded with books; a stereo, a TV. There was a man sitting on the couch with his head in his hands.

"Leonard Wescott," said the Traffic man to Schenke in a low voice. "The husband. I don't think you'll get much out of him, he's about at the end of his rope, poor bastard. All we got, he just came home from work and found her—the wife. I don't know where he works. She's in the bedroom."

Schenke went into the bedroom, automatically edging past the door to avoid touching it, and after one look said, "Oh, Christ."

Death at its best is never pretty, and this hadn't been a nice death. It was hard to say if she'd been pretty or plain: she was, now, just a starkly dead, starkly nude body. She was arched back on the double bed, spread-eagled and tied by both wrists and ankles to head and footboard. There was a thick gag across the lower part of her face, and her open eyes bulged horridly above; her face was a suffused angry red. There were red weals on the body, across hips and stomach; at the foot of the bed, across one leg, lay a crude homemade-looking whip, a length of wood with a leather thong nailed to it.

Behind him Shogart let out a sigh. "A nut," he said. "A sadist."

"We'll want the lab on it right away," said Schenke. The bedroom was only about twelve feet square, and there was just one good-sized window. He went over to look. Outside the window was a little iron balcony. The window, an old-fashioned double-hung one, was all the way up, and the screen had been crudely hacked out, a great uneven hole mute witness to un-lawful entry.

Shogart went downstairs to call out the lab, and Schenke stood in the living room looking at Leonard Wescott. "Mr. Wescott, are you up to answering a few questions?" Wescott raised his head slowly and Schenke showed him the badge. "I'm a detective from head-quarters, sir."

Wescott might have been nearly handsome at any other time: a lean tall man about thirty-five, regular features, thick dark hair. Now he was ravaged: his mouth taut with pain, eyes agonized and blank on Schenke. "What—is it?"

"Never mind," said Schenke. You wouldn't get much out of him until he was past the shock. But the lab was going to need a good deal of time here, room to work. If there was some relative to come take Wescott away for the night, it would be helpful. Schen-ke looked on the desk for an address book, found one, and began turning pages with his pen. He'd just dis-covered there wasn't any Wescott listed, at least, when the Traffic man said, "Oh-oh," and he turned to find Wescott in a dead faint on the floor. Well, that solved

a little problem; they called an ambulance and sent
him down to Central Receiving.

Schenke hung around watching the lab men, called
out on the overtime; finally he and Shogart went back
to the office. Shogart took himself off right away; it
was twelve-fifty. Schenke typed an initial report and
left it on Mendoza's desk; he got away from the office
at one-forty, forgetting the paperback book.

When Hackett came in on Wednesday morning Mendoza was reading a report; without looking up he
thrust another one at Hackett and said tersely, "Read
it and weep. New nasty one showing up overnight—
torture rape, looks like. I hope the lab can hand us a
lead."

"Oh, my God," said Hackett, reading what Schenke
had to say. "Had we said, business a little slow? My
God, what a thing. What else have you got?"

"*Nada.* Lab report on that O.D.'s car—likewise the
autopsy. He was an O.D., by the way, and there's
nothing in the car to interest Narco. We'd better start
to poke around on this one—see if the husband can
talk to us, anyway." Other men were coming in; they
heard Palliser greeting Lake, Landers saying something
in a joking voice, Grace's quiet laugh.

"We haven't had one of these in quite a while. Let's
hope we can land on him before he has the urge
again," said Hackett. "I see none of the neighbors
heard anything—she hadn't time to scream, maybe?"

"Apparently not. All Schenke got was the bare
facts—the husband passed out. Whatever we get on it,
it'll be from the lab." Mendoza stood up and pulled
down his cuffs; he seemed to have forgotten the lady in
the morgue for concern over this. But as they came out
to the anteroom, Sergeant Lake was talking to a tall
man just inside the door; he said expressionlessly, "Mr.
Bradley, Lieutenant."

"Look," said Dennis Bradley. "Look." It was mean-
ingless; he looked at Mendoza with wild eyes. "You're
the one in charge here?" He hadn't shaved in a couple

of days and he was hoarse, probably from too many nervous cigarettes. "Look, what can you tell me? What the hell are you doing, about my wife? To find her? I can't understand—middle of the city, you'd think—but all this damned time, since Sunday night, my God, and—nothing! What are you—"

"We're doing all we can, Mr. Bradley, which I'm bound to tell you isn't much," said Mendoza. "I called you last night to say her car's turned up. It's possible the lab will find something there to give us an idea— it's being examined now."

"Yes—all right, I see," said Bradley. He took a deep breath.

"There's an alert out county-wide—a lot of people are looking for her."

"The radio said something about the FBI—"

"Regulations. They're standing by in case it looks as if your wife's been taken out of the state, that's all."

"You—don't think that's so?"

"No," said Mendoza. He wouldn't say so to Bradley, but he didn't think Joyce Bradley was anywhere this side of life, now: not after three days; not after seeing that stain of blood in the car. So the rapist killer had the elementary cunning to ditch the car out there; it just said that in all probability he'd ditched the body somewhere else, in a spot remote enough that it hadn't been found yet—conceivably never would be. "I should have a report from the lab on the car sometime today," he said politely, and then added suddenly under his breath, "*¡Porvida—media vuelta!*"

"What?"

"We'll keep you informed, Mr. Bradley. We do sympathize with how you're feeling, believe me." Mendoza sidestepped around him and Hackett followed out to the hall. "Hell and damnation, what can we say to him? Sympathize—my God, yes, but what is there to say?"

"And what hit you just now? Something about the car?"

"Maybe I'm losing my grip, Art. Going senile. It

should have struck us all when we laid eyes on that car yesterday—sitting there all by itself on a lonely road in the wilds. Just not thinking simple enough—or thinking period. So he left it there. Walking five miles back to civilization?"

"Oh, ouch," said Hackett. "You're right, we should have seen it. You think he had help—somebody to pick him up in another car?"

"Probably. And if you want to exercise your imagination, you can sit down with a county map and hunt for all the places where a body might lie for months without being found. In the middle of the city, he says. Sometimes the city can be a better hiding place than the boondocks."

"I can think of a few places without trying," agreed Hackett. Mendoza was unusually silent on the way uptown in the Ferrari. When he parked in a red zone at the corner of Scott Avenue he didn't move immediately, lit a cigarette.

"The lab's still at work," he said. The mobile lab truck was parked two spaces up. "They'll be thorough on this one. Got photographs on the body *in situ* and so on last night, and going over the rest of it now. Let's see what they're picking up."

Over a good many years, he and Hackett had gone together to look at the scenes of violence, the corpses, the blood and mess human nature in the raw sometimes left behind. They could look at it with equanimity, but never quite got reconciled to it, even across the years of experience.

At least it had stopped raining. The old apartment house was quiet as they went in; there was a rank of mailboxes at one side, and Mendoza stopped, eyeing the door opposite which bore a small brass plate labeled *Manageress.* He pushed the bell and had the badge out to show when a nondescript middle-aged woman opened the door.

"Oh," she said, looking at it, "oh, more cops. Isn't this a terrible, terrible thing? Mrs. Wescott! And nobody hearing a thing—I didn't sleep a wink all night, thinking about it! Imagining how he must have got in—I always tell people, use the chain on the door, I thought Mrs. Wescott always did—"

"Have they lived here long, Mrs.—" Any question would start her talking.

"Mauser, Miss Mauser. Going on seven years, a nice quiet couple, and he's handy to fix faucets and such, never bothers me for anything. Nice people, rent always on time—she was awful sorry she couldn't have children, she'd've liked a family, I guess if they had they'd have moved, bought a house, but the way it was, this is handy to his job. He's one of the bartenders at the Ambassador Hotel, I guess makes pretty good money. I hear he was all broken up, no wonder, they was crazy about each other, you could tell, even being married I guess nine or ten years. What I can't get over, nobody heard anything—" She rambled on, but hadn't anything else to offer. They climbed stairs, feeling her gaze on their backs.

In the left front apartment, Scarne and Horder were busy, and predictably yelped at the detectives to stand clear. "We haven't vacuumed the middle yet. A million prints here and we'll have to sort them all out," said Scarne. "Find everybody known to've been in this place the last six months, to compare. I got the husband's prints first—they had him knocked out, poor bastard. But you'll be damn interested in some of what's showed already, Lieutenant."

"*¿Qué?*"

"Come in here." Scarne led the way into the bedroom. The bed was still in a tangle of rumpled blanket and sheets, and at head and foot the ropes still hung, sinister, where she'd been tied down. "First, the window. That's how he got in—you can see there's a drainpipe right alongside that balcony. Balcony not made for use, just show, but it'd be a convenient handhold as he climbed up. I think the window must have been up a little, but even if it wasn't, it's loose. He cut out the screen—I think with a dull knife—and the piece was right out there on the balcony where he dropped it. He's in, in about thirty seconds."

"Yes. And it was still raining, wasn't it? Of course we don't know what time it was."

Scarne was enjoying playing detective. "The husband got home a little after ten and found her, so it was before then. So, maybe it was still raining and that's why she didn't hear him. But there's a lot here to tell us what happened. First off, look at that." He pointed to a straight chair in the corner by the bed. "I've packaged 'em all up, but all her clothes were right there, all neatly folded up—underclothes, dress, stockings, shoes. He didn't rip them off her, she'd undressed herself. And in here"—he led the way to the small square bathroom off the bedroom—"look, night-dress and robe hanging on the back of the door, slippers underneath. I think she was getting ready to take a bath, or had just had a bath, when he got in. She was in the bathroom, came out to find him here, or he found her."

"*Lógica.* And?"

"And," said Scarne, back in the bedroom, "this line. Have a look." It was thin, tough white cord; the ends looked slightly frayed; it was heavily knotted around the bedposts. "Ordinary clothesline, and he found it right here. The rest of it's in the service-porch, hanging up on a nail. I'll put it under a microscope and we can probably show where the ends match up, where he cut it. With the same dull knife."

"*¡Pues hombre!*" said Mendoza. "Right here? That is damned queer. What about the knots?"

"Ordinary knots. Just pulled tight with ordinary strength. Now this pretty thing I think he brought with him." Scarne picked up the homemade whip. "It's been printed, nothing but smudges. You can build it up."

"After a fashion," said Hackett. "I've got a few reservations. A lot of people think the nuts will do anything, on impulse, but in my experience they're sometimes more—er—cunning than the sane ones. Of course a nut like this kind sometimes isn't nutty all the way—just a kink. You read it that he swarmed up here on the chance he'd find a woman alone, and did?"

"It could be." Scarne shrugged. "I'm just showing you the mechanics. It's your job to figure out who he is and how he picked her."

Mendoza drifted back to the living room. "These windows," he said, "look out front and side. The bedroom window's on the side. This is the second story, but from across the street—" He tried the view from each window. "There you are, Art." This was a mixed block, apartments and single houses, and across both the streets out there, front and side, were one-story single homes. "Nobody to look in a second-story window. She might not have been in the habit of pulling the curtains."

"And even if she did," said Hackett, "they're old-fashioned window shades and just thin glass curtains, you could still see in fairly well."

"Very possibly, enough to be sure she was alone," said Mendoza. "Or, of course, he could have known the husband's working hours. All right. He got in and then what? She didn't scream."

"Probably didn't have time," said Scarne. "Say she was coming out of the bathroom, after something, before she put on the nightdress and robe—or before she took the bath. He grabbed her and knocked her out right away. Then he looked around and found the clothesline, used it to tie her up so he could take his time having fun with her. God, these nuts. Oh, and the gag—I've got it at the lab, but I took a look around last night and I think I can tell you where he got that." He opened a top drawer in the old walnut chiffonier and showed them a neat pile of men's handkerchiefs. "Five handkerchiefs wadded up in her mouth and a couple tied together to hold them there, round her head. They look like the same kind here—ordinary dime-store stuff, but heavy quality."

"My God," said Hackett. "Improvisation."

"We'll be running some tests," said Scarne. "I went over the body before the wagon came. If we've got any fresh sperm, we can give you the blood type. There were some teeth-marks—and saliva will give us a lot more. The autopsy should add something. And all these latents—I've been all over the rug here with a vacuum, see what might show in that. Hair, whatever."

And a lead sometimes showed up from something as small as that: these days the lab often did provide the answers. Mendoza and Hackett left them to it and went on to Central Receiving. Parking in the lot, Mendoza glanced over there where last Sunday night Joyce Bradley had been jumped beside her own car, but didn't say anything.

Upstairs in the Emergency wing the R.N. on duty said doubtfully they could see Mr. Wescott for a few minutes. "He was in shock when he was brought in last night. He's had another shot an hour ago—you may not find him very responsive."

Wescott was lying flat and still on the hospital bed, only a sheet over him. He turned dull eyes on Mendoza and Hackett, blinked at the badge.

"Mr. Wescott, we're sorry to have to bother you at such a time, but if you could answer a few questions—"

"Yes," said Wescott listlessly.

"You were working last night. Are those your regular hours?"

"Yes. No. Split shift—twice a week. Tuesday, Thursday. I'm on"—he swallowed, paused as if to think—"eleven to four, seven to ten."

"Do you usually come home at four those days?"

"Wescott put a hand to his head. "No. I mean yes—usually do, but Lila—Lila wasn't feeling so good—coming down with a cold. Didn't want her—bother fix dinner, I dropped into an old movie awhile, had dinner at the hotel. Wasn't until—I came home—"

"I see," said Mendoza. "But a good many people would know your hours. Anyone who knew you—the staff at the hotel—even regular patrons there." He brushed his mustache back and forth.

"Knew?" said Wescott blearily. He half raised his head. "Friends—my God, my God, nobody we knew would—*that!* I never thought—easy, break in that window. Always telling her, keep the chain on, don't let strangers in—and then—oh, God, oh, God, I can't stand it—" Wescott turned over, face to wall, and began to sob.

Galeano had just come back from escorting a couple of witnesses down to R. and I. to look at mug-shots, and thought at first he was the only one in, the big room was so still. Then he noticed Jason Grace sitting at his desk absorbed in a paperback.

"Goofing off again, Jase?" Grace didn't even look up. "Interesting book, hah?" asked Galeano.

Grace jumped. "What?"

"I said—" The phone rang on his desk and Galeano picked it up. It was Central Receiving reporting as per instructions. Mrs. Rittenhouse had died five minutes ago. Galeano put down the phone and said, "So now it's homicide. And not much to go on." Grace was reading again. "Goofing off," said Galeano, and started out again. Tommy Widgeon, living on Crawford Street, would probably attend the nearest public school—but junior high, or high? How old was he?

He went to Crawford Street first, found Mrs. Buckler home and asked. It was the junior high; Tommy was fourteen. Galeano drove up there, went in and asked to see Tommy. The dignified-looking woman at the desk in the main office looked upset at the badge, and Galeano said, "He's not in any trouble, I just want to ask him a question."

"Well, I hope not, officer. Tommy's never been in any trouble I know of. You can see him here, if that's all right?" She consulted lists, used the phone, and five minutes later a tall thin black youngster came in. Galeano introduced himself and Tommy shied like a startled horse. He looked like a very young fourteen, baby-faced, immature.

"Wh-what you want, sir?"

"Just a couple of questions, Tommy, take it easy. You heard what happened to Mrs. Rittenhouse?"

"Yes, sir. It's just awful. She's a nice lady."

"Well, when you were in the backyard there yesterday, did you see or hear anything from her house?"

"I wasn't there. I didn't see anything, honest."

"Mrs. Buckler says she saw you there about twelve-thirty."

"Oh. Yeah. I'd forgot that. I was there to get the pump for my bike tires. Just a minute. I keep it there on account our garage is pretty full, and Mis' Rittenhouse don't mind. I do her grass and all for her. I didn't see anything. Honest. It was only a minute."

"Well, thanks." Galeano hadn't really hoped for anything, but you had to ask.

"D-do you know how she is, sir?" .

"I'm afraid she died, Tommy. She was hurt pretty badly."

The boy stared at him, his eyes rolling, and then he burst into tears. "Oh, gee, oh, gee, that's awful—just awful!" sobbed Tommy. "She was a nice lady—such a nice lady—" The woman came over, casting Galeano a reproachful glance, and he got away hurriedly.

Higgins was off on Wednesday. He hadn't anything to do; there wasn't any yard work to speak of at this time of year. The house felt too empty of his family: the family he'd been without so long, and acquired ready-made—Mary, and Bert Dwyer's good kids Steve and Laura. The only one home, with Mary out grocery shopping, was his firsthand family Margaret Emily, who was seventeen months old. She was prattling happily in the playpen over her stuffed animals, and paid Higgins no attention at all. The little Scottie Brucie was asleep in his basket.

Higgins wondered if anything new had gone down, if any leads had turned up in the old cases. That Huber—

Well, with Margaret Emily to think about, you worried about the Hubers.

He called in after a while to ask, and Lake said he didn't know but he'd find out. He called Higgins back ten minutes later and said, "He made bail. Supposed to show up for a hearing on March fourteenth."

"Like hell!" said Higgins. When Mary came home,

he was still swearing. "One like that on the loose again! And the more I think about it, I think he was trying to grab that kid—right off the street, and her mother there! And I put it in the report, damn it, but these damn softheaded judges—I swear to God, I don't know why we bother to catch these louts—talk about a damn exercise in futility—"

"Calm down, George," said Mary. "You'll be getting high blood pressure."

Alison was simply ignoring Mairí's dire comments; after the bout of morning sickness she was feeling fine, and fired with energy about a new house. They said you had to build one to learn from mistakes, and she'd made a lot of them in the house on Rayo Grande. It had been a mistake not to have a fireplace, and bigger bedrooms; and now they had Mairí, it would be nice for her to have a little suite of her own. And more space all around a house—Alison even thought, vaguely, about room for a pony; nice for the twins, and they could hire somebody to look after it.

And as she said to Luis, it was doubtful if either of them would ever really get used to having all the money, both of them growing up without much. Real estate prices now—and all the real estate salesmen seemed to think there was something peculiar about her specifications.

"Now this may be just what you're looking for," said Mr. McNair gaily. He beamed at Alison approvgly, a client interested in property in that price range. He was the fifth one she had talked to in the last two weeks, and she'd decided to stay with him instead of shopping around. His realty firm advertised that it supplied property coast to coast, and surely could come up with something she liked within a forty-minute freeway drive of LAPD headquarters. "This is a prime investment, just on the market—very nice area of Flintridge, five bedrooms, maid's quarters, three-car garage, cabana and oversize pool—"

"I don't want a pool," said Alison.

"You don't want a swimming pool?" He was incredulous.

"Definitely not. None of us can swim. And besides it's dangerous. Attractive nuisance, my husband says—children climbing a ten-foot fence to fall in and drown. No pool. And at least an acre, because that's what we have now. And I don't mind an older house—you get bigger rooms as a rule."

He sat leafing through papers and said, "Well, there's the older place in Altadena—they're anxious to get the estate settled. It's a bargain at a hundred and forty thousand—"

"Well let's go look at it," Alison, repressing a shudder.

He sighed. He was a spare, shortish man with a shock of white hair. Alison was already confounding him as a client, but for that kind of commission— "My car's just outside," he said.

The place in Altadena dated from somewhere around 1890. There was an acre of neglected grounds overgrown with too many trees and shrubs; the house was a tall three-story mansion complete with gingerbread round the eaves. There was a double parlor, a black marble hearth, seven rather small bedrooms, and one enormous bathroom with a walnut-encased tub and pull-chain commode.

"No," said Alison.

"Remodeling—" said McNair. "You could do a lot with it."

"I expect so. But I'd rather not have to."

"I wonder if you'd be interested in that Tudor estate in Brentwood. You said—er—within reason, no price limit. It's three acres, and the house is a little larger than you want—"

Alison guessed at what the taxes would be, three acres in Brentwood, and said she'd like to see it. He sighed again and switched on the ignition.

A report came up from the lab at three o'clock and Mendoza took it out to the detective office to see who

was in. Palliser was sitting there talking desultorily
with Wanda Larsen, and cocked an eye at Mendoza.

"Something? At least we're making some progress.
The witness on that liquor-store heist from Saturday
night finally came in—he had a bang on the head and
concussion, you remember—and picked out two mug-
shots. Everybody else is out hunting them."

"Good," said Mendoza. "The lab made the slugs out
of Morrison. It's a thirty-eight S. and W., old gun but
in good condition—if we come across it, they can tie it
up. They also picked up some prints off the door to
Morrison's office, three good latents. They were in our
records. One Steven Suttner, pedigree of statutory
rape, one count of burglary. I won't say it's a likely
background for the fairly aggressive character who
took Morrison off, but we have to look where indi-
cated."

"Right away," said Palliser, getting up. "I'm on it."
He took the report. "Last address four years back. Not
so hot."

There was a copy of Suttner's mug-shot appended;
he was a fairly distinctive fellow, if not a movie star:
big ears, a bumpy forehead, a bulldog jaw. Palliser
thought about short-cuts, and drove up Western to that
automobile agency. The two salesmen were there
alone, looking morose.

"You found out anything?" asked Albertson.

"Maybe something. I'd like to ask you—"

"There's a rumor around there'll be a merger, this
agency closed out. I guess we go looking for new jobs,
damn it," said Jay.

"Too bad," said Palliser. "Would you take a look at
this photograph? Do you think this could have been
the man who shot Mr. Morrison?"

Albertson and Jay looked at the mug-shot and
turned astonished glances on Palliser. "Are you trying
to kid us?" asked Albertson. "That's Steve! He was
right out back, he couldn't have—"

"You picking on Steve just because he'd been in a
little trouble once?" Jay was inclined to belligerence.

"Dick knew about that, some parole officer got him to hire Steve, and he's been O.K., good steady mechanic. What makes you think—"

"Well, I don't, now," said Palliser. The lab couldn't know; it just gathered facts. Suttner, with the little record, leaving prints on the door here quite naturally. There wasn't even any reason to question him: all the garage mechanics had alibied each other for the shooting, that had been established.

He was annoyed at the waste of time. He went back to the office and told Mendoza.

Galeano looked in as they were exchanging comments and said, "Like to hear a funny story? There was an old bum came up from Carey's office awhile ago and identified that hit-run victim. Another ditto, which of course is what he looked like. In case there were any relatives to notify—or pay for the funeral—I went over to where he'd been living. Kind of a loft over a row of stores on the Row, about fifteen derelicts camping there. He had one suitcase. Odds and ends of old clothes, and a diploma from Harvard—he was an accredited attorney. Dated 1942."

"*¡Cómo!*" said Mendoza, amused. "Anybody to notify?"

"I don't know. There were some old snapshots, one with a name and address on the back—woman in Hartford, Connecticut. We can ask," said Galeano. "You heard that the Rittenhouse woman died? And by the way, it's started to rain again."

"I think I'll knock off early," said Mendoza. "Everything at a standstill." He looked moodily at the little pile of clothes still sitting on the chair beside the desk. "Sooner or later—famous last words—*¿de veras?*" He stood up and reached for the black homburg on the rack. "Have fun with the heisters, boys."

Five minutes after he'd left, Hackett and Landers came in with one of the identified heisters, a black giant looming over Hackett; they stashed him in an interrogation room and Landers went to get some coffee. He was sporting the start of a black eye; the suspect hadn't been cooperative. "And why the hell he couldn't pick on somebody his own size," said Landers bitterly, "I wouldn't know. It's raining again."

"We had heard," said Palliser.

Lake looked in. "The boss coming back?"

"Pulled rank and took off early," said Palliser.

"Why? Don't tell me that missing report's showed up at last." Hackett was amused.

"What missing report? No, I've got Bainbridge asking for him."

"I'll talk to him . . . Doctor? Hackett. The boss has left. What's on your mind?"

"I'm not about to tell a long story twice," said Dr. Bainbridge irascibly. "What's he doing, taking off at this hour? Well, it'll keep, but you tell him I'll see him tomorrow. I've got something really recherché for him. But really. Something really old-fashioned."

"Old-fashioned?" said Hackett blankly.

"That's what I said. I'll see both of you in the morning. You'll be interested, and it'll make some work for you."

"That's all we need," said Hackett; but Bainbridge had slammed down the phone.

It was raining in a tentative sort of way. When Palliser got home, to the house on Hillside Avenue, and got out to open the gate, Trina leaped at him lovingly and nearly knocked him over. He wrestled her into the kitchen and went to put the car in the garage. "I thought you were going to be so smart and train her by that book," he said when he came in again.

"Don't expect miracles in a month, darling," said Roberta tranquilly. "I was getting somewhere, working with her three times a day the way it says to—she was getting fairly reliable at heel and sit—but all this rain, it's impossible, I can't take her out as often." Trina, sitting on Palliser's feet gazing at him adoringly, was an outsize German shepherd and not full-grown at ten months. "Oh, damn," added Roberta, "there's the baby, and the potatoes just ready—"

"I'll see to him," said Palliser hastily. "You get dinner on—I'm starved."

It had stopped raining again on Thursday morning, but not to clear: the sky was still lowering and overcast. Southern California sees so little rain on the average that its citizens welcome it, but tire of it rapidly; only the farmers would still be happy with this siege.

Mendoza came in a little late. It was Hackett's day off, but he'd been curious about what Bainbridge had, and come in just to find out about that.

"Something old-fashioned!" said Mendoza. "What the hell does he mean by that?"

"I couldn't say. We caught up to those heisters from last Saturday. There are two autopsy reports in— Morrison and your mysterious lady."

"*Bueno.*" Mendoza sat down, got out a cigarette and triggered the flamethrower. The phone buzzed at him and he picked it up. "Robbery-Homicide, Mendoza."

"At long last," said Lieutenant Carey, "there's a report on your female out of the phone booth. Just now, from Wilcox Street. At least I think that's who it is—description fits just fine. I've got two daughters on the way down to look at the body. Would you care to join the party?"

"*¡Claro está!*" said Mendoza. "I'll meet you at the morgue!" He rushed out, leaving his cigarette in the ashtray. Hackett stubbed it out, and the phone buzzed again.

"Robbery-Homicide, Hackett."

"Isn't he there yet?" demanded Bainbridge.

"Something just broke. I don't know when he'll be back."

"Well, he'd better be in by ten. It doesn't matter a damn to me, but other doctors have regular hours to keep. I'll see him at ten o'clock—you tell him to be there."

"I will if I see him," said Hackett, intrigued.

4

CAREY WAS WAITING IN THE CORRIDOR OUTSIDE THE
double-door entrance to the morgue, with two young
couples. "Mr. and Mrs. Aiken. Mr. and Mrs. Raybeck,
Lieutenant Mendoza."

"I don't see how this could be, but Chuck and I'd
better make sure," said the older one, Raybeck. "The
minute we talk to the police, chasing us down here—"
The other one just nodded; the two girls looked frightened and bewildered. Carey and Mendoza took the two
men into the cold room and the attendant pulled out
the drawer. The men looked at the body and drew
identical quick breaths.

"My God, it is!" said Aiken. "How can it be? It's
her, but how—what happened to her?"

"You do identify her, sir?" asked Carey formally.

They both nodded, looking unhappy and puzzled.
"My God, how can we tell the girls?" said Raybeck in
a subdued voice. "What did happen to her?" They
looked at each other, two men of the same general
type, mid-twenties, office men by their dark suits,
Aiken sandy and younger, Raybeck dark. "Yes. It's
my mother-in-law, Mrs. Olga Anton. What—how did
she die, Lieutenant?"

"We're not exactly sure," said Mendoza. "I'll have
some questions to ask, Mr. Raybeck. We'd better
break the news, do you think?"

They went out to the two girls and broke the news;
the girls started to cry and exclaim. "I thought it'd turn
out to be the right one," said Carey to Mendoza,
"when Wilcox Street called it in. She wasn't exactly the
ordinary type the mugger leaves behind. What did
happen to her, Mendoza?"

58

"At the moment I haven't any idea," said Mendoza. Carey went away, and Mendoza approached the mourners. "There are questions we have to ask, you understand. We'll be more comfortable in my office, if you'd feel up to coming there now."

"Yes, sure—where do you mean?" Aiken was uncertain, shaken.

"What about the—body? We'll have to—" Raybeck looked pale.

"You can claim the body any time," said Mendoza, not mentioning the autopsy. "Say half an hour, in my office." He added directions. Observing the girls, he judged they were fairly sensible types; shocked and grief-stricken, not given to hysterics.

He took five minutes, sitting on the bench in the corridor, to glance over the autopsy report, which he'd brought along. It told him what had happened to the lady they now had a name for, but it didn't tell him why. She had died of a depressed skull-fracture of the left temple region, probably inflicted by a weapon of some sort: the surgeon suggested a hammer. There were other injuries: contusions on left shoulder and arm, left little finger broken, bruises on left hip and leg. A dim picture filled in the dimmer one already in his mind; she'd been halfway inside that phone booth, maybe looking for change in her purse, when the mugger came on her. He'd hit her, she put up a hand to defend herself, then took the second blow on the head and fell. Straightforward enough; and now maybe the relatives were going to tell him that she'd lived right around the corner from Figueroa and Adams, but somehow he doubted it.

He drove back to Parker Center, and five minutes after he sat down at his desk Hackett brought them in.

The two girls were alike enough to be obvious sisters, and they looked like the mother, roundish faces; regular small features, blue eyes: good-looking girls, both dark, both well-dressed in conservative dark colors, a dress and coat, a pantsuit. They'd stopped crying, were sober and quiet. The men were uneasy.

"Just what is this, anyway?" asked Aiken. "What happened to her? It's—you all act as if you'd been expecting us, I don't—"

"In a way," said Mendoza, "we have. Mrs. Anton's body was found early last Monday morning, and we've been trying to get her identified."

"Monday—" said the older girl. "Oh, my God, Fred, all that time, and we never—but what *happened?* An accident—she'd have had identification—"

"It looks as if she was attacked on the street. Killed—probably not intentionally—in the process of robbery. She was found at the corner of Figueroa and Adams. It happened between eleven Sunday night and two on Monday morning." Approximate times, by the autopsy. He made a steeple of his long hands and rested his chin on them, watching the two couples.

"Fig—but that's impossible!" burst out the younger girl. "Down there—after midnight? On the street there alone? That's impossible!"

"Why, Mrs. Aiken?"

"It just is—how can I tell you—Sue—" She turned to her sister who looked up from tightly clasped hands, shaking her head blindly.

"She didn't drive. She never had learned. She was living up in Hollywood. She wouldn't be out alone at night."

The two men started to speak and Mendoza lifted a hand. "All right—we don't know anything. I'd like to hear anything you can tell me. Suppose you just go on and tell me about your mother's background, her habits, her friends—whatever occurs to you."

They looked at each other. "All right. Th-thank you," said Sue Raybeck meaninglessly. "Well—she lived in Plainfield, Illinois, till last year. That's where —we're from. You see, I met Fred when we were at college, at Northwestern, and when he got the job here we came—excuse me, I mean we were engaged then, we were married back there and came to live here—"

"I'm at JPL Electronics," said Raybeck. "Do you want all this? Sue, don't you think—"

"Go on," said Mendoza.

"Well,"—she seemed a little steadier with something to talk about—"that was two years ago, and Ginny came out to visit us last year and got engaged to Chuck—Mother came out for the wedding in March, we couldn't all go back there, and of course Dad's been gone five years. And it seemed—with both of us settled here, there aren't any other relatives, we persuaded Mother to move out here. It seemed—you know, the sensible thing, all of us together, and the nicer climate, and she had enough money to be independent, Dad left her a good annuity. She didn't want to at first, they'd lived there all their lives—well, so had we, but it *was* only sensible—that old-fashioned little house, all the yard to keep up, it was better she should— And she finally did, she sold the house and came out here. Last June."

"Mmh. How old was she, by the way?"

"Fifty-five, why?"

"Dad was ten years older," said Ginny Aiken. "But you don't understand how impossible it is, Mother down there—at night, alone. She couldn't have been. Her apartment—we gave a lot of thought to that because she doesn't drive, wouldn't know her way around at first—not that distance mattered so much, both Sue and I have cars, but—"

"Don't dither, darling," said her sister. "The apartment's on Los Feliz, Lieutenant, she could get the bus up to Hollywood. But I guess what—we're both trying to say, she didn't know many people here, she didn't really go out much—it was mostly to see us, she'd be at our place or Ginny's once or twice a week for dinner, once in a while we all went out to dinner, or one of us'd take her shopping and to lunch—like that—she didn't like the Methodist church up there, she said it was too big, the people not friendly, and she didn't go very often. She never went out alone at night, never."

"Apparently," said Mendoza, "she went out last Sunday night. She was dressed to go out somewhere. A black velvet dress and coat." He'd put the clothes away before they came in; they were upset enough. Nice, well-bred, well-educated people: the girls had obviously been genuinely fond of Mother.

They said simultaneously, "Her best dress!" "But we saw her on Saturday, she was at our place for dinner, and she never said a word about going out anywhere!" said Sue Raybeck. "I don't understand this at all—Mother, g-getting killed like that down there—"

"She hadn't any friends here she went out with at all? Men or women?"

"Of course not men—" Ginny looked a little shocked. "Oh, the woman who lived across the hall, she'd met her, they'd gone out to a movie once, shopping, but Mother didn't like her too much, she said she seemed a little"—she gave a tearful chuckle—"*fast*. I mean—you've got to see—M-Mother was—was a little bit old-fashioned some ways."

"You understand," said Mendoza, "that we'll want to examine her apartment. If you'd give me the address—a key?"

"Neither of us had a key. We had to get the manager to let us in—it isn't as if Mother wasn't quite well, we didn't get really worried until yesterday, when we couldn't get her on the phone—she wasn't out much, and when she didn't answer and didn't answer we got worried—she could have had a fall, or—and Fred said—and then when she wasn't there, we thought we'd better ask—if there'd been an accident, or—"

"I never thought it'd really turn out to be—anything," said Raybeck. "An accident—she'd have had identification on her. I joked about it, bad news travels fast, but Chuck said—be on the safe side—my God, none of this makes sense."

"Yes, well," said Mendoza, "we'll want to look at her apartment. Do you recognize this ring?" He handed the diamond ring to Sue, who clutched it and uttered a little sob.

"Yes, of course, Daddy gave it to her on their thirtieth anniversary—six years ago—"

"I'd be obliged," said Mendoza, "if you feel up to it,

if you'd both look over the apartment and—mmh—see if anything's missing. Out of place. Say this afternoon."

"Yes, of course. If you—find out anything, how it did happen—"

"We'll be in touch with you. Thanks very much," said Mendoza, and stood up. They filed out silently, Ginny starting to cry again. "Well, Arturo?"

"Mysterious lady still mysterious," said Hackett. "What the hell was she doing down there, anyway?"

Mendoza picked up the flamethrower and regarded it thoughtfully. "I thought I had a small idea—no, it won't jell. I want to see that apartment."

"You don't suppose the burglar got in and took her all the way downtown to mug her?"

"I do not. Places tell you this and that about the people who live in them."

"Indubitably. But anybody can get in the way of a mugger, right time, right place."

"Judgment—" said Mendoza.

"From on high?"

"Don't be silly. Most people—the kind of woman she seems to have been—exercise some judgment. Some reason. Lock doors, don't wander down strange streets in the dark, don't let strangers in. But most people also have moments of aberration."

"Well, at least we know who she was. And what happened to her, though there's about one chance in a million we'll ever drop on the anonymous mugger. And it is now," said Hackett, "half past ten, and the only reason I came in this morning was to hear Bainbridge's story. I would guess he's sitting out there having kittens—never a patient fellow at his best."

In fact, Bainbridge had been enjoying himself, showing his companion around Robbery-Homicide, asking about all the latest cases; he was interested in the torture-killer, and said ghoulishly he'd look forward to the autopsy, do it himself. "We haven't had a case like that in a while. I'm trying to remember if there was a full moon that night—that sets 'em off sometimes. And if you don't get him, he'll pull another, you know."

"We'll hope to get him, Doctor."

"Lab should give you this and that. I suppose you're looking at all the sex pedigrees in Records and sorting out possible suspects— That's the routine approach," he explained to the man at his side. "Then, if the lab has turned up anything concrete—"

"You said you had a story to tell us," said Mendoza.

Bainbridge chuckled. He was balder and tubbier than ever, ensconcing himself in the chair beside the desk, getting out a cigar. "Oh, have we got a story to tell you!" he said, nipping off the cigar end neatly. "I'm just the introducer—this is Dr. Adam Ferguson. Old buddy of mine, in private practice. It's his story."

Ferguson said seriously, "And I feel as if I'd got into a case history by William Roughead. Really, I was quite at a loss, I didn't know what the proper procedure would be, and knowing that Bainbridge is attached to the police—" He was a tall cadaverous man with shrewd eyes and curly gray hair. "There was the publicity, too, I didn't want a Roman holiday. I thought the technician had made a mistake at first, but—"

"Start at the beginning, Doctor?" said Mendoza patiently.

"Oh, yes. It's these patients of mine—Mr. and Mrs. Beebe. They've been patients off and on for twenty years—he's got a bad heart, she's got arthritis. Sixty-eight and sixty-seven. I know the daughter too, but since she got married she lives in Hollywood, I suppose goes to someone else. The Beebes run a little independent market on Third Street, and have an apartment over the store. Little, ordinary, quiet people," said Ferguson. "Last people in the world you'd expect—er—anything dramatic to happen to."

"And something did?" said Hackett.

Ferguson adjusted his glasses and opened his mouth to continue precise speech, and Bainbridge chortled happily. "Arsenic! Shades of Madeleine Smith, arsenic! He calls me and asks what to do about it, old couple fed arsenic in the creamed tunafish, of all the damned funny things, and of course the first thought that came to me was the daughter—first thought anybody'd have —but he says not, though God knows he's not a detective."

"Neither are you," said Ferguson mildly. "If you'd let me tell it in order— The daughter, Helen Travis, called me last Sunday afternoon—got my answering service. She said her parents had been taken ill suddenly, she had to call an ambulance. I saw them at the receiving hospital, and really, I couldn't make it out at all. It had come on so suddenly—severe cramps, purging, nausea—they were both beyond speech then, but Mrs. Travis told me her mother had said they were both perfectly well until after lunch. She'd called Mrs. Travis for help when she realized it was something serious. Naturally I took samples for testing—I'd have suspected an internal virus of some sort except for the suddenness—but I hardly expected the results the lab— Well, I suppose if you had asked me point-blank, I could have said that the symptoms of arsenic poisoning are just the symptoms the Beebes had, but as for suspecting such a thing—"

Mendoza was intrigued. "How did the arsenic turn up?"

Bainbridge chortled again. "And that was just a fluke, too. It wouldn't have turned up at all, ordinarily. Who the hell thinks of testing for arsenic these days? Or, you know, any day, come to that. We can look back at some of the classic cases—Seddon, Maybrick—and think what idiots those doctors were not to suspect, but hindsight— You don't expect poison in the soup at home But just as it happened, young Hodges is in charge of that lab, and I suppose he's been conditioned to suspecting the worst."

"Who's Hodges?" asked Hackett.

"One of my former bright young men. He's a good autopsy surgeon, but he wanted to get in the technical side. Said he was tired of dead bodies staring him in the face, and of course mostly the violently dead ones. So he gets himself a job as superintendent of the lab at

Central Receiving, and there he is when old Ferguson came wandering in with his samples—"

"More samples," said Ferguson fussily. "Nothing definite had showed up from the first tests."

"Of course not, Hodges or nobody else knew the story. When you came down personally and asked for any ideas on this little medical mystery, Hodges reverted to his police experience right off and thought of poison. At least that's the only reason I can think of why he should have run a test for arsenic. Anyway, he did."

"And I'm damned if I can imagine why anyone should want to poison the Beebes," said Ferguson. "It's senseless. To say the daughter did it, that's senseless too. Perfectly nice respectable woman, fond of her parents. They're ordinary harmless people."

"It didn't kill them?" asked Hackett.

"No, they're both still in the hospital. I don't like the way his heart's acting—we barely pulled him through. She's still very weak, but I think she'll make it."

"Another little mystery," said Mendoza. "And where did whoever get hold of the arsenic, Doctor?"

"Hah!" said Bainbridge gleefully. "That's easy, Luis. Looking at all those old cases, we feel all superior—just think, back then you could walk into a drugstore and buy laudanum, arsenic, whatever, without a prescription—now, oh, no, not these enlightened days. Oh, no? Hodges got interested and broke down the ingredients. He thinks he's got it pinned down to a brand. Stuff called Mouse-Noh, you can buy it over the counter at any garden-supply place, lots of pharmacies."

"Mouse-Noh?" echoed Mendoza, taken aback.

"To get rid of mice, Croesus," said Bainbridge. "I don't suppose it occurs to you that in a lot of places down here in the inner city where the peasants live, there are mice running around. After garbage and so on."

"I lived down here for quite a while, Doctor, and we never had mice. My grandmother kept a cat."

"Some people don't like cats."

"Well, the point is," said Ferguson, "I suppose you'll want to do something about it. Er—collect the evidence, inquire into it."

"It's attempted homicide, we surely will. Can we talk to the Beebes? They might have the best idea of who had any motive."

"Possibly tomorrow," said Ferguson. "But the daughter can tell you what the mother said, and I suppose you'll want to see their apartment. I've retained the samples, if you—"

"The technicians' report will be enough," said Mendoza gravely. "Thanks very much for coming in, Doctor—we'll be looking into it."

"And I'll be damn interested to hear what you find out," said Bainbridge.

"So will I," said Hackett when the doctors had gone. "Here's another funny one, all right. But it's my day off after all, I'm going home."

He went home, and Angel was just taking a cake out of the oven. "Oh, good, you're back," she said. I've got some shopping to do and it's so much easier without the baby." Mark was in kindergarten these days, on the whole successfully, though there had been some trouble with the principal because he already knew how to read, which was apparently a deadly sin on the part of parents. "I might," she added, "stop to see Alison first, if she's home and not out looking at mansions."

She took off in her car, and Hackett went down to check on baby Sheila, peacefully napping. Comfortably aware that since yesterday he was down to two-ten again, he had a piece of Angel's cake. It was raining again.

Bainbridge had, of course, been quite right about the routine. The lab could give them mechanical facts, on Lila Wescott's murder, but unless the facts included identifiable prints on file in somebody's records, that didn't give them the killer's name and address. It might look like the hard way to go at it, but it was the only logical way. As well as hunting for the various heisters, they were now doing the legwork on that. Palliser and Landers had been down to R. and I. this morning and got a list from the computer of all the men in their files with pedigrees of rape and rape with violence, and they were now out looking for those men, looking at them and questioning them when they were found. Galeano had a list of his own, of men with records of B. and E. who lived in the general area of the Rittenhouse homicide. The rest of them were out looking for heisters.

Mendoza went out to lunch at Federico's and found Landers and Conway there. They had, said Landers, wasted the whole morning wandering around looking for these louts, and found only one where the address in the files said he'd be, and he had an alibi for Tuesday night, he'd been visibly at work at a drive-in theater where he took tickets. Conway was sitting drinking black coffee and sneezing; he was coming down with a cold, and felt, he said, like hell. Mendoza wished them luck.

It was only as he was paying his bill that he discovered Jason Grace sitting alone at a front table, over cold coffee, reading a paperback. "Just the man I was after. Sometimes you get feelings about things, Jase. You can forget about the rapists for a while and come take a look at Olga's apartment with me."

"Olga?" Grace shut his book and shoved it in his pocket.

"The mysterious lady in the phone booth."

"I heard you'd got her identified." Grace followed him out and climbed into the Ferrari, and Mendoza gave him a rundown on Olga Anton as they drove up into Hollywood.

"I don't think there'd be any point in having the lab go over the apartment. It's not likely anything happened there, though you never know. But you can read between the lines, what the daughters said, the kind of woman she was. Respectable, straitlaced—small-town Middle West. Damn it, she must have known a few people here. And she'd dressed to the nines to go out that night, but she hadn't mentioned any plans to the girls the day before."

"And she would have, likely," said Grace. "So something came up in a hurry, just that day. Somebody called her and said, I've got a spare ticket for the ballet, or the ice show."

"Possibly. Yes, that could be. In fact, it's about the only answer. But how did she come to be alone on the street down there? Whoever the somebody was, it's likely they were in a car. But we don't even know that, of course. And whatever happened—the friend taken ill, a flat tire—somebody would have known she was missing before the daughters."

"I can't imagine a reason for the somebody not telling them, I misplaced Olga downtown," said Grace sleepily. "But we're theorizing ahead of facts here."

"I know, I know."

The apartment on Los Feliz was one of the big new ones, and Mendoza knew, looking at it, that it would be useless to ask questions of other tenants here. People who lived in these places were not neighborly; it wasn't like the smaller apartment buildings of whatever price range, where notice was taken of people coming and going. The people who lived here would be of two sorts: youngish couples and middle-aged couples with money and no kids, the men executives of this and that kind, absorbed in their own lives and friends and much entertaining and gadding about; and moneyed elderly people, retired, also with their own social lives.

There would be somewhere around a hundred apartments in the elegant eight-story building, with its graceful Norman-French facade. There was a vast underground parking area underneath, mosaic tile steps up to a plush carpeted lobby, a rank of elevators, a rank of mailboxes, opposite that a door labeled *Manager* which was opened at Mendoza's knock to reveal a small businesslike office and a cold-eyed fat man in a funereal black suit.

"Oh, yes, Mr. Raybeck called to say you'd be coming." He inspected the badge very thoroughly before taking them up in an elevator, unlocking the apartment door. "I'm sure I'm very sorry to hear about Mrs. Anton. She was a nice quiet tenant. If you'd just close the door behind you, please, thank you."

"All business," said Grace. "Nice place. What do you figure the tab is?"

"Two fifty to three hundred, a single in front. Daddy must have left her a nice annuity. I wonder what he was in." Mendoza stood in the middle of the room, rocking slightly heel to toe, looking around.

It was a quietly elegant, comfortable room, and everything looked very new. Cream and brown color scheme, queensize couch, three chairs, shag carpet, small walnut writing desk under one window, shotsilk drapes over nylon, a large anonymous seascape over the couch, no other pictures. He looked into the kitchen off to the right. Natural birch cabinets, sterile white tile counters, everything electric, the curved bar and stools that was the modern version of a breakfast nook. It was all very neat and tidy, no dirty dishes left out. He went back through the living room into the bedroom. All the rooms were a good size. In there, he contemplated the flowered quilted-satin spread on a made-up double bed, the modern walnut chiffonier, low chest, pair of bed-tables: ruffled shades on matching lamps.

"She didn't," he said, "bring anything with her from Plainfield, Illinois."

"Should she have?"

"I don't know," said Mendoza. He looked into the bathroom. Here were more personal touches: a few cosmetics in the medicine chest, not cheap quality but not the most expensive: a shower cap, bath salts, two bottles of cologne on the counter-top—White Shoulders and Chantilly. He went back to the living room and found an address book in the desk drawer, was looking through it when the daughters arrived. He asked them to have a look around; they would know her jewelry and clothes.

"She was probably wearing more jewelry than was found on her. That ring was very tight, it's probable he couldn't get it off and left it."

"She'd gained a little weight lately—she was saying just last week she'd have to have it made larger," said Ginny. They started to look in the bedroom, Mendoza following them around. In various boxes in the top chiffonier drawer was quite a lot of jewelry.

"Dad was always giving her things—she liked jewelry," said Sue.

"What business was he in, Mrs. Raybeck?"

"Oh, insurance, he had his own firm. Everything seems to be here, except—" She looked through more boxes. The jewelry was, to Mendoza's expert eye, nothing spectacular: bits and pieces, the several rings all good stuff but no large stones, one brooch with diamonds and pearls, pearl earrings, a brooch with sapphires, and a good deal of good costume stuff. "Well, you know, Ginny, if she had on the black velvet, she'd probably have worn that jade pendant with it. She usually did, and it's not here. And I can't find her jade earrings either, or the bracelet. So that's probably what she was wearing."

"Can you describe them, please?"

"The pendant's light green jade, a carved peacock and flowers, it's about two inches across, on a kind of rope chain—that's fourteen-karat gold. The earrings are carved jade roses with a little diamond chip in the center, and the bracelet's just plain tubes of jade, four of them, with gold links. They were s-supposed to be symbols of love, luck and l-long life," said Sue, and gulped into her handkerchief and wiped her eyes.

Mendoza sighed mentally: mass-produced stuff, if it showed up in a pawnshop it could never be positively linked to Olga Anton. "Would she have been wearing another ring?"

"Oh, I never thought—oh, yes, she would. Ever since Dad died she always wore his signet ring on her right hand, she had it made to fit her. It's eighteen-karat gold, I think, with his initials in script—HXA."

"X?" said Mendoza.

She laughed. "Yes, it's funny—we never could imagine why they gave him such a middle name, it was Xenophon."

And that ring would be clearly identifiable; they'd get these descriptions out on the hot list to all pawn-brokers at once. The professional heist men were after cash, the professional burglars usually had their own private fences, but the casual street-muggers—after money to support a habit, or just disinclined for the eight-hour job—usually dumped any small valuables on the pawnbroker. It was a pity they were four days late on it, was all. "Thanks very much," said Mendoza. "We may want to look around here again."

They nodded. "The rent's paid until the end of the month," said Sue. "We'll have to sort out her clothes and—" She looked around. "It's just—so *sudden*. All of a sudden, Mother gone. It looks so—awfully bare here, without her, doesn't it, Ginny?"

It had looked bare anyway, reflected Mendoza. He asked about the other tenant Olga Anton had got acquainted with here, and they told him it was Mrs. Albright in Thirty-six across the hall. He and Grace went over there and pushed the bell, and a sharp-faced Negro girl opened the door.

"Mrs. Albright's in Europe," she informed them smartly. "Since the middle of February. I just come in to dust and get the mail."

"So she didn't go off to the ballet on the spur of the moment with Mrs. Albright," said Mendoza in the elevator.

"She could have with somebody else. What I don't see," said Grace, "is what happened to the somebody."

"*¿Cómo dice?*"

"Well, they said she'd never go out alone at night. So it looks as if she had to be with somebody, even a couple of somebodies, and probably in a car. And whatever happened, they'd know, as I said before. So there wasn't any somebody. It comes back to Sherlock Holmes."

"Try that over again, slower." They got into the Ferrari. It was raining again.

"It's what Holmes always said," said Grace. "When the impossible is singled out, whatever remains, however improbable, is the truth. It looks to me as if she did decide to go out alone somewhere, for once. Maybe just out to a restaurant for dinner, or a movie. And I'll add something else. Because she hadn't been around much here, except with other people, and didn't drive, she didn't know the town. She might not have realized that wasn't such a good area to be alone in, at night."

"Now that could be on the nose, Jase. But against it, I'll say—Figueroa and Adams? There isn't a good restaurant—the kind she'd pick—within miles of that area. She had a choice of thirty, a lot closer to home— probably the ones in Hollywood she'd be familiar with. And what else? A scattering of eighth-run movie houses, a few that only run Mexican films, porno houses—no place Olga would have been attracted to. Any ideas on that?"

"*Nada*," said Grace sadly.

"Well." Mendoza had brought the address book along; he lit a cigarette and began to look through it. "How long had she been here—eight months? She hadn't made any new friends that she cared enough about to write down addresses, phone numbers. Plainfield—Plainfield—Plainfield—Aurora, Illinois—Geneva, Illinois—Plainfield. That apartment—" He was silent, and then switched on the ignition. "Let's go back to base and see if we've turned up any hot suspects on the torture-killer."

They hadn't. Higgins had brought in one out of Records with a suggestive pedigree, three counts of robbery and rape with violence—nobody asked what he was doing walking around loose—but he had, surprisingly, an alibi: he'd been at the hospital on Tuesday night waiting for his wife to produce a baby. Everybody but Wanda was out hunting more possibles, and she complained to Mendoza that they wouldn't let her go along, get more street experience. "I'm a policewoman, not a glorified secretary," she said bitterly. "Oh, there was a lab report just came in."

Mendoza took it and a minute later uttered a gratified. *"¡Que bien!* The lab coming through. They picked up some latents on the Bradley car, good ones. Now we see if they show in Records."

But nothing came in about that until five minutes to six. Higgins, Landers, Palliser and Galeano had trailed back with nothing to show for the day's hunt; they'd talked to a number of men with the good—or bad—records to be X on Lila Wescott, but with nothing to say for sure enough to haul them in. Conway, sneezing steadily, had come in half an hour before and was huddled miserably at his desk. Higgins told him he was spreading germs around and ought to go home.

Mendoza had just picked up his hat when Sergeant Lake came in with a report from R. and I. The latents from the Bradley car had been in their files; they belonged to Lee Collard, Negro, five-ten, a hundred and sixty, black and brown, forty-one, no marks. He had a pedigree of petty theft, burglary (one count) and B. and E. (one count). He was off parole, and the address was a fairly recent one.

"Progress," said Mendoza. "Leave him for the night watch. Tell them to call me if he comes apart and tells us where they left Joyce."

He drove home through an increased downpour. After a couple of dry winters, they were getting it this year. Garaging the Ferrari, he found the shaggy dog Cedric unconcernedly nosing around the backyard; with his tremendous fur coat, Cedric was impervious to rain. He bounced in joyously with Mendoza and shook himself vigorously all over the kitchen, and Mrs. MacTaggart uttered some very Scottish noises.

Mendoza wandered down to the living room and found Alison, cozily wrapped in an amber robe, stretched out on the sectional with a thick brochure labeled Red Carpet Realtors Current Properties. All the cats were curled up around her. Mendoza bent to kiss her. "Have you located a mansion?"

"No. They've all got swimming pools. Status symbol," said Alison.

"I want a drink. You?"

"Some crème de menthe." El Señor had a sixth

sense about drinks, and woke up with a start to pre-
cede Mendoza back to the kitchen, floating to the
counter-top and demanding his share in a loud Siamese
voice. "That cat," said Mrs. MacTaggart. Mendoza
poured him a half-ounce of rye in a saucer and took
his own rye and Alison's drink back to the living
room.

"That place in Brentwood," said Alison, and wrinkled her nose. "It belonged to some recording star, Mr.
McNair was surprised I didn't know his name. *¡Qué
atrocidad!* We'd have had to hire a butler."

"*¡Dios me libre!*" said Mendoza. "I'm not that ambitious—like a nice quiet life myself."

It was Shogart's night off, and Piggott and Schenke
were just as happy about that. Maybe he'd been a
good cop in his day, but he'd never adjusted to the
streamlining of bureaus at headquarters, and was a
drag to the younger men.

They didn't have to wait for a call, had this to go
out on right away—the suspect on Joyce Bradley,
latents found in her car. The address for Collard was
Ditman Street in east L.A., so they both went; not such
a good area for a lone white man to be in after dark.

It was an old ramshackle apartment building, and
they got no answer at Collard's door. They tried the
apartment across the hall, and a fat brown woman
opened her door a cautious two inches.

"Mr. Collard? I don't know nobody else lives here,
we just moved in."

They tried the apartment down the hall, and a
smiling Chinese fellow said, "Mr. Collard? Yes, he is
living this place, nice polite man, no wife. I do not
know where work, but nights, yes. Not here at night."

"Well, that throws it back to the day watch," said
Piggott philosophically. They went back to the office
and settled down to wait for any calls. After a while
Piggott asked, "Did you like that book, Bob? I thought
it was interesting—quite a character. A good man."

"What?" said Schenke. "Oh, that book—damn,
where is it? I left it right here—somebody must have

swiped it. Yeah, very interesting, Matt." He was aware
that when Piggott said, a good man, probably the book
was just as uninteresting as he'd found it, as far as he'd
got.

"Hey," said Piggott, "I want that back."

"It'll probably turn up." And then the desk buzzed
them—another heist.

On Friday morning, with Galeano and Glasser off,
the day men were just coming in at eight o'clock—
Hackett, Higgins, Palliser, Landers, Grace—out of a
continued thin drizzle of rain. Mendoza came in at
eight-ten, shedding coat and hat. There was all the
continued routine to work, the eternal legwork; the
rain just made it more annoying. But before he had
glanced at the night report Sergeant Lake swung
around from the switchboard.

"Lieutenant! Sheriff's office—that nurse just turned
up, the Bradley woman, and she's alive!"

"*¡Parece mentira!*" said Mendoza. "I don't believe
it! Where, for God's sake?"

5

"I WOULDN'T'VE BEEN OUT HERE AT ALL, EXCEPT FOR
the roses," said Ben Armidjian. He was still looking
shaken and dazed. "My God, I never had such a
shock. They all shoulda been cut back in January, but
it's tough to hire decent workers, we been three—four
men short, and a place like this, there's a lot of work
to keep caught up. And all this rain—but this morning
I think, it's just a drizzle, I can get something done,
and I come out. My God, here I am cutting roses a
mile and a half from the main building, and there she
is—like a corpse come up out of a grave—not that
that section's laid out in graves yet—my God—I heard
about it on the radio, but I never thought—"

Mendoza, Hackett and Higgins stood at the edge of
a tamed green rolling piece of land that was part of
Rose Hills Memorial Park. Here and there along the
gravel paths were large rectangular beds of rose trees;
embedded in the lawns the discreet bronze grave-
markers.

The ambulance had gone, but Armidjian said she'd
still been alive when the paramedics came, and the
ambulance. It was right over here, she'd crawled up
out of that gully. "I figure she musta been left somewhere over there, down from the other road maybe,
that's the boundary of our grounds there and it's all
wild down to the city line. My God, I wonder how long
she'd been there—"

They followed him to where the gully ran down, the
neat green lawn this side, tangle of underbrush that.
"She was right there," said Armidjian. "My God, I
thought I was hearing things, please help me, she says,

77

please help me—and when I got to her she was passed out, but still breathing—"

There were marks in the muddy underbrush at the edge of the gully; they could see where the paramedics had knelt, where the stretcher had been put down. All the rain— "But you can see a kind of trail," said Higgins, and plowed down the slope into the gully. "Look at that."

A desperate little trail it was, of a body crawling full-length, painfully and slowly, through the tangle of wild mustard and sumac. It led up the other side of the gully, into deeper undergrowth beyond, and the first thing they found was the belt from her nurse's uniform, just a wisp of bloody white nylon. They went on backtracking the faint marks, and found a shoe; there was blood on it, under the mud: the plain flatheeled white shoe she'd been wearing on duty. Twenty-five yards on, under the deep shade of live oaks now, they came on the other shoe, and a muddy, bloody wool scarf.

"*¡Dios!*" said Mendoza. "Five days—five and a half—"

"I'll say that girl's got guts," said Hackett softly. "Look at that." Under the trees, out of the rain, the track was clearer. She had come up against a steep rise of ground here, and tried to get up it, fallen back, and laboriously crawled around where the slope was gentler. Down from there they found a little bloody wad caught on a low oak branch: two handkerchiefs soaked with blood. Thirty yards on from there they came to the beginning of her trail, a thickly grown muddy hollow at the bottom of a steep hill. Up the hill a little swath was cut in the brush, and in the hollow, rain trapped there, were still reddish discolorations on the wet earth.

"She was thrown over from the road up there," said Mendoza. "Guts you can say, Art. She'd lost a good deal of blood in the car. But she kept trying, by God—she wouldn't give up."

"Muddled," said Higgins. "Was she trying to get

back to the road, figured maybe she'd be spotted quicker there, and crawled the wrong way? In the dark she couldn't tell—no lights out here—and she couldn't have known the cemetery was that way."

"And it ties up in a sense," said Mendoza. "The car was left, what, five miles from here but in the same general area." The road up there, Sycamore Canyon, marked the boundary of the city of Whittier. He looked up there.

"After five days of rain, there won't be anything to see," said Higgins. "But I suppose we have to be thorough. I don't pay five hundred per for my suits— let me." He swarmed up the hill, sprawling flat once when he slipped, and vanished over the brow of the top. Five minutes later he came slipping and sliding down, catching at branches to slow himself, and said, "Nothing. It's a blacktop road, not much of a shoulder, and not a sign of tire marks. Of course."

"I hope to God she makes it," said Hackett. "She fought hard enough. Five days, and that downpour most of the time—" He hunched his wide shoulders.

"More to the point," said Mendoza, "if she makes it, there's a good chance she can tell us a lot about him—at least give us a good description. Let's get back to civilization and find out how she's doing."

But as they came into the Robbery-Homicide office they found Landers and Palliser just in with a lanky black fellow. "Collard," said Landers. "He was home this morning."

Lee Collard was scared and shaking, a curious slate-green with fright; his eyes rolled at the detectives. "I don't know what you want with me, I done nothing— what you think I done?"

They herded him into an interrogation room and made him sit down. "Last Sunday night, Lee," Higgins began it. "What did you have in mind, rape or robbery, when you jumped that nurse in the hospital lot?"

"I never! I never done such a thing!"

"Now come on, Lee, we know it was you."

"You don't know, on account I never did. I don't know what you mean—nurse, that nurse—it said on the radio—I don't know nothin' about that at all!"

"Let's not waste time, Lee. Your fingerprints were in her car—we know you were there."

Panic flared in the rolling eyes, but also a vast surprise; his mouth fell open and he began to shake harder. "They wasn't—they couldn't be, no way—I never see her car, I don't know anything about that—"

"So where were you instead?" asked Hackett. "Last Sunday night about eleven-fifteen?"

"I—I—I was at work Sunday night, like always, just— What time you say?"

"Eleven, eleven-fifteen. Where do you work?"

"Eleven—thass too late," he said numbly, "too late. We close down ten o'clock, we don't get much business after—I never did that! I never—"

"Where do you work?"

He was looking at them like a trapped animal, the rolling eyes coming back always to Higgins' grim craggy face. "I—I—where do I—uh—it's called the Golden Knight, I'm in the parking lot—but it shuts at ten, I mean we go off then—I never hurt nobody, I don't know nothin' about that nurse—"

Mendoza caught Hackett's eye and they left him to Landers and Palliser. "Question of time before he comes apart," said Higgins in the hall.

"I wonder," said Mendoza. "That's a popular restaurant."

"What's that got to do with it?"

"Bradley will be at the hospital—I want to talk to the doctors anyway." Hackett tagged along with him.

"Are you thinking what I'm thinking?"

"The lab," said Mendoza, "just collects facts. And facts can sometimes be misleading."

At Central Receiving, they asked for the doctor first, and waited ten minutes in a sparse small office before he appeared, a little fierce-looking man with bushy eyebrows. "I'm Lafleur—you wanted to see me?" He was brusque, but at sight of the badge said, "Oh—sorry, I thought you were reporters. Of course you want to know about Joyce. I can give you five minutes, we're still working on her. It's a Goddamned miracle she's still alive, that's all I can say. What? Yes, of course I know her—a damned good theater nurse, damned fine woman. A miracle. I don't know why she's still alive."

"Do you think she'll live, Doctor?"

"We'll try our damnedest to see she does, but I'm not saying one way or another yet. She lost a lot of blood—she was stabbed a number of times in the body, I think raped, and she's got a dislocated right shoulder, a compound fracture of one ankle, and bruises all over her—but chiefly, of course, she's suffering from exposure. She's in a coma now, and I won't guess how long it might be before she's conscious—if ever. I suppose you'd like to talk to her, but you won't be able to for a while yet."

"We'd appreciate being kept informed. Is her husband here?"

"He is. We're not letting him in either."

Bradley was sitting in an alcove down the hall, smoking nervously. He gave them a shaky grin, and said, "They won't let me see her. That doctor's saying she might not make it, but she will. I know she will. Nothing gets Joyce down for long. When she's made it this far—"

"I believe you, Mr. Bradley," said Hackett. "That girl of yours has got guts."

"You bet," said Bradley proudly.

"Mr. Bradley, do you know the Golden Knight restaurant?" asked Mendoza.

"What? Why? The—why, yes, we've been there, it's a nice place. I took Joyce there just last—that is, a week ago last night—it was our anniversary. Why?"

"Damnation," said Mendoza mildly. "A little complication, that's all. We'll be holding the good thoughts for your wife."

"Coincidence?" said Hackett in the car. "That could play hell with a court case, Luis. If it can be shown his prints could have got into the car innocently—"

"Which they may have," said Mendoza. "Let's get him calmed down and ask some more questions."

But in the absence of the two tough cops, Hackett and Higgins, Collard had calmed down a little for Landers and managed to come up with some answers. After he'd left the job on Sunday night, he said, he'd gone to a pal's place for a while. He was off work the next night, didn't have nothing to do, so he'd gone to see Ranny. Another pal was there, and they'd just hung around, playing cards some and listening to records, till maybe four A.M. Ranny Eggers' house on LaVerne Avenue, and there'd been another pal there, Joey Fisher. They'd both say he was there. Landers had gone out with Palliser to see if they could locate the pals.

There were things Mendoza and Hackett could be doing, but they waited around a little to see if that alibi could be checked right away. Higgins had gone back to the routine legwork. It was getting on for noon then and they were just thinking of lunch when Landers came in with Palliser on his heels.

"I think we can write off Collard," said Palliser after he'd heard about the Bradleys' visit to the Golden Knight. "Damn it, he looked so hot, prints usually the best evidence we get. But the coincidences do happen. Both these pals are decent enough types, working regular jobs and no pedigrees. They both say Collard showed up about a quarter of eleven on Sunday night and they were all together until four in the morning. Collard's pedigree doesn't include any violence, and he hasn't been in any trouble for two years, since he got out the last time."

"Yes," said Mendoza. "Frustrating, but I think we write him off. Just coincidentally, he was the one to park the Bradley car a week ago last night, and left his prints in it. Which X apparently didn't. Damn. And it's a coincidence too that they were driving her car that night and not Bradley's. Well, these things will happen. I just hope Joyce goes on hanging on, and eventually can tell us something."

They went out to lunch, after which Landers and Palliser went back to hunting the possible rapists. Conway had called in to say he was staying in bed, with aspirin to keep him company.

"I just don't understand it at all, and I'm sure I don't know what to tell you," said Mrs. Helen Travis. "Maybe it's a blessing in disguise at that, seeing they're going to be all right, because we've been after Dad for years to sell that place and retire. Well, when I say all right, the doctor says it's weakened Dad's heart some more. Anyway, I don't think they can go back to keeping the store. The property ought to be worth something."

Mendoza and Hackett were seeing a good deal of Central Receiving Hospital in the last few days. They were back again now, talking to Mrs. Travis in one of the little waiting rooms, in another wing and higher up than where Joyce Bradley lay in a coma. "That day they were taken ill, did either of them say anything— mmh—relevant about it?" asked Mendoza.

"Relevant—" She seemed to meditate on that. She was a placid, stout woman in her late forties, dressed practically in a heavy wool brown pantsuit, stout oxfords. Her brown hair was plentifully streaked with gray, and she wore no makeup at all. "Well, you just never saw two sicker people, that's all. I dropped everything when Mother phoned, I could tell she was terribly sick, and anyway she's never been one to ask for help easy, you see what I mean, and so I knew they really needed me. I hadn't seen them all week, we live up in Hollywood, and we don't go to the same church, that is, they're both Methodist but one here and one there, you know. I came down, and oh, my, they *was* sick—I was scared to see how sick, I called an ambulance right off. But—I suppose that was what you meant—before it came, I was asking Mother when it come on and so forth, and she said they'd been feeling fine till after lunch. But now the doctor saying somebody poisoned them, and police asking—well, I can't make that out at all, there'd be no earthly reason anybody'd do that, everybody likes Mother and Dad."

"The doctor said we could probably talk to her. And we'd like to go over the apartment."

"I don't see why not. I'm going down there myself right now, redd up a little more and see everything's all right. They're just old locks on the doors and I've been nervous somebody'll break in and steal the stock. I'd be that glad if they got shut of the business, though they've been there forty years, but the way it is down here now—not like when I was growing up here, for sure. She's still awful weak, I guess you shouldn't talk to her too long. But I'll be at the store, I could show you whatever you want—you got the address? Well, I'll say good-bye for now then." She plodded off down the corridor, and Mendoza and Hackett went to find a nurse and Mrs. Beebe.

She looked a good deal older than sixty-seven, lying in the rumpled hospital bed, because she wasn't wearing her false teeth, and she was still under some kind of dope, her mind hazy and slow. She didn't understand who they were. She gazed foggily up at them and murmured, "Poison—silly. The fish was fine."

"Mrs. Beebe, can you understand me?" said Mendoza. Evidently Dr. Ferguson had tried to question her too. "Were you out on Sunday morning? Away from home?"

"Church, 'f course."

"And did you have any callers that morning? Any customers at the store?"

"Not open—Sunday. Don't believe in. Dad says—all go to hell, open Sundays."

"Did anyone come to the apartment?"

"Sunday? Before—so sick. Just leaving for church—Hermy was there. Told doctor—prob'ly the milk. On the turn—shouldn't've used."

Mendoza brushed his mustache, looking at her frustratedly. "Have you had any trouble with anyone lately—you and your husband, that is—with customers? Any arguments?"

She shook her head drowsily. "Milk. Sorry—Dad so awful sick, worse than me."

"Who is Hermy, Mrs. Beebe?" asked Hackett.

After a moment she said, rousing a little, "Thought—Dad a bit hard on her. Times—not so easy. She'll pay. People mostly do." She gave them the slow smile of a sleepy baby. "Good—all you people—take care of us so good," and she turned over and went peacefully to sleep.

"Damnation," said Mendoza. "And this is another one where we're late on the job. No use to turn the lab loose on the place, after the doctor and the daughter have been meddling around with pots and pans and dishcloths. I suppose the dutiful daughter—she strikes me as a practical housewife—cleaned the whole place up as soon as the ambulance left."

But they had to take a look at it.

It had stopped raining, this time for good; a high wind had blown the overcast away, and it was getting steadily colder.

The Beebes' humble business was down on Third Street, almost within spitting distance of headquarters, as Hackett put it. It was an old block of tired buildings; the Beebes' was the only single one, separated from its neighbors on one side by a narrow alley, on the other by a slightly wider driveway. It had begun life as a single house; now the entire ground floor was given over to the little grocery store. The hand-lettered sign hanging in the front wondow, *Closed for ilness,* was eloquent. There wasn't any front yard; the street had been widened years ago, right up to the sidewalk. At the end of the drive was a single old frame garage.

They walked down the drive looking for a back door, and Mrs. Travis hailed them from an upstairs window. They climbed a rickety wooden staircase and she let them into an old-fashioned square kitchen.

Mendoza looked around it and sighed. As he had thought, it was neat and clean. Everything old, from the black gas range to the square wooden table, but scrubbed and polished.

"I don't know exactly what you want to see," she said. "You can see for yourselves, they've been comfortable here but with the district changed so I'd be glad to see them out of it. They'd get something for the property, Dad owns it outright, and goodness knows Ed and I'd be more than happy, have them with us, we've got the extra room since the kids are both married." The upper floor here had been made over, a long time ago, into a good-sized apartment, two bedrooms, a living room, a dinette area off the kitchen, long hall and old-fashioned bathroom at the end.

"Mrs. Travis, according to Dr. Ferguson the arsenic was in some tunafish they had for lunch. I wonder if you'd know, had your mother prepared lunch after they came home from church, or—"

"Now that I can tell you, for whatever it's worth. She'd fixed it before. She usually did, that new minister is terrible longwinded and Dad does like his noon meal right on time. It was creamed tunafish, and as I told the doctor—that was before he went to talking about poison—it was perfectly fresh, I saw the can right there in the wastebasket myself where Mother'd put it after she got the white sauce together. And I know she'd opened it that morning because Dad always empties the wastebaskets first thing, he's fusssy about it. So likely Mother got the creamed tuna fixed before they left for church, that'd be about ten-fifteen, and left it in the double boiler all ready to heat up while she made the toast, after they got back. And that's where it was—what was left of it—when I got here. Of course I was busy looking after them and then I went to the hospital, of course, and after Dr. Ferguson saw them and I knew they was in good hands, I came back here to clean up. They hadn't—well, you know, they'd been terrible sick. And I was just about to throw out the rest of the tuna when the doctor called and wanted some of it, whatever they'd been eating, he said it might be bad, but it wasn't. The can wasn't bulged at all."

"Your mother mentioned a Hermy. Would you know who that is?"

She nodded. "Mrs. Howstatt—Hermione Howstatt. She's one of their regular customers, lives right around the corner. They've got a lot like that, and I will say a lot of people'd be sorry to see the store close, it's

handy for people here. Some old folks who don't drive
any more, can't get around easy—that's one thing
about Dad, he never had any trouble passing the test—
most of their trade's always been right in the neighborhood."

"Your mother implied that this woman owes them
money."

She nodded again. "Likely so. A lot of people
would. That's another reason they always had a steady
trade, even some people with cars can go farther. Big
markets, it's strictly cash, or these food stamps which I
don't hold with. But Dad, he knew how families get
tight for money sometimes, and he'd let people run
bills. Not long, and only people he knows are honest."

"I see. Well, we'd better check on that." It was the
first place Mendoza could think to look. "Does he keep
books?"

"They'll be in the store."

The store, downstairs, took them both back vividly
to the past: a past more sharply evoked by smell than
sight, the combined smells of the typical old-fashioned
grocery store, unground coffee, licorice, wieners and
luncheon meat not sealed in plastic, the old wood in
walls and uncovered floor, maybe of time itself. There
were shelves all round and a counter in the middle,
with an ancient cash register on it. Mrs. Travis reached
under the counter and produced a tome of a ledger.
"Dad always keeps the books up to date. But what
that could tell you—I just think you've all got to be
imagining it, nobody'd want to hurt Mother and Dad."

Hackett leaned on the counter. "You know, Mrs.
Travis, the locks here—anybody could get in without
any trouble. They're old pin-tumbler locks, just
straight warded keys. Almost any key would work
them—hasn't there ever been a break-in here?"

She looked worried. "I know," she said. "Ed used to
go on to Dad about it. No, we never had any trouble,
but then like I say a lot of people around know Mother
and Dad, they've been good neighbors to people,
they're respected. But the way the district's changing—
Dad did get a locksmith up once, but it'd have been

awful expensive, new locks. They're never both out at once except to church on Sundays, and they got those steel prong things to put under the doorknobs, so nobody could force their way in."

"But," said Hackett, "the steel rods were not under the doorknobs when they were out."

"Well, acourse not," she said.

"It seems," said Mendoza, who'd been looking at the last few pages of the ledger, "that ten or eleven people owed bills here. Mrs. Howstatt, a Pete Byrnes, Charles Drucker, Mrs. Miles, Mrs. Farley—nothing very big, eleven dollars, fifteen, eighteen, twelve—"

"Sure, like I said. That doesn't mean anything. It couldn't have anything to do with their getting sick. There's no sense in saying they were poisoned, who'd want to do that? Well, if you'll excuse me I've still got work to do upstairs, you look around wherever you want." She vanished up the narrow wooden stair at the rear of the store.

"*¿Dónde estamos ahora?*" said Mendoza. "There is no handle to this thing, Art. Who would want to? And I've been feeling haunted, and now I know why. Does all this remind you of anything?"

"I don't think so specially, what?"

"Coffin Corner," said Mendoza. "That haunted house over on Old High Street."

Hackett burst out laughing. "My God, you're right. But these people aren't nuts, Luis. Just like the doctor said, little ordinary people. Harmless. No handle is right."

Mendoza got up and wandered around the store, looking aimlessly at the packages of cereal, detergent, dog food, baby food, jams and jellies, cookies, packaged bread. He stopped over at the side and said, "Well." Hackett came to look, and there among the cleansers, soap, dishcloths and disinfectant, were two cartons labeled Mouse-Noh. The cartons were red and white, and bore a prominent warning on the bottom, Poisonous, keep out of the reach of children, if accidentally swallowed—

"Oh, I forgot to say," said Mrs. Travis, appearing suddenly again on the stairs, "if you're going to be talking to those people, I'd be obliged if you don't mention what the doctor said about poison. It couldn't be poison, but people might get funny ideas if they thought so. And if you find that Mrs. Howstatt at home, all I can say is you'd better leave the door open and be ready to get out, she'd talk the hind leg off a donkey."

Sergeant Lake was alone in the office at three-thirty, except for Landers and Higgins who had a suspect in one of the interrogation rooms. He was just starting a crossword puzzle, feeling more contented with life than he had for some time—the diet seemed to be working, he was down seven pounds and his pants didn't feel so tight—when the switchboard light flashed on and he plugged in. "Robbery-Homicide, Sergeant Lake."

"This is Frome, Traffic," said a hard businesslike voice. "Say, have you got a dick up there with an Italian name? I don't know what."

"What? Well, we've got a Nick Galeano, would that be him? Why?"

"Well, I don't know. Just a second." There was a pause, and then Frome said, "Yeah, he thinks that's the one."

"He's off today," said Lake. "What's this about?"

"*I* don't know," said Frome. "The things that happen on the job! All I know is, I get chased up to this school, and here's this kid saying something about a dead lady, he wants to tell this dick something—says the dick talked to him before, but he doesn't know where to go. Well I'm not a detective but I make like one and deduce if it's something about a dead lady your office'd be handling it. Only this Italiano isn't there, so what do we do now?"

"Well, we've got other detectives here," said Lake. "What dead woman is the kid talking about?"

"Somebody named Rittenhouse. You know anything about it?"

"Some," said Lake. "What's the kid's name?"

"Widgeon—Thomas Widgeon. He looks fairly dumb," said Frome.

"You'd better bring him in," said Lake. "There'll be somebody here to listen to him." And just what this was—

Grace came in before Frome arrived, and Lake told him about it. "That's funny," said Grace. "So he saw something after all, or remembered something. We'd written that one off—the lab didn't come up with a thing there, there were no leads on it at all, might have been any casual sneak-thief. I'll talk to him, Jimmy."

When the hardbitten patrolman brought Tommy Widgeon in, Wanda Larsen had come back to her desk, and Grace eased the boy over there into a chair. Wanda was good with kids, and Tommy looked scared to death. He had to be urged to sit down and then he sat bolt upright; he was shaking a little.

"My ma's gonna be awful mad," he said.

"Take it easy, Tommy. You remembered something—maybe something you saw at Mrs. Rittenhouse's place that day?"

"No, sir. I mean, yes, sir. I'm scared to tell but I'm scared not to because of going to hell like preacher says. I—I—I just didn't know what to do—I couldn't think about anything else, and I thought, tell Ma, and then I thought—I thought I'd just have to tell you anyway and Ma—" His mouth was trembling badly, and he tried to control his squeaky shaking voice. "It ain't easy for Ma—she works awful hard, I tried to help but I couldn't get many jobs, only—only—only Mis' Rittenhouse was nice and paid me to cut her grass. Ma said do a good job. Mis' Rittenhouse had some more money than most folk because her grown-up son got a good job and send her money, but she couldn't afford pay out for no-good work. I—I—"

"You're doing fine, Tommy." Wanda gave him a warm smile, encouraging. He gulped and fixed his eyes on Grace.

"Basketball," he whispered thinly. "It was the basketball. I—I grew a lot last year, I got to be pretty good at it, and the coach—the coach said I should be on the first team, see, that's the team that goes to play different schools and they put all about it in the school paper—and I like basketball, it's great, I mean besides that I just like to play. But you got to have the uniform, see. With the school colors and all, it's twenty-four dollars. And the coach, he said to tell Ma there's a special f—f—something, a fund?"

"Yes. For the uniform, if a boy can't afford it."

"Yes, sir. So I did. But Ma, she don't believe in taking charity, not no way. She wouldn't even take the gov'ment money when my dad died. The foreman tried tell her it wasn't no charity, but she wouldn't. She says it's something to do with a person's pride, you take charity so you got no pride left and then you got nothing. That's what she says. And she said I couldn't do like that, take charity about the uniform. But she didn't have twenty-four dollars neither, so I couldn't go on the team."

Grace looked at Wanda, and she looked at him, and then she picked up the phone and turned her back on both of them. Tommy gulped down a sob and brushed a dirty hand over his face.

"So what happened next?" asked Grace gently.

"I—I—I wanted be on that team! I wanted to the worst way—I knew I'd be good, I could maybe win some games for us! And I—came home—that day, lunch time—"

"You don't have lunch at school?" Grace, playing for time, looked at Wanda and she nodded.

"Yes, sir, Ma puts one up for me, she's at work all day, she sews ladies' dresses in a factory. But I—came home—because I'd thought—I'd kind of thought—maybe Mis' Rittenhouse'd let me have it, I thought I could tell her I'd work it out, take care her yard real good as long as it took, work it out like that, and that way nobody could say it was charity—and I knocked on her back door but she didn't come, and I wanted see her and ask, I went in, the door wasn't locked—and she—and she was asleep in the chair right there in the kitchen, and she had her purse in her lap, I see some money in it, and the devil he just tempted me, just that one second, take it and go and nobody ever know—" He was talking faster and faster now. "And I reached out and she woke up and saw, and she was mad, I was scared and she said dirty little thief and I knew she'd tell Ma and I just didn't know what I did but then she fell down and I saw some blood on her and I—and I—"

Somebody came into the room; Grace didn't turn to see. "Did you knock her down, Tommy?" He was remembering that she'd been a good-sized stout old lady, and the lab hadn't found any blood anywhere except on her.

"I had—I told—the other one, sir—the Italian one—I went there first, get my bicycle pump. For my bike tires. I had it—I guess I hit her with that—and I was so scared, I knew she'd tell Ma and Ma'd about die, think I could do such—and then—and then, when I got home from school there was a police car and Mis' Buckler said— I never wanted to hurt nobody! I never meant to— She was such a nice lady!" Tommy burst into loud sobs.

Grace turned. "I see why you called Juvenile," said the pretty blonde in uniform. "I heard most of it, I think. Officer King. What a mess, isn't it?"

"Say it twice," said Grace. As a rule he was a mild-mannered man, and as a reasonable man he knew you couldn't generalize about people from the standpoint of race or economics or education or religion or anything else; and he wasn't so convinced about environment versus heredity, either, because the same environments produced heroes and villains. If you wanted to be strictly logical about it, maybe the only answer was reincarnation and karmic debts and credits.

He stood up abruptly and looked at Tommy, bowed over weeping like a baby. A good boy and a good mother. And that earnest fundamentalist Matt Piggott would say indeed, the devil tempted him just that one second. A life spoiled, in one second? You couldn't know that until the life was lived.

He said, "For the first and probably only time I'm

just as happy we've got these lenient rules in. What'll happen?"

"You know," said Juvenile Officer King. "He's what, thirteen, fourteen?—a hearing, and probation until he's twenty-one. He sounds like a good boy, from a pretty good background. The prognosis, as they say, may be hopeful. Which isn't always the case."

"No," said Grace. He thought of plump brown Celia Ann at home. You could try your damnedest to raise the kids right, but sometimes things happened.

"You'll be getting in touch with the mother," said Officer King briskly.

"And I never in all my life hated a job worse," said Grace.

Galeano had enjoyed his day off. In between looking up the heisters and rapists, he'd been wandering around down by that Ford agency, talking to people in other businesses there, trying to get some idea of who had known Morrison, might have known about that money, and it was a tedious job. He was ready to give up on it; they'd never get anything there. Possibly they'd never know who shot Morrison.

He'd ridden down in the elevator with Grace the night before, and Grace had asked him if he knew who owned this paperback. "It's interesting, I could hardly put it down." Galeano didn't, but he borrowed it and started it over dinner in his bachelor apartment, with a couple of glasses of wine first. He found it interesting too—what a character that fellow had been!—and he finished it about three o'clock on Friday afternoon.

Marta was off this afternoon; he knew her schedule. He called her and persuaded her to go out to dinner with him. She had to be back at the restaurant by seven; they'd have an early dinner at that little Italian place.

She agreed, very correct and ladylike, and then she said, "You are very good to me, Nick. No, for me. Almost you make me think the world is not such a bad place to be."

"That's fine. Sure it isn't. Pretty good place, by and

large. And take it from me," said Galeano, "when a homicide dick can say that, after all he sees on the job, that's a testimonial. I'll pick you up at five."

She laughed and said, "Then, *auf Wiedersehen.*"

"What do you think?" said Landers.

"I think he's hot," said Higgins. "But very." He lit a cigarette and sat down at his desk. In the course of questioning the suspect he'd pulled his tie loose, he needed a shave at this time of day, and his gray suit was stained from where he'd swarmed up that bank this morning; he looked like the complete tough cop. Facing him, despite the black eye, Tom Landers was the complete contrast; people would be telling him he didn't look old enough to be a detective until he was a grandfather; he was slim, fresh-complexioned, innocent-looking. But they were both experienced, intelligent cops, and they liked what they had just turned up.

They had left him in an interrogation room while they talked it over.

"I like him the hell of a lot," said Higgins. "And one big reason, Tom, is his address."

"Oh, yes," said Landers. "Me too."

"And his pedigree," said Higgins. "And the fact that he hasn't got a car."

"Um-hum. But unless he comes apart, have we got enough to charge him on? What about the lab evidence—did you see the report?"

"It came in this morning. Kind of disappointing," said Higgins. "No latents except for the husband's and hers. Blood and hair from the blankets and sheets—Type O, the commonest, and pubic hair, black, Caucasian. Sperm on the sheets—she'd been raped all right. We've got enough to ask for a search warrant on his pad."

"Do any good?"

"I don't know, damn it. But I like him for it."

"Oh, so do I," said Landers.

Mendoza wandered in looking preoccupied and said, "Joyce Bradley's still hanging on. Guts you can say, in spades. Let's hold the good thoughts. Why are you still here?" It was five minutes past six.

"We've got a hot one," said Higgins, "for Wescott. I'll put it to you, Luis. Tell me if we hold him." He got out the Xerox from R. and I. "Rodney Niemeyer—skip the description, he's a big strong bastard forty-three now, pedigree of rape, robbery-rape, assault with intent, three counts of rape with violence altogether. Committed to Camarillo, in for two years, let out, another rape count, sent back to the loony hatch, in one year, out. He's living in a cheap apartment on Delta Street."

"*¡Como!*" said Mendoza.

"Yeah. Job as a short-order cook at a hamburger joint downtown," said Higgins. "He takes the bus, hasn't got a car. He's a loner and a nut, Luis. All the signs. He just sits there saying no, I don't know nothing about it, but I like him for Wescott. You can see."

"Mmh. The address. Six blocks from Scott Street." Mendoza knew this sprawling town by heart.

"Do we hold him? Just overnight, all we can, and get a search warrant for the apartment? Something might show."

"*Es posible.* I like him too. Get the warrant, just on the chance. Where does he say he was Tuesday night?"

"No alibi. In his apartment, alone. I don't think. Out roaming around and spotting that apartment, woman alone, as you deduced."

"Hold him," said Mendoza. "See if anything shows in the apartment. Did you hear that we'd cleared one up?—the Rittenhouse woman. I just met Jase going out. He was a little sad about it. The hell of a thing all right. Human nature—we do see a lot of it, boys."

6

Higgins took Niemeyer down to the Alameda jail; they could hold him twenty-four hours without a charge. Mendoza got the machinery started on the warrant, and they knocked off for the day.

On Saturday morning, with Lake and Landers off, and Sergeant Farrell sitting on the switchboard, Mendoza got in a little early and started to look back over all the odds and ends of this week, the various reports on various cases. They had been busier. Morrison, that looked like a dead end, the routine had turned up nothing. Hackett had been going to have a closer look at the son, see if he looked likely, if it had been a personal kill. There were still various heist jobs; just as the luck fell, sometimes they dropped on the heisters, sometimes not. Rittenhouse. Along with the routine legwork, they had to spend time at the clearing-up; there'd been an inquest on Morrison yesterday, with Palliser there to give evidence; there were inquests scheduled on Monday on Lila Wescott and Olga Anton. Nothing had come in from the pawnbrokers about Olga's jewelry.

He called the hospital. Joyce Bradley was holding her own; she had rallied slightly, and they were now saying she would live, but she was still unconscious.

He took up the night report and had just read about a new body found by Traffic in an alley off Jefferson, when the men began to come in. Farrell brought in the search warrant. "Just sent up."

Grace came into the office and said, "I'll be taking a little time off. Clean-up. The Widgeon boy—I said I'd sit in a little conference with Juvenile and Mrs. Widgeon. That poor damn woman—at least Juvenile

96

will be doing the paperwork on it and making the court appearance."

"Small favors," said Mendoza absently. The Traffic men had put a name to the body: Lenny Fritch, a known fag said to have a pedigree. There was a routine lab report: Huber, who was Huber?—attempted robbery, and he'd had an unregistered car. The lab now reported that they had traced it by the engine number and it had been stolen two months ago in New Mexico. Mendoza got up and went out to the communal office to share the new jobs. Another heist at a drugstore, a mugging with the victim in the hospital, a brawl in a bar with a man stabbed to death.

"And we've got that search warrant," he added to Higgins.

"More legwork," said Galeano, glancing over the report. "On the mugging, what's to do?—take us a month of Sundays to haul in everybody with that kind of record, and barring a definite description—but I suppose somebody'd better see this guy."

"And there seem to have been about twenty witnesses to the stabbing—Schenke got names and addresses, I see," said Palliser. "What a life. Well, the sooner we get on it the sooner we can get to the paperwork. And I don't doubt something else will be coming up. How's that nurse doing?"

"Fine—we'll probably hear something from her eventually."

Hackett, hearing about Niemeyer for the first time, said, "Jackpot. But will we get enough to make a charge stick, if he doesn't come to pieces?"

"There's the lab evidence, they can match up the hair and sperm," said Higgins. "Maybe something on his clothes—the reason I said, a warrant."

"So let's go look," said Mendoza. They all crowded into the Ferrari and went out to the address on Delta Street. It was an old three-story house cut into cubbyholes of rental units, larger apartments on the first two floors, single rooms on the third. They rang doorbells, looking for a householder to serve the warrant on, and raised only one tenant in a second-floor apartment, an elderly man in a bathrobe who said, "The owner don't live here, catch him, he lives Pasadena or somewheres, just comes once a month collect the rent, his name's Goss is all I know."

They had Niemeyer's key, and the tenant could tell them which was his room. They went in and Hackett said, "Don't break a blood vessel, Luis. Some people don't mind living in the middle of mess."

"*No lo niego,*" said Mendoza. "You take what's on top, I'll look at drawers." The single room was in monumental disorder, clothes strewn about at random as well as hanging in a makeshift closet curtained off; there were dirty paper plates, Dixie cups, magazines, newspapers, a few paperback books, all over the place. Underneath all the mess was sagging single bed, sheets gray with dirt, a couple of straight chairs, a table with an electric hot plate, a battered and dirty coffeepot sitting on it, and a small black and white TV, a plywood four-drawer chest.

They started to look around silently, and Higgins said presently, "How in hell anybody can live like this—"

"Not the average citizen, George," said Hackett. He was looking at the paperback books: they were mostly cheap pornography. Mendoza uttered a little exclamation. "You found something?"

"Come here to be witnesses." He'd just got to the bottom drawer of the chest. The others held underclothes, socks, shirts. This one was nearly empty: a little pile of miscellany in a heap, unfolded. "Pretty," said Mendoza, and lifted them out one by one: women's panties, brassieres, a pair of high-heeled shoes, a garter-belt, more panties.

"I haven't seen what the head doctors said about him," said Higgins distastefully, "but this kind of nut's so often what they call the fetishist. Little collections like that. Could even be souvenirs of women he's raped—not every rape gets reported."

"But this could be something definite, George." Mendoza singled out one pair of panties and held them up. They were white nylon briefs, and at one side of the front panel was a demure L in pink lace.

"Now that I like," said Higgins. "That's very gratifying."

"Provisionally. A good many female names start with L, but it's something."

They went on looking, but that was the best find they made. He only had one suit; the other clothes were old slacks and shirts, some torn, mostly dirty. They didn't know what he might have been wearing on Tuesday night, so they bundled all the clothes up to hand to the lab. They stopped off at Scott Street on the way back downtown.

Wescott had been released from the hospital; even if he'd gone back to work he wouldn't have left yet. They had to wait, after pushing the bell; in a few minutes he opened the door.

"Mr. Wescott, we'd like to show you something," said Mendoza. "If we can come in?"

Wescott stepped back silently. He wasn't planning to go to work, evidently: he was unshaven, wrapped in an old terry robe, and he looked haggard and ill. The apartment was subtly changed from even a few days of neglect; there was a pile of dirty dishes on the counter in the kitchen, a film of dust on the furniture in here, and the open door showed the bed unmade.

He had followed Mendoza's glance. "I—'ll have to leave this place," he said. "They let me out of the hospital, but I—couldn't stay here—I came back last night, start to pack—slept on the couch."

At a second glance, Mendoza thought they shouldn't have let him out of the hospital. He seemed to have dropped ten pounds; he looked dazed, and his eyes were unfocused. "Mr. Wescott," he said sharply, "would you look at these, please." He displayed the white nylon panties with the initial. "Could you say whether these belonged to your wife?"

Wescott looked. Slowly he nodded. "Lila—had some like that, pretty much. Yes, I think so. Why?"

"Are you sure?"

He took a breath and held it. "Leave me alone," he said. "I can't—I've got to think about—things. A funeral. I haven't called her mother yet—don't know how to say—"

"Mr. Wescott, we'd like a definite answer. Can you identify these as your wife's?"

"Yes," said Wescott. "Yes. If that's—" He turned away.

"Thanks so much," said Mendoza.

"So that ties him in tight," said Higgins in satisfaction. "Solid evidence. That's good."

Wescott turned. "Have you—have you arrested somebody—for Lila?"

"Let's say we have a good suspect," said Mendoza. "Thanks." They were all feeling gratified about this: four days' work on it, and it was the kind of thing that could have dragged on for months, but here was the hot suspect with the evidence building nicely.

Mendoza dropped Hackett and Higgins off in the lobby and delivered the clothes to the lab, asking priority on the job. "You're always so eager," said Scarne. "Rome wasn't built in a day."

"We can only hold him until six," said Mendoza, "and it'd be nice to know sooner whether we'll have enough to make a charge, Bill. Otherwise it could get complicated. We let him go and two days later you tell us he's the one we're after, and he's flown the coop."

"So what are we looking for?" Scarne wrinkled his nose at the pile of clothes.

"Maybe blood, hair, sperm, to match the Wescott kill. Anything to put him in that apartment. You gathered in a lot of this and that there."

"We did. If there's threads off that carpet, anything like that, I can probably match them up for you. I'll have a try for the hair and sperm first, that'd be definite."

"And don't forget the deadline." Mendoza ruminated, watching him carry off the unsavory bundle. Saturday morning. He might raise somebody at the D.A.'s office, but there was no point until they had something definite from the lab. But he wanted a look at Niemeyer for himself; Hackett and Higgins had gone over to the jail to question him again. Mendoza went to join them.

He was a little surprised at his first look at Rodney Niemeyer: not exactly the crude lout he'd expected. Niemeyer, sitting hunched at a table in an interrogation room, was not bad-looking, a tall broad-shouldered man with graying black hair; at first glance, you wouldn't pick him as the deviate of any kind, as a mental case. But appearances meant so little sometimes.

"We'd like to hear some answers, Rodney," Higgins was saying. "About your little collection of female dainties. Where'd you get them all?"

Niemeyer looked at him from under his eyebrows and was silent.

"Those pretty white nylon panties with the pink L," said Hackett. "What's the L stand for, Rodney?"

Niemeyer shook his head and said nothing, Mendoza leaned on the wall and watched him.

Conway was still nursing his cold at home, so with Landers off they were two men short. The overnight cases would make some new work; they divided up the legwork and got on it. Galeano went down to R. and I. and pulled the file on Lenny Fritch, who was a longtime fag with a string of little counts, petty theft, D. and D., purse-snatching, possession of narcotics, There was a next of kin listed, his mother, at a recent address; Galeano went to find her, brought her down to the morgue and got the body formally identified. She didn't do much carrying on; he suspected she was slightly under the influence at the moment. He'd take a bet that Fritch would turn out to be another O.D.; he'd been a known user. Wait for the autopsy.

Palliser and Glasser had taken the brawl in the bar; with Grace tied up at Juvenile, seeing there were about twenty witnesses to cover, they'd taken Wanda along. Galeano, remembering that paperback, left it in the tray on Wanda's desk and sat down to type an initial report on Fritch. When he finished that he went over to

Central Receiving to see the man who'd been mugged last night. His name was Rassky, and he was a projectionist at a movie house on Fourth; he'd been on the way to his car after work. The mugger had got about four bucks and his wristwatch.

"Describe him?" said Rassky. "How would I do that? It's dark, it's cold, and I'm anxious to get home to bed—I think I'm going to quit that job, I don't mind the hours but they only run Mexican movies and I don't know a word of Spanish—all of a sudden this guy comes at me behind and I go down, bang, and that's all I know."

"Did he have a weapon of any kind?"

"Yeah, I think he did—that I can say. He sure didn't hit me with his fist. It felt like a hammer, I tell you, but I wouldn't know what."

The casual mugger there wasn't any way to look for, but Galeano had one small thought. A hammer? The Anton woman, the doctor said, could have been killed with a hammer. Also probably by the casual mugger.

He went back to the office and wrote a report on that. He felt a little lonely, there all by himself; usually there were several men in at once, or they were out hunting in couples. It was getting on to twelve o'clock, and he was starting out for lunch when Farrell hailed him and said there was a new call just in.

Galeano, in spite of being a bachelor—largely of inertia, and he was thinking differently now, serious about Marta—was a strongly family-oriented man; he approved vaguely of happy families; and what he found himself looking at next left a bad taste in his mouth.

It was a house up on Berendo Street, and the ambulance was just arriving. The house was bastard-Spanish stucco with a mean little front yard and a twelve-year-old Chevy in the drive. Inside, there was a sparse collection of ugly old furniture in five small rooms, a woman bleeding and unconscious on the living-room floor, the paramedics working on her, and a stout square man in a tight navy suit complaining loudly.

"Carelessness—sheer carelessness, and most inconsiderate, that's the kindest thing I can say! I'm always reminding Edna to lock the doors and windows at all times, the shocking crime rate these days—and in broad daylight! Broad daylight, I can't be away from the house an hour to run a few errands—and that was Edna's fault too, forgetting to buy razor blades—without this happening! Some robber getting in—the back door was wide open! Wide open! *And* the front door! Criminal carelessness—though that may have been the children's fault, they're even worse than Edna—"

Galeano showed the badge and squatted down beside the woman. She was thin, dark, nondescript, in a faded print housedress and cotton stockings. "What's the verdict?" he asked the paramedics.

They shrugged. "Looks as if she's been stabbed. Couple of deep cuts in the chest, but she'll live, I think. Couldn't see a knife around, he probably took it with him." They got her onto the stretcher. "His name's Buller."

"Mr. Buller," said Galeano, getting up, "just a few questions. This is your wife?"

"Yes, yes, of course. Careless! And where the children are—I do not like them gadding about all over, they had strict orders to stay close to home—and I come back to find this—this muddle! This unforgiveable upset!"

"Mr. Buller, your wife seems to be pretty badly hurt. She's being taken to the emergency hospital."

"Yes, yes, I daresay."

"Does it look as if anything's missing here?" There was an old TV in the living room, but the sneak-thief wouldn't have been thinking so big. Galeano, ignored by Buller, walked through the house quickly, glancing around: no drawers open, everything fairly neat. In the kitchen, he looked out to a side yard. There was a clothesline with some clothes on it, a big laundry basket. No marks on either front or back door, but both unlocked. He thought she'd probably been out in the yard, hanging up clothes; the thief took the chance to sneak in, and she came in and caught him. Maybe the neighbors had noticed something.

"And just where have you been?" Buller's voice rose again. "You know I told you to stay around!"

"We were just over in the Snyders' yard." A thin young voice. Galeano went back to the living room.

"I do not want you associating with that family. They are riffraff, as I've told you before."

There were two children: a girl maybe thirteen, a boy a year or so younger. They looked like little white rabbits, wary and defensive; obviously afraid of him. "We saw the police car," said the boy. "What happened? Is—is Mother all right?"

"There was a robber, and all her fault for leaving the doors unlocked. How often have I told you all—"

Galeano gave up on it. As far as he could see the sneak-thief hadn't got anything, probably been scared off, just striking out with the knife. Edna's bad luck. If anything was missing Buller would let them know in a hurry. Ask the neighbors, write a report.

The neighbors on one side were out; Mrs. Snyder on the other side said that was terrible, a thief hurting poor Mrs. Buller, but she'd been at the back making the beds, she'd got all behind this morning, and hadn't seen a thing. There was a thin girl about twelve, who said she'd been in the backyard with Joe and Linda just fooling around, they hadn't seen anything either.

Galeano was starving. He stopped at the first decent-looking place he passed on the way back and had a hamburger. Then he went back to the office to write the report.

"It is," said Mr. McNair, "a prime piece of property. Very sound investment."

"Well, I'm afraid I just don't see us living here," said Alison. She looked around at walls of glass, the paved courtyard beyond with Grecian statuary and a row of Italian cypresses down the drive. "I don't care much for modernistic architecture, and my husband —" She could hear what Luis would say.

Mr. McNair sighed. "I could show you a place in

Westwood. Just the size you want and only five years old, two-story Spanish, a balcony on the master suite—"

"And a pool," said Alison.

"I'm afraid so. You know, Mrs. Mendoza, any house of the size you want, in such spacious grounds, is almost sure to have a swimming pool."

"I suppose if it came to that," said Alison thoughtfully, "we could have it taken out. Dug up, and—"

Mr. McNair groaned involuntarily. "But you couldn't seriously consider—destroying so much resale value—"

"Well, really," said Alison, "we're not intending to move every two years or so. I want a place to *settle* in. Permanently."

"Mrs. Mendoza," he said patiently, "estate-size properties such as you have in mind are rather rare anywhere in the city. You'll have to compromise some of your specifications, if you want that much space and square footage."

"Oh, I realize that. But I'm afraid this won't do," said Alison. It was rather a pity: there'd be a glorious view at night, over all of Santa Monica. But Luis would take one look at this place and say something about people living in glass houses. "Have you got anything else to look at?"

"Oh, there are a number of places to show you," said Mr. McNair. He didn't sound very enthusiastic, but he was game, thinking about the commission.

Mendoza was feeling vaguely dissatisfied about several things; he couldn't pin it down. He didn't feel at all inclined to go and help out on the legwork. He hoped the lab would come through with that definite evidence on Niemeyer. He sat at his desk and thought about Lila Wescott, and Olga Anton, and Morrison, and Tommy Widgeon, poor little devil. And about the arsenic. "Coffin Corner," he muttered, and presently got up and went out to the communal office.

Nobody was there but Wanda. She was sitting at her desk eating a sandwich and reading a paperback. She apologized for the sandwich hastily. "There's so much paperwork to catch up on, I thought it'd save time—"

"So you find a good book to spend your lunch hour on." Mendoza grinned at her and went on out. He picked up a rather tasteless sandwich in the canteen and proceeded down to Third Street, to the Beebes' little store and immediate neighborhood. Mr. Beebe's rudimentary bookkeeping had included addresses for the customers who owed back bills; and Mendoza didn't really think that anybody had mixed the Mouse-Noh in the creamed tuna for such a reason, but at least it gave him some people to talk to who knew the Beebes, knew the area. Possibly something would emerge.

He saw Pete Byrnes, who was a widower living in a tiny apartment with a parakeet. Byrnes had been sorry to hear the Beebes were so sick, salt of the earth they were, good folks. "Don't know what I'd do sometimes, they didn't let me have a bit on credit till next month's check comes. I got the money I owe now, and I was wondering if they might need it—doctors and hospitals awful expensive now."

Mendoza saw Mrs. Farley, a meek old lady bent over with arthritis and nearly blind. She'd been sorry to hear about the Beebes, such good kind people they were, not many like them these days, Mr. Beebe even delivered her groceries sometimes when she was feeling too bad to get out. "I owe them a little money too, I reckon to pay it up as soon as I get the Social Security, might be they need it."

He saw Charles Drucker, a cheerful rosy-cheeked man with one leg, who had a shoe-repair shop a block away from the store. He'd been sorry to hear about the Beebes, and it was damned inconvenient the store being closed, he usually went there for most everything.

Mendoza told himself he was wasting time. Nothing was going to emerge. Obviously the only contact the Beebes had with these people, their neighbors in general, was merely commercial, if casually friendly. Ordinary quiet people indeed, the Beebes, living humdrum lives, never out except to church on Sunday. He felt unreasonably annoyed at the Beebes.

He'd left the Ferrari on the street almost in front of the store. There was no chance that the immediate neighbors on either side could tell them anything: one was a tailor shop, one a cleaner's, and both would be closed on Sunday. The second-story space of both those buildings was leased for storage: nobody would be there on Sundays or most weekdays.

He got out his keys to unlock the car, and paused. A woman was peering in the front window of the store. She turned away, caught his glance, and asked immediately, "Oh, do you know the Beebes? Are they still in the hospital?"

"Yes," said Mendoza. "You're a friend of theirs?"

"Oh, yes, not as *old* a friend as some people here but I can certainly say a *friend*." She chuckled. She was a vast-bosomed, ample matronly woman in her sixties or older, with three chins and brightly hennaed hair. "I was so *relieved* to hear they're better, Mrs. Miles was telling me, such dear good people, I was so *sorry* to hear they were sick, food poison somebody told me. They're still in the hospital, you said?—I must go and see them, they'll be lonely there, especially if they're getting better, and only the daughter to come see them—I always feel so *sorry* for people without big families, I had ten myself and a good many brothers and sisters, and it does make a difference. I always say with a big family there's *somebody* to sustain and cheer you in sorrow, but if there's only one or two, well, what *have* you? And just as the Bible says, bread on the waters, and goodness knows the Beebes have been so *kind* to me, I always say—"

Mendoza opened the car door, recalling Helen Travis's warning. "Would you be Mrs. Howstatt?"

"Why, yes, that's me, how did you know? I don't recollect seeing you around here before. Yes, I'm Mrs. Howstatt, it's a funny name, isn't it, and I thought twice before taking it—he was my third, you know—but after all a name's not that important and I was born Smith— Well, I can see you're in a hurry, I'll tell the Beebes you were asking about them—"

Mendoza switched on the ignition and fled. That vague old windbag was the one who'd been at the Beebes on Sunday morning; but if she'd provided the arsenic, he couldn't see why. It was more likely that somebody had got in while they were at church; but again, why, and who?

There was just no handle to it.

He started back for the office, but changed his mind halfway there and ambled up Glendale Boulevard at random. Go back to his desk and sit there fidgeting waiting for the lab to call.

Morrison. Probably that was dead-ended; shove it in Pending. The new bodies might present more of the tedious routine to do, or get cleared up right away. He hoped Joyce Bradley was doing better. Another mugging on the street last night, and no way to catch up to those, unless one of the pawnbrokers could tie up some loot, or one of their informants had a grudge or needed a few bucks for wine or dope. Olga Anton . . .

Hackett would tell him it didn't matter a damn, was extraneous; and of course it was. By all the earmarks, Olga Anton had run into the casual mugger too, and died of it, which did sometimes happen. But how in hell had she happened to be down there?—that upright, sufficiently affluent woman with her elegant apartment, loving family, and carefree life?

That apartment . . . He'd had a dissatisfied feeling about that too, for no reason. And for no reason now he went on up to Hollywood, turned on Hillhurst and again on Los Feliz, and parked in front of that place.

The cold-eyed manager recognized him, but examined the badge again before he took him upstairs. Mendoza stood in the middle of the living room and lit a cigarette, and a number of vague, slightly unrelated thoughts wandered through his mind. That little old-fashioned house, living there all those years. Mother a little straitlaced. I always say with a big family you've got somebody. Plainfield, Illinois.

The girls had been here, starting to sort things out.

Very likely the funeral was scheduled for Monday or Tuesday. In the bedroom, there were things from the closet laid out on the bed; in the kitchen, all the dishes and silver left in cupboards and drawers—they would belong to the apartment. The living room undisturbed too: only her personal things to take away, from the bedroom. He sauntered back in there.

The dresses were mostly plain, practical everyday dresses: nylon prints, navy blue, black. No pantsuits, he noticed. One heavy lined wool coat, heavier than she'd ever need here; that was a relic of Plainfield. Neatly folded underwear, plain white nylon; stockings. He looked into the closet: a few clothes still hanging there, and neat on a rack on the floor, six or seven pairs of shoes: those very small shoes.

The black velvet dress was the best, the most sophisticated, she'd had. Mendoza would take a bet it hadn't been her choice; he saw her shopping with the two girls, oh, Mother, it's perfect for you, so becoming, and the small-town Middle-Western housewife a little doubtful. But she'd been a good-looking woman, a pretty little woman. The girls responsible for the silver hair-rinse too? Fifty-five. Married at nineteen, and it had been a happy marriage. Dad's signet ring.

That old-fashioned house, and then this apartment. She hadn't brought anything from Plainfield but her clothes.

He opened drawers and rummaged. He wasn't looking for anything; that was at random too.

Probably they had told themselves they were thinking only of Mother's welfare. A nice new apartment, not so much housework; she should take things easy, enjoy life in the nicer climate. So much better to have Mother living here, all be together. But had it? The young people were considerate kind young people, but the men were working, the girls would have friends and interests of their own, and what had it been— thought Mendoza, straightening from the bottom drawer of the chiffonier—but dinner at Sue's, dinner at Ginny's, once a week, the occasional shopping trip and lunch, the occasional dinner out?

She had said the church here was too big, people not friendly. He wondered how big a town Plainfield was. He eyed the newspaper on top of the chiffonier idly, and then his interest sharpened. A plebeian sort of paper for this apartment: a tabloid, with the sensational stories, human-interest stuff, sometimes scandal, the cute animal photos. No, the small-town lady hadn't liked the big town, or probably this apartment. No personal touches here—and most women had a kind of nest-building instinct.

He opened all the drawers of the lefthand bed-chest, one by one; they were empty. He didn't know what he was doing here.

Nest building. Alison looking for a bigger house, more property. A Tudor estate, a Victorian monstrosity. God alone knew what she'd find in the end. But she was sensible enough in the general way, he didn't think she'd settle on anything impossible, though you never knew, of course, with a redheaded Scots-Irish girl.

He opened all the drawers of the righthand bed-chest; they were empty. The girls had done an efficient job: the piles of underwear, stockings, handkerchiefs, scarves, probably from these drawers. An open suitcase on the floor where they'd begun to pack. Only the white drawer-lining left—he slammed the bottom drawer, and it bounced open again slightly—new furniture, not like solid old stuff—and he heard something shift inside.

He opened the drawer again. The lining paper had slid forward, and there was something under it—a thin sheaf of something. "*¡Ca!*" said Mendoza, and took out the liner. There were three letters in the bottom of the drawer.

"*¿Y qué es esto?*" he said to himself interestedly, and went back to the living room, sat down on the couch, lit a cigarette and looked at the top letter.

It was handwritten on fairly good quality paper, with a matching envelope. The writing was in ink, round and careful; there was no letterhead, just a date three weeks back. "Dear lady, It was nice that you answered my advertisement in the paper. I want to be honest and open all the way, so I will say at first I am 59 and a widower, two years, with one boy 28 and married, two kids. I have a well paid job and will have a good pension when I retire, and I own a nice two-bedroom house here which is all paid off. I have been lonely since my wife died because my boy Jim lives in Arizona—"

"*¡Diez millones de demonios desde el infierno!*" said Mendoza. He picked up the second letter.

It was typed, on an old machine with elite type, and bore a date a month back. "Dear Mrs. Anton, your sincere and welcome letter arrived today. As you say it is difficult for those in our circumstances to make new friends in new surroundings. Of course you want to know something about me, I am 54 and single, without dependents, and have a good job with the Board of Education. I like going to the theater and am partial to folk music and old-fashioned dancing—"

"I will be eternally damned!" said Mendoza. "The lonely hearts ads—I will be—" He went back to the bedroom and snatched up the tabloid, riffled through it to a double page of small print laid out in ads. *Tucson area, gent. 45, nonsmoker, like meet Christian lady 35-40 for companionship. South. Calif., gent 56, widower, Christian, social drink and smoke, like meet lady 45-50. L.A., gentleman 60, lonely widower, owns house and car, good job, like meet Christian lady for friendship.*

"By all the archangels in heaven!" said Mendoza. He gathered up the tabloid and the letters and started back for the car.

When Hackett came in at four-thirty the office was humming. There were four citizens in, presumably to make statements, talking to Wanda, Galeano, Glasser and Grace. The one sitting beside Galeano's desk had a loud arrogant voice and was laying down the law about something. One of the interrogation rooms was in use and Hackett deduced that Palliser and Higgins were talking to somebody there, on the brawl in the bar or something.

He shoved open the door of Mendoza's office. "We can put the Morrison thing in Pending, Luis. We both had the bright thought, drama student Gordon setting Daddy up, but it's a dud. By everything I've heard from Morrison's casual dates, teachers and students at the Pasadena Playhouse, Gordon and his father were pretty close, real pals. And Gordon's closest pals, the ones he shares the pad with, were all correctly in class when Morrison was shot. I think—"

"Yes. *Probablemente,*" said Mendoza. He was sitting at his desk shuffling the well-worn deck of cards. It wasn't once a year he sat in a hand of draw now, but he still thought better with the cards in his hands. "You know what, Art? She was lonely. Olga. Those two well-meaning girls fetched her out here away from everybody she knew, and planted her in that damned impersonal apartment. So nice for Mother. And she didn't know what to do with herself."

"What?" said Hackett.

"She was only fifty-five. Still healthy and enjoying life. Or she had been. Very likely back in Plainfield she had scads of friends, interests—her house, the yard, the church. It could be there'd have been, in time, some congenial widower. But here, she was lost."

"What are you talking about?"

Mendoza laughed and put down the cards. "Believe it or not, Art, she'd been answering letters in a lonely hearts column. I don't know which, but quite likely in this tabloid paper—it was in the apartment. The letters I found by accident. I don't know if those ads are screened in any way, I shouldn't think so. In this tabloid there's only box numbers given. But, cynic though I am, I might guess that most of them are sincere enough—there must be a lot of lonely people in the world, and you don't always run into the congenial companions just by chance at church, or walking in the park." He shoved across the letters, and Hackett looked at them.

"Well, for God's sweet sake!" he said.

"Mmh, little surprise. She must have been feeling damned lonely and lost, Art, to do such a thing. We can deduce that she wasn't a letter writer, or she'd have occupied herself keeping in touch with all the old friends back there, to fill up her time. She'd probably never got in the habit, she'd always had her friends right around her. Now here she was out here, alone to all intents and purposes—seeing her daughters once or twice a week, and that was about it. Not a reader either—she didn't bring any books with her, no library books around. And she'd have been—she was—very, very cautious about it, you notice." Mendoza sat back in the desk chair and swiveled around to look at the Hollywood hills stark against a vivid blue cold sky. "The proper small-town lady. You can have a look at those ads. Christian, non-smoker, non-drinker, lonely widowers. As a kind of last resort, I think, she tried that as a way to meet somebody, maybe somebody to introduce her to a circle of new friends. But she wasn't foolish enough to give her name and address out blind. You notice those letters are addressed to a box number—she got a post-office box, probably at the Hollywood station. And she'd have been very careful about the ads she answered." He laughed. "I wonder if she got any more letters. She was ashamed of it, you see, the way she hid those under the drawer-liner. But, I would deduce, these three letters are the ones she hung on to, the men she'd picked out as sounding the most likely—mmh—congenial companions. And if anything had ever come of it—say she liked one of the lonely widowers, they got on fine, and enjoyed going around together, even decided to get married—she'd never have told the girls how she met him. She'd have said, at church, or walking in the park."

"For God's sake!" said Hackett. "This—are you tying it up with the homicide? That she got in touch with a Bluebeard in the lonely hearts column?"

"That's damn farfetched," said Mendoza. "I don't know, Art. All I will say is, I'd like to chase down the writers of those letters and ask some questions. About whether it had come to anything. If they'd ever arranged a meeting."

"Yes, I see what you mean," said Hackett. "Has the lab called yet?"

"Not yet," said Mendoza, and Bainbridge walked in and sat down beside the desk.

"Mostly," he said, "it's a damned dull job, Luis. Just sometimes the little surprises turn up. I've got one for you now."

"On what?" Mendoza was shuffling the cards again.

"On your torture rape kill." Bainbridge got out a cigar and nipped the end off. "You found out anything about the arsenic, by the way?"

"Not yet. You've done the autopsy—what showed?"

"Well," said Bainbridge, "I don't know anything about the woman's background. You will. Not every victim is simon-pure innocent just because of being a victim. Oh, she died of suffocation, by the way—the gag was rammed down her throat. Bruises and some bites on the body—really nothing out of the way—"

"What the hell do you mean?" asked Hackett. "That whip—"

"Well, yes. I suppose we're all grown-up," said Bainbridge. "But, yes, she'd been flogged, but not to draw blood. What interested me, and what'll interest you, is that she'd been actively cooperating."

They stared at him. "Can you mean what I think you mean?" asked Mendoza.

"Oh, yes. Vagina in a tumescent state—very definitely she was sexually aroused. She died, in fact, in an orgiastic state," said Bainbridge, and puffed his cigar.

"*¡Diez millones de demonios desde el infierno!*" said Mendoza for the second time in two hours. "But that's—"

"Goddamnit, it was a break-in!" said Hackett. "Rape by violence! The evidence was clear on that—"

"That's what you said," said Bainbridge. "Interesting, isn't it? You know about the evidence. And we've all had some experience of human nature. There could be answers. Could be she was a nympho."

"Good God, with a violent rapist?" asked Hackett.

"I could quote you case histories. It happens."

"My God, that husband," said Hackett. "He'd be— he'd go over the line if he—"

Mendoza picked up the cards again. "Well, we're getting the little surprises, aren't we?"

7

Higgins and Palliser came in, attracted by argument, and agreed with Hackett. "Of all the damned queer things," said Higgins, "that's the queerest we've ever had, and when I say queer—"

"The vernacular, yes," said Mendoza. "It reminds me of the old joke—"

"We've heard it, we've heard it."

"—When rape is inevitable, relax and enjoy it. But you're wrong, Doctor—she wasn't a nympho or the husband would have known it, or would he? What this does tell us is that she'd probably slept around a good deal, for one thing." Bainbridge nodded shortly and the others looked at him inquiringly. "I don't have to spell it out for grown-ups. The average woman, faithful to one husband, reacts to the rapist with disgust and fear—the woman who's played around with a lot of men just isn't capable of the same reaction, to the same extent. They do say, the husband's always the last one to suspect. But the other thing this says is even funnier, isn't it?"

"She liked it—she was getting a kick out of it," said Hackett slowly.

"*¡Cómo no!*" said Mendoza softly. "The Freudians have the word for it. And that, you know, must have been one hell of a surprise for the rapist."

"My good God above!" said Hackett, and began to laugh. "Surprise! You really think—"

"Case histories," said Bainbridge. "You'd be surprised, even you sophisticated cops, the things that can happen in that field. It's very possible it was a surprise to her. I'll say this, I don't think there was any inten-

116

tion to kill her—that was probably an unlucky accident."

"You think," said Higgins incredulously, "that he
got in and jumped her, tied her up and so on, and then
she discovered she was enjoying it?"

"That's what it looks like."

"Look, if she'd been playing around," said Hackett,
"why couldn't it have been one of the boyfriends? She
knew her husband wouldn't be home— Hell, but—"

"Yes, there was the break-in," said Mendoza. "It's a
queer one, but when you think about it, it doesn't
change the nature of the case. Not really. It's still a
break-in and rape. Damn, I wonder if the lab's got
anything—" Mendoza picked up the phone and told
Farrell to get him the lab.

"On Niemeyer—but this puts him right out of the
picture," said Higgins with a scowl.

"Oh, does it, George? Can it? Nothing of the sort.
He's still damn well in the picture. It crossed my mind
this morning, he's really not a bad-looking fellow, well
set up. I won't say that if somebody black as the ace of
spaces, generally resembling King Kong, had jumped
her, she wouldn't have screamed and struggled, but
given experience and—mmh—the kink she apparently
had, I can see her relaxing to the inevitable with
Niemeyer. Or one like him. I still think he's a hot
suspect."

"Well, put like that—"

"Scarne? Have you got anything for us?"

"No," said Scarne. "Sorry. No sperm samples to
compare. The hair doesn't match with any we picked
up off the bed. Nothing on the clothes to place him in
that apartment, but he could have been wearing different clothes."

"Damnation," said Mendoza. He put down the
phone. *"Nada.* And it still doesn't say anything definite. He could, as Bill points out, have been wearing
other clothes, and subsequently got rid of them. He's
got kinks, but he's not a fool. But we haven't got enough
to charge him, we'll have to let him go."

"You seriously think he's still the best bet?" asked Palliser.

"I do—chiefly on account of his address. Proximity. This is just a complication, and another thing, you know what it would mean in court." Mendoza slapped the cards down viciously. "The intent may have been rape, gentlemen of the jury, but how could it have been actual rape when the victim was taking pleasure—"

"This really is the damnedest," said Palliser.

"And the only other thing it says," added Mendoza sardonically, "is that Lila was damned discreet. If she'd had boyfriends calling there when hubby was at work, that apartment manager would have known, the neighbors, there'd have been gossip. But that's got to be the answer. Yes, I still think Niemeyer is the hottest suspect, but I doubt if we'll ever nail him for it." He was annoyed, and amusedly they saw that he was annoyed at Lila. "Women!" he said. "Doesn't it come somewhere in Chaucer, nine cocks to satisfy one hen! And because she was a tramp on the sly, with a kink, we'll never nail anybody for it. Oh, we can try. Leave him alone tomorrow, haul him in again on Monday and lean on him some more—but even if we get him to admit it, with this damned complication, we'd be lucky to get him recommitted to Camarillo for a while." He got up and reached for his hat. "I'm going home. Thanks so much for your invaluable help, Doctor, I don't know what we'd do without you."

"Well, at least," said Hackett philosophically as the outer door shut behind Mendoza, "it makes a funny story to tell our wives."

Saturday night was usually busy for Robbery-Homicide, and that one was no exception. The night watch left a report longer than usual: two heists, another mugging, another hit-run, a freeway crash with two dead. Except for the heists, that wouldn't pose much legwork, they could hope.

Palliser was annoyed, reading Schenke's report on the first heist. "I will be damned, here that pair is again, at least the descriptions—elderly men, a long

gun. A dairy store this time. I will be damned. I'd
better hear what the witness has to say, just to see if he
can add anything. And there are still six witnesses to
see on that bar knifing—"

"What was that?" asked Galeano.

"Oh, argument over a girl. Two young louts—of
course they were both Italian—getting into a knife
fight."

"These foreigners," said Galeano, yawning. He'd
really intended to get up early and go to Mass this
morning, but he'd forgot to set the alarm. He reflected
that if he ever did get Marta to marry him, probably
she'd see he got to Mass regularly every Sunday. Very
strongminded girl, you got past her nice soft exterior.
Well, he wouldn't really mind.

Palliser went out to find the proprietor of the dairy
store, who said amiably he didn't mind coming in to
look at some pictures, he'd know that one fellow again
anywhere. "Seventy-five if he's a day, and a big
hooked nose. The other one must have been just as
old, and a thirty-ought rifle, of all things—"

"Are you sure about that?"

"Yeah, yeah, I know a deer rifle when I see one."

Palliser settled him down with some books of mug-
shots, but without much hope that he'd recognize any.
He didn't think the senior citizens would be in records,
when the other witnesses hadn't spotted them: they
sounded fairly distinctive characters.

Galeano, that good workhorse detective, plodding
on at the routine, called the hospital and was told that
Mrs. Buller could be talked to; she was out of danger,
would be released tomorrow. He went to talk to her;
he was prepared to be sorry for the downtrodden wife
of that bully, but he just felt exasperated with her—
there wasn't much to choose between them. She looked
at him suspiciously out of little cold eyes and took her
time about answering questions; it was like pulling
teeth to get anything out of her. She said in a wooden
voice, yes, that was what happened, the thief got in
when she was hanging up clothes, and no, she couldn't
say what he looked like, it had happened too fast.

"Didn't you get any kind of look at him, Mrs. Buller, when he struck at you with the knife?"

"No," she said, and shut her thin lips tight together.

Galeano thanked her. There wasn't much in it, but the paperwork had to be done. And he'd no sooner got back to the office than he had Buller in, loud and angry, to report that there was nothing missing from the house. "You asked me to look, to be sure. I know we have to cooperate with the police, but all this has been such a confounded nuisance—wasting time, and all due to one moment's carelessness!" He fumed and fussed at having to wait while Galeano typed a statement for him to sign, and presently fumed and fussed his way out.

Grace strolled over and said, "That's a pleasant customer. Not very concerned about his wife in the hospital, is he?"

"Oh, it was all her fault, not locking the doors," said Galeano. "Wouldn't you know he works at the local Social Security office? Typical petty bureaucrat."

"Human nature, human nature," said Grace. "Did you hear what Bainbridge came up with on that Wescott woman?"

Hackett and Higgins, basely taking advantage of seniority and leaving the new legwork to underlings, had thrashed out the little surprise on Lila, coming grudgingly to accept Mendoza's opinion. If there was, they agreed, one subject Luis knew backward and forward, it was females. "Come to that," added Hackett, "it was damned queer about that Anton woman answering the lonely hearts ads. Last thing you might have expected one like that to do."

"I didn't hear about that," said Higgins.

Hackett was telling him about it when Sergeant Lake relayed a call, passed on by the main desk downstairs. It was a Dr. Hooper at a clinic up on Virgil, who wanted to report that he had a patient in the office with a gunshot wound in him. The patient

had offered an explanation, but the man was a stranger
to Hooper, who was correctly reporting to the police as
per regulations. "Thanks very much, Doctor," said
Hackett. "Serious wound?"

"Well, that's the other rather peculiar circum-
stance," said Hooper. "The wound is some days old,
badly infected, and when he hasn't asked any medical
attention until now, I thought there was—"

"Something fishy about it," said Hackett. "Hang on
to him—we'll be right with you. George, you don't
suppose this guy could be the one with Morrison's
bullet in him?"

"Let's go and see." Higgins was interested. "What
the lab figured out, that sixth bullet had to go somewhere."

At the clinic, they found Hooper waiting for them:
he was a serious, spectacled young man. This was one
of a number of private emergency medical clinics
springing up over the county; the police were aware
that most of them were profitable abortion mills, but
these enlightened days there was nothing illegal about
it any more, by the letter of the law. The patient was
still here; he would be sent to the hospital for further
treatment, the arm was in a badly infected state, a
threat of gangrene. Hooper had, at the patient's re-
quest, had his nurse call the nearest relative.

As they all crowded into the little treatment room,
the patient glanced up nervously and said, "Who're
you?" He was lying flat on the metal table with his
shirt off: a wiry, dark fellow in the thirties with a
tough broken-nose face, and a lot of hair all over him.
There was a thick bandage on his upper left arm.

Hackett showed him the badge. "Oh, now, boys," he
said, and gave them a wide friendly grin, "the doc
didn't need to call cops. I'm not a gangster, fellas—I
told him how it happened, it was a damn fool thing to
do but it was strictly an accident, see? I was checking
over my gun, see if it needed oiling or anything, and it
went off—coulda swore it wasn't loaded, but it sure
was, and it got me right here, just a nick I thought. I

never said anything, thought it'd be O.K., put some stuff on it myself, but the last couple of days it's been giving me hell and I thought I better let a doctor take a look at it. Everything's O.K., nobody tried to murder me."

"That's good," said Hackett. "Have you got a permit for the gun?"

"Gee, I don't need one, this state, unless I'm going to be carrying it around, do I? Well, if I do, I'll sure get one, don't worry, I'll see to it."

"What's your name?"

"Morton. Daniel J."

"And what's the gun?" asked Higgins.

"Uh," said Morton. "Well, it's a thirty-eight."

The doctor touched Hackett on the arm and he turned. "I thought possibly you might want it," murmured the doctor, and dropped something into Hackett's hand.

"Hey," said Morton weakly. "Hey."

"Well, Mr. Morton," said Hackett, looking at the hardly damaged slug with interest, "that's the neatest trick of the week you just pulled, getting a thirty-two slug into yourself out of a thirty-eight. Would you like to change the story a little?"

"Oh, hell," said Morton. "Oh, damn it to hell." He shut his mouth then and wouldn't say anything else, so they left him there and told the doctor there'd be an ambulance to ferry him over to the guarded wing at Emergency. They were still waiting for that when a girl came into the little lobby and said, "Is there a Dr. Hooper, somebody called to say my brother was here and kind of sick. What's wrong with Danny?"

"Well, surprise, surprise," said Higgins. "Don't you work at Jeanie's Cafe on Western, miss?"

"Yeah," she said. "Why? Oh, I seen you—you were the cop came asking questions about that guy." Suddenly her rather vacant eyes sharpened. "Say," she said uncertainly, "that isn't—isn't anything to do with Danny, is it? What's wrong with him? He isn't in any trouble again, is he? I sure thought, we come out here

and kind of start over like, everything'd be different."
She looked ready to cry. "He is in trouble, isn't he?"

"He surely could be," said Higgins. "Miss Morton—
the day that fellow was in the cafe, for lunch—was
Danny there then? You told me you couldn't remember if anyone else was there."

She looked surprised. "I don't. But when you said
anybody I thought you meant customers—Danny
wasn't a customer, he'd just dropped in to borrow a
few bucks off me."

Higgins looked at Hackett and shrugged expressively. "Where'd you come out from? Where was he in
trouble before?"

She began to cry in a hopeless kind of way. "I
thought some place new he could kind of start over. I
thought— Well, Denver. And Colorado Springs. And
Boulder."

The ambulance came and the doctor let her go into
the treatment room. They heard her say, "Danny, you
damn fool. Why can't you stay out of trouble for once?
I got that good job lined up for you—"

"We work our tails off on the legwork," said Higgins, "and then catch up to him just by a fluke. Oh,
well, at least we've got him. I hope."

The girl, whose name was Janet, said tiredly they'd
been sharing an apartment on Fourteenth Street. She
didn't have a car, neither did he. She got into Hackett's
Barracuda without protest, and let them into the bare
little apartment. "I didn't know anything about it," she
said when they spotted the gun in plain sight on top of
a chest in his bedroom. "I never knew he had a gun, he
never left it out before." They couldn't poke around
without a warrant, but she got curious then and went
looking herself, and turned up a pile of cash under his
socks. They asked her to count it; it added to nine
hundred and ninety bucks. "He just bought a new
suit," she said. "I asked him where he got the bread,
he said he got lucky at poker."

Hackett gave her a receipt for the gun and the
money. They went back downtown and dropped off the

slug and the gun at the lab, and sent a query to NCIC on Danny Morton. In twenty minutes the answer started to come in, and it was a long one; he had a pedigree back to age thirteen, mostly B. and E., robbery, armed robbery, assault with intent.

"Well, let's see if we can wrap it up," said Higgins. They drove down to Central Receiving. By this time Danny was tucked up in bed with some painkiller in him, but rational enough, and resigned. There was an old man asleep in the other bed; they drew the curtains to this area and looked down at Danny.

"We've got the gun, and the rest of the cash," said Higgins. "Would you like to tell us about it, Danny? It won't make any difference whether you do or not."

"Oh, hell," he said. "I might as well. I was just so damn surprised, that's all—I never had to let off a gun in a heist before, not ever! You show it and the people hand over. I mean, that's the way it always goes." He sounded plaintive; rules had been broken. "I was in that place Janet works when the guy was there eating. And when he paid, man, he had a sheaf of the long green in his billfold like you wouldn't believe. I chased after him and saw where he went, that Ford agency, and you know it was raining like hell, I could see him through the window, he went into an office inside and I couldn't see was anybody else there at all, so I just kind of pulled my hat down and buttoned my coat up high—"

"You had the gun on you."

"Yeah, that's right. I went in, and Jesus, there's two other guys there, but I was *in* then, so I just kept going, figured to do it fast—and then, my God, there he was sitting at a desk with that billfold in front of him and a gun right there—I hadn't hardly said, hand over, when he started shooting—I was never so surprised in my life!"

"So you shot back," said Hackett.

"I never meant to—it was like defending myself, damn it. I grabbed the billfold and ran, but one of his slugs got me, damn it, I didn't think it was bad, but the doc says now it's got poisoned. Damn it to hell, if that guy'd been reasonable he didn't need to have got shot," said Morton reasonably. "I never meant to shoot anybody."

He agreed to sign a statement and when they left was eating lunch with every sign of enjoyment.

These days Mendoza was apt to be late on Sundays, if he came in at all, but nothing was ever said in front of him about it; he was a little touchy about going back to the arms of Mother Church. He came in at nine and looked over the night report, but didn't stay long.

He was amused and annoyed at the complication that had turned up on Lila Wescott, but nothing about any female would surprise Mendoza very much. The annoyance to it was that, whether that had been Niemeyer or some other character with the kink, Lila's reaction would effectively shoot down any legal case against him.

And it was a little thing, but he was more curious about Olga Anton and her venture into the lonely hearts column.

The three letters she had kept, and probably answered, all contained names and phone numbers. Alan MacDonald, William Kindler, Herbert Telford. Mendoza sat down with the five phone books and spent ten minutes matching them up. MacDonald on Laurel Street in South Pasadena, Kindler on La Mirada in Hollywood, Telford on Lamer in Burbank. With any luck, on Sunday they'd be home, the lonely widowers. He started out with the nearest one, Kindler. The house was a neat old frame place, newly painted, with a very green lawn and trimmed bushes in front. The door was opened almost eagerly, and Mr. Kindler wasn't at all upset to find a cop on his front porch; he'd have welcomed anybody to talk to, and he talked readily. He was a cheerful little man as friendly as an innocent pup.

He said he'd been kind of ashamed of putting that ad in the paper, seemed silly in a way, but he'd been so darned lonesome since Ethel died—no relatives, the boy so far away, and they hadn't been much for socializing, hadn't many friends. He didn't figure Ethel would mind, if he found some nice, good woman to be friends with, maybe even get married again. And he'd had quite a few letters, he said, his eyes twinkling.

"This one you're asking about, this Mrs. Anton, she sounded like a nice woman. I kind of hoped I'd hear from her again, but I didn't. I was fixing to ask her out to dinner, maybe. But maybe she found somebody she liked better. Well, I wrote to some more of 'em, and I've met one of those, Mrs. Ella Langstrom, she's a widow, lives in Santa Monica, seems like a real nice lady. But why're you asking about Mrs. Anton—police? Nothing's happened to her, has it?"

"An accident." He was a transparent little man.

"Oh, I'm sure sorry to hear about that. Maybe that's why I never heard from her again."

The address in South Pasadena was a house of the same vintage, not so well maintained, and MacDonald was an older man, not so voluble. Like Kindler, he was sheepish about the ad; but lately he'd been feeling lonely, no family, the wife dead. The letters he'd got, only a couple had sounded like decent sensible women. Mrs. Anton had been one of them, but he'd never met her. "We talked on the phone, and I wanted her to come see my place, but she didn't drive and my car's on the fritz, have to wait for payday to get it fixed up. But what's a cop doing, asking questions about her, anyway?"

Maybe it was a wild goose chase, thought Mendoza, but it was the only thing, you could say the only surprising thing, that had turned up on Olga, and he wanted to follow it up. And he thought pessimistically, possibly these three letters hadn't been the only ones she'd followed up, and if she had run into a Bluebeard via the lonely hearts, his name wouldn't be one of these. But being on the hunt, he continued on over to Burbank.

That address was one side of a stucco duplex, and there was a man in tan work-clothes cutting the lawn in front with an old-fashioned hand mower. He looked with curiosity at the Ferrari and Mendoza: a middle-aged man with a bald head and fat face. "Mr. Telford?" said Mendoza.

"No, I'm Kidwell. Telford's my landlord, lives the other side. Out somewhere right now. You come about the car?"

"The car?"

"The Buick he's advertising. It's in pretty good shape, he figures get more for it, selling it private, than they'd give him on a turn-in. He just bought a little newer one. Awful the way prices are, he tells me, as if I didn't know, he said he guessed he'd have to find a rich widow, support him in his old age." Mendoza laughed dutifully. "You can probably catch him later on, he did say he wasn't going out tonight."

"Thanks very much." Mendoza started back downtown and stopped at Federico's for lunch. Here he ran into Hackett and Higgins, who told him about Danny. "That one we'll get tied up tight, with the ballistics evidence," said Higgins. "I'm still wondering about Lila."

"I'll give you three to one on Niemeyer," said Mendoza. "But that we'll never get tied up. These things happen, boys."

They got back to the office together, and Lake told them there'd been another shooting, just awhile ago. "Nick and Tom went out on it. God knows when they'll get lunch. And that doctor's been calling you. Three times since ten o'clock."

"Which doctor?"

"Ferguson. He said you could reach him at Central Receiving till three."

"So get him for me, Jimmy." Mendoza sat down at his desk and picked up the flamethrower, idly admiring his new ring as he pulled the trigger. Presently the phone buzzed at him and he picked it up.

"Dr. Ferguson? You wanted to talk to me?"

"Oh, Lieutenant—I'm glad you called, I've been trying to reach you. They've been poisoned again," said Ferguson baldly. "We had the hell of a time with them, just barely pulled them through, and even now I wouldn't be too sure of the old man, with that heart of his. He—"

"Again? In the hospital? *¿Qué demonios?*" said Mendoza. "How the hell could that happen? You mean, more arsenic? With a crew of doctors and nurses around?"

"I'm just trying to—er—sort it out," said Ferguson. "I thought you'd like to do some investigating yourself."

"You're damned right I would. I'll be right there. We might just as well," said Mendoza caustically, banging down the phone and getting up, "move my office over to Central Receiving. *¡Por Dios!* Somebody wandering around Emergency with a carton of Mouse-Noh, and nobody taking any notice? I do ask you! This goes beyond a joke."

"The Beebes?"

"The Beebes. Fed the arsenic again, and I'll find out more about it this time if I have to camp out there. Come on, we may have to question a lot of people."

Over at Central Receiving, they found Ferguson talking with two white-clad nurses in the corridor outside Mrs. Beebe's room. "Well, Doctor, I thought you were supposed to look after patients here," said Hackett genially.

"We usually do. I've just had a report from the lab which may tell us something, I think."

"The suspicious Hodges," nodded Mendoza. "All right, what happened, Doctor?"

"They were both taken ill about the same time, just before the dinner hour yesterday. The same symptoms, cramps, nausea, etcetera. They—"

"They're in separate rooms?" asked Higgins.

"Yes, of course. Mrs. Beebe is in a two-bed room, Mr. Beebe in a four-bed. The floor nurse called me at once, I'd left orders to be informed of any change, though they'd both rallied well by then. I got here about seven and it was touch and go with both of them most of the night. It wasn't until about three A.M. I felt they'd both pull out of it, and of course I couldn't begin to investigate the circumstances until an hour ago. At least the same staff is in now."

"And you've got Hodges' report on the samples you sent to the lab. What," asked Mendoza, "does the perspicacious Hodges tell us?"

"The arsenic seems to have been contained in some chocolate substance. Hodges suggests soft-centered chocolate drops," said Ferguson.

"Very imaginative. So, the obvious question, did they have any visitors yesterday afternoon?"

"Just what I was asking," said Ferguson. "This is Mrs. Vincent, the station nurse in charge, and Mrs. Purdy, who has charge of Mrs. Beebe's room among others. What about the visitors?"

The nurses both started to talk at once, stopped; they were both middle-aged, and looked excited. Even to experienced nurses in Emergency, the Mouse-Noh would be exciting. "Well," said Mrs. Vincent, "I can tell you the daughter wasn't here. She called about noon and asked us to tell her parents she wouldn't be in until evening visiting hours, it was something about a birthday party—one of her children, I think."

"And of course she knew they were getting better, wasn't worried," said Ferguson. "Mrs. Purdy?"

"No, she didn't come, I know her by sight of course, and her husband. There was only one visitor came for Mrs. Beebe yesterday afternoon, I saw her come in, I was taking some orange juice to the other patient in the room. I don't know who she was, but Mrs. Beebe knew her—and I don't know if she did go to see Mr. Beebe, but as I was going out I heard her say she was going to."

"What did she look like?" asked Hackett and Higgins together.

"Oh, she was a big blowsy woman with dyed red hair and a rather loud voice. She had on a green dress—"

"Hermione Howstatt!" said Mendoza as if it was an oath. *"¡Porvida!* Hermione Howstatt—now by God I want to talk to that woman, and this time she'll do some talking to the point!" He wheeled and marched down the corridor, his two senior sergeants after him.

Galeano and Landers were privately wondering why they'd ever chosen this job. It didn't look as if they'd get any lunch today, or anything else on the new body.

The body was one Mike Deasy, he'd been shot once in the middle of the forehead, and he was lying on the floor of the living room of a house on San Marino Street, an ugly old box of a house on a block of old houses. There were three witnesses and they all told the same story. His wife, Ann Deasy, said he'd been watching TV and she and her two friends had been talking in the kitchen, sitting over coffee. Mrs. Jernigan and Mrs. Eichenhorn, they lived next door, one on one side and one on the other. And the doorbell rang, Mike said he'd get it, and then they heard a shot and rushed in, and Mike was on the floor and this strange man rushed out past them. They tried to grab him, but knowing he had a gun, maybe didn't try too hard, and he ran out the back door and down the yard through the vacant lot on the next street, and was gone. Period.

Galeano called up a lab truck. The women were excited, naturally, and Mrs. Deasy inclined to fits of sobbing, which was understandable, but a few facts emerged.

"Do you know anybody who might have wanted to kill your husband? Now I don't want to upset you any more, Mrs. Deasy, but the sooner we get something to go on—" Galeano was tactful, sympathetic.

She sobbed harder and then gulped and sat up in the straight kitchen chair. Duke and Horder were busy in the living room. "I suppose," she said. "What do you want to ask?"

"Where did he work? Any trouble there?"

She shook her head, dabbing her eyes. She was about thirty, a washed-out blonde with china-blue eyes and a long nose. "He's a plumber, he works for ABC Plumbing on Vermont. I always said he'd get into trouble with the gambling. He was always down there, gambling. Where they have those gambling houses."

"Gardena."

"Yes." She hiccupped. "I always said so, didn't I?"

"And so did we." Mrs. Jernigan was little and dark and emphatic. They were all about the same age. "He'd had men come dunning him before—what Annie put up with!—him losing the rent money, the grocery money—and some of those big gamblers, I've heard they got connections to the Syndicate."

Which was unfortunately true, but this didn't look like a professional hit. It could, however, very well have been somebody Deasy owed a gambling debt, somebody with a short temper and little patience. They asked for a description and got a unanimous one.

"He was tall and blond, and he had on brown slacks and a beige turtleneck sweater," said Mrs. Jernigan promptly.

"Yes, but I thought it was more off-white," said Mrs. Eichenhorn.

"I'm afraid I didn't get a good look at him," sniffed Mrs. Deasy, "I was running over to Mike, but I guess that's about what he looked like."

They were sure he hadn't touched anything. Well, the back door—the solid door had been standing open— "I'd been cooking cabbage," sobbed Mrs. Deasy, "for Mike's lunch—" He'd just had to push the screen door open. Galeano got Duke to dust the screen door. He and Landers went out into the backyard, but there wasn't any trail to be seen, and just a low hedge at the end of the yard, which he could have jumped.

The wagon came for the body, and they started to question neighbors, but nobody had seen or heard a thing. It was a cold day, most people inside. Mrs. Eichenhorn's husband worked nights and had been sound asleep in the house on that side of the Deasys'; Mrs. Jernigan was divorced.

They reasoned that he had left a car in the next street over, having cased the neighborhood and spotted that vacant lot. And about then they found themselves

surrounded by about thirty-nine kids, all shouting at
the tops of their voices, we seen the police car, what's
happened, hey, Joey, it's your house, look, it's Joey's
house, there's an ambulance— And a great concerted
wordless moan went up as the covered stretcher came
out.

The women somehow got the kids quiet. Four were
the Deasys', three Mrs. Jernigan's, another four Mrs.
Eichenhorn's; the rest had just been there in the play-
ground up the block when they spotted the cops down
here. But by then they'd probably effectively spoiled
any possible trail left through the backyard, which the
lab men hadn't seen yet.

"This is just going to be a bastard," said Galeano
wearily. "Spend the next month down in Gardena
trying to find out who Mike owed what, and come up
with damn all."

Landers agreed. It was four o'clock. Duke said the
gun was an automatic, they'd found the ejected car-
tridge case. Probably a .25; if they ever came across
the gun, that would be something solid, but it was all
they had.

Galeano said he had to have something to eat, damn
it. Landers generously offered to write the report; that
would take him to end of shift nicely.

Before he went up to the Robbery-Homicide office,
Landers rode down to R. and I. and sought out his
bride. She was standing on a ladder rearranging tomes
of mug-shot collections. "Hello, darling. You haven't
brought in any witnesses? Good."

"Why?" asked Landers.

Phil laughed. She looked very delectable in her trim
navy uniform, with her cropped flaxen curls and tilted
nose; she'd look even more delectable in, say, that blue
dress with the pearl necklace and earrings. "All day,"
she said, "detectives have been bringing witnesses to
look at mug-shots, and nobody's made any hits at all. I
never saw Captain O'Callaghan look so cross. Your
poor Sergeant Palliser just looked resigned."

"One of those days," said Landers. "Look, I've got
a report to write and then I'm going home. Suppose we

both get dressed up a little and I'll take you out to dinner."

"Heavenly. At The Castaway."

"Naturally." The place with the spectacular view, up in the hills above Burbank, where they'd been sitting when they got engaged.

"It should be gorgeous tonight, it's so clear," said Phil. "I'll see you at home. Six-thirty."

Which was something to look forward to.

Mendoza and his sergeants emerged from an interrogation room at five-thirty feeling mentally bludgeoned. They looked at each other tiredly.

The session had begun with Hermione Howstatt welcoming them into her dingy apartment gaily, examining the badges with surprise. "But what do all you nice policemen want with me? Of *course* you can come in, I always say if it wasn't for the police where would we all be?" It had ended down at headquarters, with Hermione in turn coy, helpful, motherly, Biblical, and skittish. Of course she'd gone to see the Beebes, such dear good people, and she was so sorry to hear they were worse again. Chocolates? She didn't know anything about any chocolates. She never ate chocolates herself, so fattening, and as they could see for themselves she didn't need to add any more weight. Mice? She'd never been troubled with mice here, not that she had a cat, couldn't abide the nasty things, but when people were *clean* they didn't have mice, it was only riffraff who were troubled. And how they could *think* she'd ever do anything to harm poor Mr. and Mrs. Beebe—never hurt a fly, she wouldn't, people were always telling her she was too generous for her own good, her own worst enemy and she couldn't imagine where they'd got such an idea.

It went on and on like that, and now Higgins said, "What a woman! Great God, Luis, what do you think we could ever get out of her?"

"*¡Sin mujeres y sin vientos, menos tormentes!*" said Mendoza viciously. "All I know is—with the small piece of my mind I retain—she's our only suspect. One of you can ferry her down to jail, and the other one get the machinery started on a search warrant. I am going home."

The garage door was open, and Cedric nosing around the yard. He leaped lovingly at Mendoza and followed him in. Mairí MacTaggart was just lifting a pan of scones out of the oven. "I will say," she remarked thoughtfully, "some of these places Alison's been telling about, they sound just fine for the bairns. Space to run about and all. I'm thinking myself, she's too particular. Now that place she saw with the iron gates and all the glass and statues, it sounded just fine."

Mendoza laughed. "Do I need to tell you, Mairí, she's not to be led or driven." He went looking, and found Alison in Terry's room, red head bent seriously over the little desk. Johnny was sprawled full-length on the floor wielding crayons industriously.

"*Amado,* I didn't hear you come in." The twins flung themselves at him.

"Daddy, I've drawed a pony, look! Mamacita says we're gonna have a pony for Terry and me to ride! I want a black and white one and I know what we'd name him, Daddy, we'd name him Arturo for Uncle Art—"

"Johnny!" said Alison.

"Would not," said Terry calmly. "Mairí had a pony when she was a little girl and it was named Donald. We'll name the pony Donald and I want a brown one."

"*¿Cuándo occurio eso?*" said Mendoza severely.

Alison said guiltily, "I know, I shouldn't have said anything. But I've been gone so much, looking at places. I know I shouldn't have, especially as it doesn't seem that I'll find anything possible. If they're not estates needing a butler and housemaids, run-down Victoriana. And nine out of ten with swimming pools and cabanas."

"At least," said Mendoza, "it's taken your mind off names for the new offspring."

"Oh, I'll give in to you there. James or Luisa. Not worth arguing over."

"I'll have a drink before dinner—"

"All right, I will too. Just a little gin and vermouth on the rocks. And really, I'm not the doting parent, Luis, but don't you think there's a little talent here?—look how good this line is, and the pony's mane—"

"Gonna have a *big* new house," said Johnny importantly, "and a pony, and a man to take care of it, and we'll name it Arturo."

"Donald," said Terry.

Mendoza went to get the drinks, and inevitably got one for El Señor as well. "I'll be going out again," he said. "A witness."

"If you weren't so wedded to the job," said Alison dreamily, "we could look anywhere. Way out of the city. Never mind, something will turn up—I feel it in my bones."

8

"That ad—" said Herbert Telford. "Say, why are the cops asking? About that?" He looked at Mendoza curiously. He had looked interested at the badge, asked Mendoza in, even offered him a drink, and he wasn't stalling now, just surprised. "What's the cops' interest in it?"

Mendoza sat back on the couch and said, "Well, now, let's trade, Mr. Telford. You tell me and I'll tell you." He thought Olga Anton would have been well impressed with Telford if they had met; he was in the middle fifties, tall and spare, with graying hair and a wide humorous mouth.

"Fair enough," agreed Telford with a shrug. This side of the duplex on Lamer Street in Burbank was modestly furnished, neat enough; he was rather dapper in gray slacks and matching sports shirt "That ad. I felt a little silly about it. But the way it was, I haven't had the chance to get to know many people here. Stop me if I talk too much, but my first marriage went sour and I didn't marry again until sixteen years back, to Ruth. We got along fine, only no kids, but she never was so strong, and about four years ago she took it into her head that she'd be a lot better, all her ailments improve, in this kind of climate. So we came out here—from New Jersey. Well, she didn't get better, she got worse, and it turned out to be something they call lupus, like the worst kind of arthritis with complications." He looked down at his clasped hands. "It was rough—I had to take care of her like a baby, nearly two years before she died. That was the main reason we hadn't made any friends here. Well, she died six months ago, and I've been at damned loose ends ever since. Do you want all this?"

"Go on," said Mendoza.

"That ad—it seemed to be a way to meet somebody. I mean, at this end of life, we haven't got all the time in the world for that, no?" He gave Mendoza a brief grin. "I had some answers, and this Mrs. Anton sounded like—well, a good bet, put it crudely. Sensible woman, about my age, used to keeping house and all that, and as I found out a real good-looker, and I gathered a little money, which I wasn't averse to—well, who would be?"

"Excuse me, you're not working?"

"I was in construction, I got into property invest-ment as I could, rental property. It's nothing big but I can live on it, especially as I can save by doing repairs myself. I cashed out back there when Ruth and I came west, and reinvested here—I own this place and three others around town, two duplexes and a triplex." He waited and went on. "I called her on the phone, she'd sent me the number, and we had quite a little talk. I liked the sound of her and I guess she liked me O.K.— I thought. We met up in Hollywood and had lunch together at the Brown Derby—that was a week ago last Wednesday—and we got on fine. She's a nice woman, I thought it was going to be just what the doctor ordered, you take me."

"What went wrong?" asked Mendoza.

"Ah, women!" said Telford. "I asked her out on Sunday night—a week ago tonight—to the Shrine, there's a light opera company on there, thing I can live without but I thought she might like it—"

"The Shrine Auditorium," muttered Mendoza. *"Mea culpa.* Figueroa and Jefferson, eight blocks away."

"What? Well, she said fine, and we went," said Telford. "First time I knew where she lived, well, I understood her being cautious, but by then we knew each other, she knew I was O.K. I picked her up at her apartment—she must have more money than I'd fig-ured, that place. Look"—he threw out a hand in helpless gesture—"I don't know why the hell you're interested, but you can see how it was. We'd met each other, liked what we saw, we aren't either of us kids, and I ask you, why would a woman answer an ad like that if she wasn't interested in just what I was—getting married again to somebody, to *have* somebody, not just the sex, my God, but that too. Anyway, like I say by then we knew each other, and when we got in the car after the show I—well, I didn't figure I was out of line, she'd been acting real friendly and joking with me. On the way up Figueroa I just put my arm around her, snuggled her up a little, and we get the light at Thirtieth, I leaned over to kiss her."

"And don't tell me," said Mendoza, suddenly enlightened. "She objected."

"Objected? My God, you'd have thought I'd offered to rape her. I'd figured she was a little straitlaced, but like I say I'd also figured why the hell would she answer an ad like that if she's not interested? She fought me, and of course I let her go, she said she didn't think I was that kind of man, and let her out right away, she'd go home alone. I told her not to be silly, but she got the door open, I was afraid she'd fall out, and I stopped, and out she got—it was a damn fool thing all round, I never meant the woman any harm, but she—" Telford stopped abruptly. "For God's sake," he said hollowly, "don't tell me she's laid a complaint of some kind, and that's why you—"

Mendoza smiled and shook his head. "No. So what did you do?"

"Well, my God, what could I do? It was dark and raining like hell—no night to be out, but I'd already got the tickets and it wasn't raining when I picked her up. I called after her, be sensible, I'd take her home, I said don't be silly—it was no place for a woman to be alone in the street, that hour. I don't know if she heard me, she'd got up on the sidewalk and was walking off. I'd have parked and chased after her, but there wasn't a place there and a guy behind honking at me. I had to go nearly a block before I found a place, and I walked back, got soaked, and tried to find her. No go. You know the street's lighted well enough for driving, but beyond the corner lights, not so hot. And I wasn't so sure if I did find her she'd come along like a sensible woman. And when I spotted two empty taxis, up on Adams, I figured she'd pick one up without any trouble. So I came home. I was—you can see—feeling damn mad about it. That damn fool woman! So she'd let me know how she felt, arm's length till we knew each other better, I wouldn't have tried anything. She's just too damn straitlaced."

Mendoza put out his cigarette and laughed. "Such a simple answer when we know. I think you've just rendered a verdict, Mr. Telford. She was just too damned straitlaced indeed. I'm sorry to tell you that she didn't get home. She was probably trying to call a cab when the mugger came along and ended up killing her. And it's puzzled everybody how she happened to be down there at that time of night. Now you tell us."

"Oh, my good Christ!" said Telford, horrified. "My God, that poor woman! My God, if I'd suspected anything like that could happen—but I couldn't locate her again after she got out of the car, and I thought, cabs all over—oh, my God! I feel as if I'd murdered her myself!" Shaken, he apologized, got up and poured himself another couple of fingers of Scotch. "To think of—damn it, she was a nice woman, Lieutenant, I liked her a lot, I was sorry she'd taken offense like that. But to think of that happening—all my fault in a way—"

"Hardly. Nice yes," said Mendoza. "Maybe a bit too much so." And he thought, the proper small-town lady, answering those ads, must have realized the implications: what else might she have expected? But proper to the last, outraged when Telford moved a bit too fast for her, she'd lost any judgment and climbed out of the car. Not knowing the town, probably thinking she could get a cab in five minutes. Poor proper Olga.

"I feel like hell about it," said Telford. "Oh, damn. The damn things that happen—she didn't need to—"

"No," said Mendoza. "She didn't. Leave it at that." At least they knew now why and how she'd got there. If they ever caught up to the mugger it would be sheer luck.

On Monday morning Conway came back in; he was still hoarse but said he felt better. It was Palliser's day off. There wasn't much in the night report; as Mendoza was glancing at it, a report came up from the lab— ballistics evidence on Morrison. The slug out of Danny was from Morrison's gun, and it had been Danny's .38 that killed Morrison.

Galeano came in and started to give Mendoza a rundown on Deasy. "Not really funny that nobody saw or heard anything, it was a small caliber, not much noise. But when I think of the damned legwork on it, trying to find his gambling pals—I just wish you'd have a hunch about it and tell us where to look."

"I seem to be out of hunches for the moment, Nick. Did you ever find that woman in Hartford, Connecticut? Something to do with that old wino?"

"Oh—that. Yeah, it turned out she was his ex-wife. She said let the city bury him, she couldn't be less interested. Well, if we're going to accomplish anything at all today—" He went out with Landers, and Sergeant Lake came in past them.

"Here's your search warrant."

"*Muy bien,*" said Mendoza. "Now maybe we'll get somewhere. Art—George! ¡*Vamos!* Let's see if we can find some solid evidence to keep Hermione in jail." He snatched up his hat and swept Hackett and Higgins out of the office ahead of him.

Hermione Howstatt's apartment was at the rear of an old dingy brick building on Miramar Street. They showed the warrant to an incurious manager, went up uncarpeted stairs and used the key. There wasn't any spectacular disorder such as in Niemeyer's room, just muddle and clutter. A lot of clothes crowded together in every available hanging space, stacks of magazines, drawers crammed with little boxes full of nearly-used cosmetics, costume jewelry, piles of underwear, night-gowns, some of it years old by the style. Cartons standing around stacked with old family photograph albums. It looked as if she'd never thrown anything away. Before they began to dig deeper, however, they came across a two-pound box of chocolates, all soft centers by the label, and in a kitchen cupboard a half-empty box of Mouse-Noh and a hypodermic syringe.

"Very nice evidence," said Mendoza. "At last." Hackett transferred all of that into a plastic evidence bag for the lab, and after that they began to look closer, go through cupboards and drawers. They found motheaten quilts, seven pairs of shoes with holes in the soles, a box full of old beaded evening bags dating from the twenties. The bathroom had shoes stacked around the walls, boxes of clothes on top of each other, and paper bags full of dime-store cosmetics, boxes of henna powder, toilet paper, Kleenex, hairpins, yards of cheap lace, a jumble of miscellany. "Talk about hoarders," said Hackett. "But the chocolates are all the evidence we need, Luis."

"Luis—look at this," said Higgins. His voice sounded a little peculiar; they went to see what he'd found. It was an old tin box with a faded painting on the lid of Venus and Cupid. He held it out mutely, and Mendoza lifted the lid.

The box was full of death certificates. The top one was dated two years ago in this county, and certified the death of Robert Howstatt of colitis, certifying physician Dr. James Pratt. The one under that was dated five years ago in Tulare: Arthur Fordham, colitis. The next one, Tulare, six years back, John Fordham, influenza. Tulare six years back, Clara Fordham, colitis. San Jose, eight years back, Alice Fordham, influenza. San Francisco nine years back, William Meecham, ulcerated colon. San Francisco thirteen years back, Alice Meecham. San Francisco fifteen years back, Margaret Meecham, senility and syncope. San Francisco, Frances Meecham, influenza. Bakersfield, Roger

Jarvis, ulcerated colon. Bakersfield, Roger Jarvis, Jr., cholera infantum. Beatrice Jarvis, cholera infantum. James Jarvis, Sr., senility. James Jarvis, Jr., colitis. Ronald Smith, ulcerated colon. Marjorie Smith—

"*¡Santa María y todos las arcángeles!*" said Mendoza in naked astonishment. "But these—*Jesus, María y José*—go back to 1929! 1929!—Marjorie Smith, twenty-two, influenza and complications—" In silence he counted; there were twenty-nine death certificates.

They looked at each other. "Oh, no," said Hackett. "It couldn't be, Luis."

"I wouldn't take odds," said Mendoza. "My God. We'd better find out, Art."

"Why else did she keep them?" asked Higgins. It was a cold day, and chilly in here, but he got out his handkerchief and wiped his forehead. "All together in a box? But twenty-nine—my God." By the time they got out to the car he had another thought. "But it's impossible, Luis! Doctors saw all these people, signed the certificates. Even in 1929, doctors weren't idiots. I can't believe—"

"Tell it to Bainbridge," said Mendoza. In his office, he told Lake to get hold of Bainbridge. "I want you, Doctor."

"Damn it, I'm busy, I can't come up now," grumbled Bainbridge.

"Not even for something—mmh—recherché? Say a mass arsenic poisoner?"

There was a little pause, and then Bainbridge yelped, "You've got her? More than one? Of course, damn it, I might have known—"

"How'd you know it's a her?"

"It always is," said Bainbridge. "I'm on my way!" He came in ten minutes later looking fiercely interested, flung himself into the chair beside Mendoza's desk, and said, "Except for the very offbeat lunatics like Cream—or the effeminate ones like Armstrong—it's usually the females who go for the poison. Who is she? How'd you drop on her?"

Mendoza told him, and he gloated over the death

certificates like a miser over gold. "Oh, beautiful—
beautiful! And all so typical—you look at any of the
classic cases, and the same things show up. The utter
carelessness for instance—or a very rudimentary cunning. That was a lunatic thing to do, walk into the
hospital with those chocolates, and yet, you know, she
could have got away with it."

"You seem to be sure she's got away with the hell of
a lot already." Hackett was incredulous. "Twenty-nine,
Doctor? And you don't think she *is* a lunatic?"

"Not in any legal sense. They never know when to
stop," said Bainbridge simply. "It's like an addiction."

"But all these doctors—you'd think at least some of
them would have suspected something!" said Higgins.
"Look at the ages—kids, young people, middle-aged
people, old people—"

"And I'll bet mostly her nearest and dearest. Very
possibly there were small amounts of insurance involved in most of them. Doctors!" said Bainbridge,
and emitted a gray cloud of cigar smoke. "Didn't I say
when I brought Ferguson in, who the hell is going to
suspect arsenic? Run a test for it? Here's an old man
weakened by a bout of flu, he gets cramps and nausea,
obviously it's an intestinal virus, and not too surprising
it should carry him off. Babies die every day of suffocation, intestinal complications, croup. Lots of people
have colitis and ulcers. Busy doctor, when he's been
attending the patient and thinks he knows the diagno-
sis, he isn't going to bother with an autopsy, and even
if he did, he wouldn't test for arsenic, of all the damned
things. Oh, this is very pretty—say, Luis, let me call
Ferguson and tell him, will you?"

"We're going to be calling more people than Ferguson," said Mendoza grimly. "And the first one is this
Dr. James Pratt who signed Robert Howstatt's death
certificate right here two years ago."

"Oh, we're going to have fun and games all right,"
said Bainbridge happily. "You're going to be busy, Luis.
Check back on all these deaths—well, 1929, I suppose
some of these doctors are dead by now— *And* get some

exhumation orders. Start with Howstatt, the most recent one. I wonder where he's buried—some cemeteries have better preservative qualities than others—"

"And I wonder if he wasn't cremated," said Mendoza. "But we'll find out, oh, yes."

"But who were all these people?" wondered Higgins, still incredulous. "The husband, sure, but all these other names—"

"Did you say she told you she'd been married three times? Typical too—it could have been more," said Bainbridge. "It falls right into the pattern—nearest and dearest. Husbands, parents, in-laws, children, anybody. Anybody a little in the way, or for the insurance—finally, for any or no reason. What's she like to look at?" They told him. "Typical too. Here's this jolly, motherly-looking woman telling the doctor how carefully she's been nursing poor Robert, and she looks the part, and when Robert's one of a couple of hundred patients, who would put it in the doctor's head that she's been mixing arsenic with the invalid diet?"

Mendoza had Dr. Pratt on the phone now and was being suave. Bainbridge demanded it when he put it down, and called Ferguson with ghoulish enjoyment. Then he sat in thought for a moment and said, "I'd better get busy on the exhumation order. Find out where he is. I'll let you know. By God, I'm glad to be in on this, Luis—very interesting! You let me know what you find out about the rest of 'em hah? We may end by digging up seven or eight of them, who knows?"

"I'm glad somebody's getting a kick out of this," said Hackett as he went out. "My good God in heaven. Did you say it reminded you of Coffin Corner? I suppose we have to check all these."

"It can't have escaped your attention, Arturo, that the Beebes aren't dead. All we can charge her with, as it stands, is bodily harm with intent to kill. If Bainbridge digs up her latest husband and finds him full of arsenic, and possibly a few of these other bodies, it'll be Murder One," said Mendoza.

And this was not a time when the impersonal computers of NCIC could be of much help. They got busy on telephones, to Tulare, San Jose, Bakersfield and San Francisco. Mendoza was being patient with the coroner in Bakersfield when Sergeant Lake came in and said a Dr. Pratt was here. Mendoza beckoned him in, finished temporarily with the coroner, and said, "Well, Doctor, did I disrupt your day?"

"Disrupt?" said Pratt. He was an elderly bald man with a mustache. "I know you've played hell with my blood pressure, Lieutenant. I didn't even remember the man's name. I had my girls hunting for half an hour in the dead files before we found the case history. You did say arsenic? Good lord. Good *lord*. Well, all I can say is, it's a good thing I'd planned to retire this year. That sort of thing doesn't do a doctor's reputation any good."

"There wasn't any question in your mind about the cause of death?"

"Good lord, no. I remembered the man when I looked at the case history. He was seventy-seven, said his regular doctor had retired. The wife seemed a nice motherly sort of woman—" Hackett gave a hollow laugh across the office, and Pratt jumped. "He had severe colitis, as a good many elderly people do, and when these symptoms showed up I naturally diagnosed an intestinal virus—"

Palliser, unaware of the new routine he'd be helping out on tomorrow, was watching Roberta working with Trina, round and round the backyard. Trina was erratic; she didn't always stop when Roberta did, but she seemed to be getting the hang of it in a vague way, to guess what *heel* meant at least. The last time Roberta took her around and stopped, Trina sat down right away, and Roberta took the lead off and hugged her. "Good girl!"

"Say, she does seem to know what you want," said Palliser. "That's pretty good, Robin. You may civilize her yet."

"It just takes patience," said Roberta, "and she's an intelligent dog after all. That book's interesting—you can train them to all sorts of things, and I should think it'd be fascinating to see one of these obedience trials. If she gets good enough, maybe we could even enter her—"

Trina, spotting the neighbors' Siamese cat on top of the fence, was making wild leaps at it, barkly furiously. "I think you're looking some way ahead," said Palliser dryly.

Galeano and Landers were down in Gardena, doing the legwork with a vengeance. There were a lot of gambling houses in Gardena, the only area in L.A. where gambling was legal, and it was a tedious job plodding from one to the other asking if the management had known Mike Deasy, who he played with, who he might owe. At least they had confirmation that the gambling was probably the motive for the murder. They had gone to see Deasy's employer first, Guy Halliday who owned the ABC Plumbing Company. He'd been more interested in the murder than sorry for Deasy.

"I don't doubt the wife's right," he said. "I nearly fired the guy more than once, but he was a good workman when he cared to work at all. Generally he didn't—a big lazy bum. And what they call a compulsive gambler. He was always begging me, let him have fifty, a hundred, in advance of his salary, he'd had lousy luck that week, dropped a bundle. Like that, see? But I couldn't give you any idea where he played or who with."

So that had sent them down here, and by one o'clock they had seen the inside of eleven houses and talked to about seventy people without finding anybody who claimed to have known Deasy. While they had lunch at the coffee-room of the twelfth place, Landers said, "Listen, Nick. Suppose we call Scarne and ask him to get a shot of the corpse's face—mask out the bullet hole. Then we'd at least be able to ask, do you know this man? These gamblers—I doubt if they know each other's names half the time."

"Good idea," said Galeano. "We should have thought of it before."

Grace came in after lunch to find Mendoza, Hackett, Higgins, Bainbridge and Ferguson having a protracted conference in Mendoza's office, the door open. He'd been out looking for heisters, and was nearly as fascinated as Bainbridge to hear about Hermione.

Conway was sitting beside Wanda's desk looking haggard and complaining that it was cold in here. "You shouldn't have come in at all," said Wanda, "you're still spreading germs. Oh, here's your book, Jase. I loved it—he was just a tremendous character, wasn't he?"

"Very interesting old boy. But it's not mine, I don't know whose it is."

Conway picked it up. "No name in the front," he said.

"I think I'll go sit in on the conference," said Grace. "This is the damnedest thing we've had in a blue moon." But as he came out to the corridor Lake hailed him.

"It's the hospital. That nurse is conscious and wants to see a cop."

"Right away, Jimmy!" Grace was pleased. When Joyce Bradley had been in his father's office seven years ago, he'd still been in uniform; before he was married, and Ginny working in an office in the same building, he used to drop in now and then to say hello to Dad. He remembered the brisk efficient girl so proud of her R.N. cap and pin. She had guts, Higgins said, describing that painfully crawled trail through muddy underbrush. That you could say. Grace hoped she could give them some idea who to look for.

She was half propped up on several pillows, the curtain round the bed, and a needle in her arm for the intravenous feeding. The nurse who brought him in said, "Now don't get to chatting and let him stay too long, you hear? You're not exactly ready to go on duty the next shift."

Joyce Bradley grinned up at her faintly. "I'll be good."

"Hello, Mrs. Bradley," said Grace, smiling down at her. "I remember when it was still Miss Parsons."

She stared up at him. She was a handsome girl rather than pretty, with a firm jaw and thick dark brows over very dark brown eyes. "Why—I remember you," she said. "Dr. Grace's son—you were in the police force when I worked for him."

"Still am," said Grace. "Only I got out of uniform. We were all glad to hear you're going to be all right. That was quite an experience you had."

"My goodness," said Joyce. "Oh, my goodness, wasn't it." Her voice wasn't very strong and she was obviously still weak, but all there mentally. "I hope I don't have nightmares about it the rest of my life."

"You gave us all a surprise, you know. We'd written you off as a goner when we found your car with all the blood in it. But as one of my colleagues put it, you had too much guts to give up so easy, didn't you?"

"I don't know about that," said Joyce soberly. "I was just too damned mad to give up, Mr. Grace, that was it. First *I* was surprised, and then I was scared to death—when he stabbed me and I knew I was bleeding pretty badly—but after he pushed me out of the car and I fell down that bank and felt my ankle go, I was just *mad.*"

"Take it easy, don't talk too much."

"I'm all right. Once they patched me up and got me fed and watered, so to speak, it's just a question of time. I remember I lay there at the bottom of that hill, knowing I was still bleeding like a stuck pig, and the rain coming down in buckets, and not knowing where I was but miles away from anywhere, and I was *so damned mad,"* said Joyce, "I told myself I'd live to get out of there just for spite. I know you're supposed to think, I've got to live for my husband and children, but I didn't. Just for spite."

Grace laughed. "We've been hoping you can tell us something about him."

"Oh, I can. I can indeed. His name's William Scully," said Joyce. "He was an orderly here up to two weeks ago, he got fired for being drunk on the job. What he was after was my paycheck—it was the end of the month, we'd just been paid."

"Well, I'm damned," said Grace. "Thanks so much."

The other nurse came in and said, "Out. Sir. This is only the second time she's been conscious."

Grace gave them an obedient salute and turned away, chuckling to himself. That was quite a girl.

He asked at the main desk, and presently they found an address for Scully in their back records: Geneva Street downtown. He tried there first; it was a single room in an old boardinghouse, but Scully had moved out two weeks ago and nobody knew where he'd gone. Grace had a simple mind, and it occurred to him that possibly Scully had been in trouble before and might show in records. He went back to headquarters to look. Phil obligingly handed him a Xerox tear sheet in three minutes. William Scully was described as Negro, six-two, two hundred, forty-one, black and brown, and he had a pedigree of D. and D., petty theft, assault and rape.

"Do tell," said Grace thoughtfully, and went up to the office. Conway was sitting at his desk reading the paperback, and Glasser was talking to Wanda between wrestling with typing a report. "Where's the brass?" asked Grace.

"They said they'd have to talk to that woman sometime," said Wanda. "They all went off together."

"Well," said Grace, "Mrs. Bradley tells us who to look for." He brought them up to date on that. "When I looked at his pedigree, it occurred to me that he's pretty big and probably mean, and I'd like somebody to hold my hand if we pick him up."

"I thought you said the address was n.g.," said Glasser.

"Well, Henry, you know my simple mind," said Grace gently. "He was working downtown so he got a room there. But the latest address on his pedigree, two years back, is Vista Street in Whittier. And he pushed her out of the car on one side of Whittier and dumped the car on the other side, so I thought we'd just have a look at that address. It might be his mother's place or something."

"You and your simple mind." Glasser abandoned the report without regret.

"You must understand by now, Mrs. Howstatt, that the game's up," said Bainbridge. "You can't wriggle out of this one, it's the end of the line. We've got you for the Beebes, with the poisoned chocolates."

She gave him a coy glance from under the painted-on black brows. "There could have been another visitor?" she said tentatively.

"No, and you know it. End of the line. We've got all the death certificates, and we're going to start by digging up Robert and having a look for arsenic. We'll find it, won't we?"

"That's not very nice," she said.

They couldn't all get into an interrogation room at once; they were talking to her in one of the holding rooms at the jail. She sat at the long table in the middle of the room, a raddled, fat old woman in a stained ancient green wool dress; a lot of fake gold chains dangled down her ample front, and she had on big green plastic earrings. The men sat facing her across the table. Irrelevantly Mendoza wondered why all the furniture in jails and courtrooms was always golden oak.

He said, "It wasn't very nice, what you tried to do to Mr. and Mrs. Beebe."

"Oh. Aren't they dead?"

"No."

"Oh," she said.

"But I don't think you'll be charged with attempted murder," said Mendoza gently.

"Robert," said Bainbridge genially, "and Arthur, and William, and John, and so on. There ought to be enough left of some of them that we can isolate the arsenic. It was always arsenic, wasn't it?"

She looked away, past them out the little window. For the first time she didn't look the jolly, motherly matron, a little silly, a little vague. Her little blue eyes with the too-lavish mascara looked a little hard. She said, "I've had a lot of trouble in my life, lost a lot of my dear ones. But I've always put myself *out* for people, that's just the way I'm made, I don't care what I can do if I can just *help* my dear ones."

"And help yourself to any little insurance left?" said Bainbridge.

"I've never had *much,*" she said with dignity. "I just feel for people, I just want to help them. Poor Robert. He was so sick, and he was old—he wanted to die, you know. He'd never have got better. I was so *sorry* for him."

"So you helped him. Why were you sorry for the Beebes?"

She made an aimless gesture, plucking at the chains. "I wasn't sorry for them. He was *very rude* to me about the money. I'd have paid it as soon as I could. I haven't much money now, but I hope I'm an honest woman. I'd been thinking of moving away from here anyway—I never have liked to stay in one place long, just a rolling stone, that's little Hermione," and she gave them a coquettish look. "And, well, I *did* think, it would cost something, you know, and if they weren't *there* nobody would know I owed them the forty dollars."

Higgins beside Mendoza took a deep breath. There was quite a long silence, and Ferguson cleared his throat.

"Would you like to say anything about any of the others?" asked Bainbridge, suddenly gentle.

She was still looking out the window. She said, "The babies were suffering something *dreadful.* Such pain, the poor mites, I couldn't bear to see them suffer." They waited, and she gave them a rather doubtful smile. "And I *was* sorry for Arthur's mother, but I won't say it wasn't a relief to have her gone—such a difficult old lady. But nobody can say I didn't do my best for all of them. All the hard times I've had—lived for others, that's what everybody always said of me. I just can't help feeling sorry for people, wanting to help them." There was another silence, and then she said brightly to Bainbridge, "I'm feeling a little tired. Not so young as I used to be, you know. Do you mind if I go and lie down now? That's a nice little room they've given me here, and the bed quite comfortable. I'll tell you some more tomorrow if I feel like it."

They watched the matron shepherd her off, and Bainbridge said, "She'll come apart now, gradually. Part of the pattern too. When they finally get caught up to, they'll often admit everything quite calmly. I've always thought, because it was never quite real to them. This kind, the mass killer, they're—at one remove from the rest of humanity. Inside every one of them is an ego a lot larger than life. They don't think of other people as real."

"That's elegant phrasing, Doctor," said Mendoza, "when all you mean is that they lack any empathy."

"I'm not thinking about the four-dollar words," said Higgins. "I'm wondering how much truth there is in any damn death certificate. And how many people like that may be walking around loose."

Mendoza laughed. "Fortunately few and far between, George. Reason they get written up in the anthologies of famous cases. But it makes me wonder about doctors."

"Now, Luis. We really are reasonably efficient most of the time. By the way, I found out about Robert. He's buried at Rose Hills. I've applied for the exhumation order. When I told the coroner why, he was damn interested. Wants to be there to have a look."

"You damned ghouls," said Hackett.

"I really think, Mrs. Mendoza, that you're going to have to build to get exactly the kind of house you want," said Mr. McNair. They were standing on the sixty-foot-long patio of a twelve-room brick mansion in Pacific Palisades, overlooking a glorious view out to sea and a fifty-foot swimming pool.

Alison sighed. She was almost coming to think so too, and she didn't look forward to it. It had been fun the first time, with the unlimited money, but a lot of work. But she hadn't seen a thing that was possible, and she was tired of going through other people's houses with the people there, and having to be polite. Also of all the swimming pools.

"Suppose you let me show you some of our excellent building sites," said Mr. McNair. He was a sticker, she'd give him that; and of course a couple of acres almost anywhere around the city would run to at least a hundred thousand, and the commission wasn't to be sneezed at.

"All right," she said. "But not here. It's all going to slide into the Pacific piecemeal, why people build expensive houses here I can't imagine. Every winter another one starts to slide."

"I can show you a prime piece of property, one and a half acres in North Hollywood. And then there's a three-acre parcel in La Cañada, with several beautiful oak trees—"

"Yes, all right," said Alison morosely, and shivered a little in the strong breeze off the sea.

The address in Whittier turned up William Scully like clockwork. A smartly-dressed Negro girl opened the door to Grace and Glasser, looked at the badges, heard Scully's name, and said, "Well, my horoscope said it'd be my lucky day. You're going to arrest him for something? Fine. My dad always says, it isn't the person you marry so much fetches trouble down, if you're lucky, it's the family they drag along behind. That no-good bum, I don't know how he and Jim ever came to be brothers. Jim, he's steady as you'd want, reliable, doesn't drink, good to the kids and me—and that Bill, a drunken bum. He gets out of work, lands on us."

"Is he here?" asked Grace.

"Be my guest. Watching TV in the living room."

It was, after all, a very tame arrest. He was surprised to see them, listened to his rights and got in the car without prodding. "Nervous Nellie," said Glasser to Grace. They'd taken Glasser's car, the little green Gremlin, and Scully filled the meager back seat.

"Just like to be on the safe side, Henry."

In an interrogation room back at the office, they started to talk to him. It wasn't strictly necessary to get an admission on this, Joyce Bradley could identify him; but they told him that, invited him to talk.

He didn't look like a very bright specimen. "Bradley?" he said. "Who's that?"

"The nurse you jumped a week ago last night," said Grace. "You remember that? You knocked her out and stabbed her and raped her, and stole her paycheck, and shoved her out of her car up on Sycamore Canyon Road."

"Uh," said Scully. "You can't prove I did that. I never did."

"Come on," said Glasser. "She can identify you. How d'you suppose we knew who to pick up?"

He sprang up from the table and knocked over the chair; they both started forward, but he was only scared. He backed up against the wall and said hoarsely, "You mean she's still alive? She couldn't be alive—she couldn't no way—"

"Well, she is," said Grace, "and she told us your name right away. Who helped you ditch her car?"

And he said numbly, automatically. "Lee Livesey. He just thought I picked it up awhile—my heap died on me last month—"

"That's fine, Bill," said Glasser. "Just keep on talking."

Mendoza's description of Hermione had taken Alison's mind off houses. "Honestly, Luis! But Dr. Bainbridge is right—it's just like the cases in the anthologies from a hundred years back, and wishful thinking to say it can't happen now. Twenty-nine—good heavens—"

"Human nature hasn't changed much in the last few thousand years, *cara*." Mendoza was stretched out on the sectional with El Señor on his chest. The twins had been read to and settled in bed. The other three cats were in a pile around Alison in the armchair. "Bainbridge seems to think she'll come out with chapter and verse, over a period of time. And God knows we'll have time—*¡caray!*—all the exhumations those doctors decide on, ferreting around for old insurance policies, and finding possible witnesses in all the places she's lived—"

The phone rang down the hall and he heaved El Señor off and got up. El Señor hissed at him and went to join his mother and sisters. "*Not* all of you at once," said Alison. "You're crowded enough now, just wait a couple of months and I won't have any lap at all."

"Mendoza," said Mendoza through a yawn to the phone.

"Sergeant Finlay, Lieutenant, main desk. I just got a call from Central Receiving to pass on to you—"

"Might as well move my office there, damn it," said Mendoza. "What about?"

"They had an attempted suicide brought in awhile ago, guy cut his wrists they said, but he reconsidered it and called for help and he'll be O.K. They say he's asking to see you."

"Did they say why?"

"Don't think they know. His name's Wescott."

"*¡Vaya!*" said Mendoza. "All right, thanks." He put the phone down, went into the bedroom for a tie, and back to the living room. "I've got to go out again. A witness."

"So I'll expect you when I see you," said Alison. After he left she shooed the cats off and went down the hall to tell Mairí all about Hermione.

9

THE NURSE WHO LED MENDOZA TO THE SIX-BED WARD was crisp and unsympathetic. "He's not bad," she said rather scornfully. "Called for help right away. I've no patience with these people who pretend suicide just to get sympathy."

Mendoza didn't think Wescott had tried suicide to get sympathy. He stood looking down at Wescott, flat and motionless in the hospital bed, both arms bandaged. The nurse drew the curtain around the bed and went away. "Well, Mr. Wescott," said Mendoza, "were you feeling sorry for yourself?"

Wescott didn't open his eyes. "Yes," he said. He was quiet, and then he did look up briefly, to identify Mendoza there. "Have you arrested somebody?"

"Not yet."

"I did it," said Wescott, "because I wanted to die—and then I thought I couldn't die, not right away, it wouldn't be right if you arrested—somebody else. I had to—tell you first. It was me. I killed her." After a long pause he added, "Aren't you going to—say anything? I killed her."

"Suppose you tell me about it."

"I've got to. It was—all crazy," said Wescott. "But —I—loved her." That was dull. A red flush mounted in his cheeks; he moved his face away from Mendoza's gaze. "She—I—she'd got these books, she wanted me to read them too. I told her it was crazy, only weirdos went for that—we'd always got along all right—eight years we'd been married—but she was all hot to—

"Porvida," said Mendoza to himself softly.

"—Gags and whips, crazy—she made me get the

156

stuff to make that whip, there was a picture in the book—she said it'd be better, more exciting. She—I—" He swallowed; his head was turned away. Basically a shy man, Mendoza realized, not given to the frank talk of such things. "She—once or twice, before, I'd hurt her—didn't mean to—she liked it. I didn't want to hurt her, but she said—and I wanted—I wanted to please her, I tried—but I couldn't use that whip. But that day—I lied about it. It wasn't so—that she wasn't feeling good. I did—come home. Between shifts. And she was—waiting for me—all undressed, and she had that rope out again—she said—really make it better, the best. And tie her real tight this time, the gag real tight—because—" He was talking to the wall, in little spurts, and incongruously he was chokingly embarrassed. "I didn't want to do like that, but she was really hot—oh, my God, I don't have to say all of it—make it real tight, she said, so she'd really feel it, and she was liking it, all excited and she got me excited too, I don't think I hurt her much, I didn't want—but then all of a sudden she wasn't breathing and I—and I—and I—"

Mendoza waited. The suffocation, any form of strangulation, would have been very quick. "And, Mr. Wescott?"

"I don't know. She was dead. I didn't believe it, I don't know how, but she was dead. I think I just blacked out. Then it was dark and I don't know what time and she was still there dead and I didn't know what to do. I guess I went crazy, I guess it was shock or something. I looked at the clock and it was seven, so I just—I got dressed and went to work. At the bar. It was like I was a robot, mixing drinks, the girls come with orders. And then quitting time and I came home and she was still there. Still dead. Just like I left her. I don't know, I guess I'd expected, back of my mind, I'd just imagined it, and she'd be all right. But she wasn't. It wasn't anything real, I was there looking at her and the rain coming down outside and I thought, I killed her, everybody'll know I killed her, and I thought I couldn't've killed her because I loved her. Somebody

broke in and killed her, it wasn't me. And—I—cut out
that screen with my knife, make it look—and I called
the police—but all the time it got worse and worse
because I knew I'd killed her." He drew a long, long
breath and slowly he turned over, flat on his back, and
looked up once, fleetingly, at Mendoza. "It was all—
not anything real, she couldn't be dead, I couldn't
stand her being dead. It was—a little better—if I could
pretend—somebody else—but it wasn't, I did it, and I
couldn't—let you arrest somebody else—because I did
it, I killed her. I loved her, but I killed her."

Mendoza stood looking down at him. "It that it, Mr.
Wescott?"

"Just so you won't arrest somebody else," said Wescott wearily. "You'll have to arrest me. But—right
now—I wish you'd go away."

Mendoza went down the corridor and found the
nurse. "You'd better keep an eye on him," he told
her.

She regarded him scornfully. "Oh, they never try it
again—once they get the attention they're after, they're
satisfied."

"Possibly, in some cases. But keep an eye on him,
please," said Mendoza.

The men on night watch hadn't time to be bored.
They'd just come on shift when there was a head-on
crash on the Santa Monica freeway, with two dead; it
took some time to be sure of identification, get names
and address of witnesses. Shogart went out with Piggott and Schenke on that and pulled his weight, but
back in the office he relapsed into silence, switching on
the traffic calls on the radio. That was no novelty to
either of them, and Piggott was trying to type up the
report; he wasn't a swearing man, but Schenke could
have sworn for him.

Then they got a call from Traffic, and Piggott left
the report half written to go out with Schenke on that.
It looked like being a little mystery for the day men to
work: a teenage girl found dead outside the house
where she lived with her parents. The mother was

having hysterics, the father nearly as bad, the neighbors were out on either side, and the Traffic men hadn't got much out of anybody before calling in.

"About all we can tell you," said Bill Moss, "is that she was supposed to be home by eight o'clock on a week night, they said she was at a girl friend's, and she was late so her father went to look out the front door when he heard a car, spotted something in the front yard, and looked, and there she was. Her name's Peggy Conyers. The neighbors say she's a nice quiet girl, only sixteen, not wild, and the Conyers nice people. I bet. Look into it, probably find she was on the hard stuff or whatever."

"You're just a cynic," said Schenke. "It look like an O.D.?"

"No, matter of fact I think she was strangled."

They looked, and that was what it looked like. She looked older than sixteen, in the glare of combined flashlights, but she was just a kid at that, blonde, huddled on the grass; she was wearing jeans and a heavy sweater, no coat—it had turned warmer just the last few hours.

They called the lab out to take pictures, and they took names and addresses. They had to call an ambulance for the mother. They weren't going to get anything from anybody tonight, so they left Marx and Horder at the scene and came back to the office.

It was a little surprise when Mendoza dodged into the same elevator just as the doors were closing. "Overtime, Lieutenant?" said Schenke.

"We just had a very funny one break," said Mendoza. "I've got a little business for the uniformed branch. And there aren't any private phones at the hospital—I want to call Art." He didn't shut the office door, and they could hear him in there on the phone, detailing a guard to chase over to Central Receiving, and then talking to Hackett. "God knows I should possess enough sophistication to have thought about it, but damn it, that cut-out screen had us all blinded, of course . . . see what you expect to see . . . *Ya lo creo,* a very queer one—in both senses of the word. Well,

I've sent a man over to watch him, I wouldn't put it past him to make another try. I don't know what the D.A. might call it . . . Well, at least one less thing to spend time on. And damn it, I was still thinking Niemeyer was a good bet. My crystal ball getting a little rusty these days, Arturo."

He came out while Schenke was still busy on the new report, and asked, "Anything interesting?"

"New body, and looks like giving the rest of you some work. Little mystery," said Schenke.

"Well, I'll look at it tomorrow—sufficient is the evil," said Mendoza, and went out.

Grace was off on Tuesdays. Sergeant Lake had been busy yesterday and would be busier today; the major piece of business now was the Howstatt thing, and there would be more long-distance calls coming in today and into the future. Mendoza had no sooner got in, talking with Hackett and Higgins in his office, than he had a call from the coroner in Tulare, and then the coroner in San Francisco. Lake had just put that call through when a local call came in for Grace, and he said, "It's his day off, sorry. Anybody else do?"

It was the Widgeon woman. There was some sort of meeting set, up in Juvenile, this afternoon, and she said Mr. Grace had been so kind, she'd feel better if he was there, but if he was off she wouldn't bother him. Lake debated; he knew Grace was interested in the case, and after all it was up to him if he wanted to spend time on it. He called Grace, told him about that; Grace thanked him and said he'd probably go to hold her hand.

Then there was a call from the coroner's office here. Lake put it through and picked up his crossword book.

It had now emerged, just this morning, that Hermione had been married to Arthur Fordham, William Meecham, and Roger Jarvis Senior. "Very likely some of the children were hers," said Mendoza. "The poor suffering babies." But a lot of sorting out was still going on.

Bainbridge called at eleven o'clock to say that Robert Howstatt's exhumation was set for Thursday morning. As far as this Robbery-Homicide office was concerned, they'd gone about as far on it as they could for the moment; they'd set a lot of other forces in motion, up and down the state, and other men were unraveling relationships, looking up marriage and birth and death certificates, talking to doctors, getting statements. Nothing had been decided about any other exhumations; as Bainbridge said, wait to see what turned up in Robert.

Mendoza, Hackett and Higgins went out to lunch at Federico's, and were talking about Lila when Galeano and Landers came up to join them. "That really is the end," said Higgins, amused and scandalized over Lila. "We're getting some weirdos the last week. Not one thing it's another. And ironic, you come to think. I mean, look at that Anton woman and Telford—her so prim and proper, she has a fit about nothing at all and slams out of that car into the arms of a mugger. And then the Wescotts—"

"Consenting adults, George," said Hackett with a wry grin.

"Only he wasn't, exactly," pointed out Mendoza. "Nothing new about human nature. But we've been having a few surprises, *pues sí.*"

"It's looking like rain again," said Galeano gloomily. "And we've wasted the whole morning, if you want to know."

"How come?" asked Higgins.

"This damned Deasy. We wanted a shot of his face to help out locating his pals down in Gardena, and Scarne couldn't get to it till this morning. We got him to mask out the bullet hole, but even so I wouldn't say it looks just like him when he was alive. It may be some help."

"Deasy," said Mendoza musingly. "Did anybody tell me about him?"

"I gave you the gist of it yesterday," said Galeano, "but you were preoccupied with Hermione."

"So tell me again," said Mendoza. Galeano obliged over lunch.

"It looks as if the only motive for shooting him was a gambling debt—we can't turn up anything else. But try to track it down! We haven't found anybody who admits to knowing him yet, and there was nothing on him, in his effects at the house, to give us any names. The wife didn't know anything, or his boss."

Mendoza finished his coffee. "Four kids," he said ruminatively.

"Why, yes, I think four of 'em were the Deasys', why?" Galeano was surprised.

"He was shot in the middle of the forehead, you said?"

"Right between the eyes. It looked like a small caliber."

"Let's see the picture," said Mendoza. Galeano passed it over.

"Don't tell me you're going to have a sudden hunch on this one. We could use it."

"I don't know if it's a hunch," said Mendoza. "Sometimes the crystal ball is a little muddy and I'm seeing things that aren't there at all. Then again, sometimes you don't really need the crystal ball, Nick."

"Come again," said Galeano.

Mendoza looked at the picture again and suddenly laughed. "Well, come on, boys, let's see if my sophistication's working at full speed again. Art, you and George can go sit on the phones and talk to the coroners." He got up.

"What's in your mind?" asked Galeano curiously.

"The result," said Mendoza, "of observing human nature at this thankless job for the hell of a lot more years than you or Tom. What's the address? You can follow me down there."

They trailed the Ferrari in Landers' Sportabout. Everybody had been warned last night when it turned warmer: more rain on the way, but it hadn't arrived yet. Now the sky was getting darker; it would probably be raining by tonight.

The Ferrari slid to the curb in front of the ugly little house on San Marino. Mendoza got out; Landers parked behind and they followed him up the front walk. Galeano pushed the bell.

Ann Deasy opened the door and said, "Oh, it's you again. Have you—have you found out anything?"

Galeano left it to Mendoza to start the ball rolling, and before he did a triumphant voice called from somewhere at the back of the house, "I've nearly got it, Annie! Have you got a pair of tongs?"

"C-come in," said Ann Deasy loudly. "Are there some more questions you want to ask?"

"I rather think so," said Mendoza genially. He strolled in past her and headed for the voice. In the kitchen Mrs. Jernigan and Mrs. Eichenhorn were standing in elaborately casual attitudes by the table. Mrs. Jernigan was holding a yardstick.

"What're the tongs for?" asked Mendoza.

"Toast," said Mrs. Eichenhorn, and at the same moment Ann Deasy said, "I dropped a potholder behind the stove, it doesn't matter." "Oh, did you?" said Mrs. Eichenhorn.

Mendoza regarded them with interest. "You're all admirable witnesses," he told them. "You all told the same story and gave the same description of the villain."

"Well, we've all got eyes," said Mrs. Jernigan smartly. "Who may you be—more police?"

"Lieutenant Mendoza. And seeing that Mrs. Deasy hasn't a helpful male on the premises any more, we may as well make ourselves useful. Nick, Tom, suppose you see if you can find that potholder."

"It really doesn't matter," said Ann Deasy uneasily.

"No trouble." Galeano and Landers moved the stove out eight inches and revealed only a thick layer of dust. "And so that leaves just the refrigerator, doesn't it?—that the three of you couldn't move. Suppose we try there." Mutely they watched while Galeano and Landers heaved the refrigerator forward. "Now isn't that a surprising little find," said Mendoza. He took the yardstick from Mrs. Jernigan and used it to edge the gun out all the way from under the refrigerator. It was a small black automatic, probably a .25 caliber.

"I'll be damned," said Landers under his breath. "My mother'd say he had second sight."

Ann Deasy burst into noisy tears, and Mrs. Eichenhorn said fiercely to Mrs. Jernigan, "You had to be so smart, think of the quickest place to hide it!"

"Well, how did we know people wouldn't hear the shot and come running around, we had to—"

"Oh—oh—oh!" sobbed Ann. "You said so easy, everybody'd think it was another g-g-gambler—"

"They did! They did!" said Mrs. Jernigan. "It wasn't till this one came—" She looked at Mendoza in annoyance.

"And how the hell did you know?" asked Galeano in frank astonishment.

"I didn't really," said Mendoza, "but it was worth a gamble. And you should both have seen it—you've been detectives long enough. How many times do three witnesses tell exactly the same story? There are always discrepancies, maybe unimportant but there. And then, you know, he'd been shot between the eyes. That didn't sound like the sudden fracas described, stranger in waving the gun. It sounded as if he'd been asleep, at least lying down, when he was shot."

"The l-l-lazy big bum!" sobbed Ann Deasy. "Gambling away the money—kids need things and I need those teeth fixed—and I could get the welfare if— didn't have any husband—and it was all your fault!" She stared angrily at Mrs. Jernigan. "You said easy, nobody suspect a thing—I shouldn't have listened to you one second—"

"My fault! Say, listen, you'd never have got up the guts to think about it if I hadn't—"

"You were both crazy!" said Mrs. Eichenhorn. "I tried to tell you it was crazy, but—"

"All right," said Mendoza, "who actually pulled the trigger?" They all fell silent at once and just looked at him, and he started to laugh. "Has anybody got an evidence bag? We'll have to take this thing in. And also you, you know," he added to the women. They started arguing all over again.

Galeano went out to the car to get an evidence bag, and Landers went next door to alert Mr. Eichenhorn to his wife's predicament. He had to push the bell five times before the door finally opened and a broad sandy man faced him yawning. Landers explained economically, and Eichenhorn said, "What?" Landers explained again.

"Now I will be Goddamned," said Eichenhorn. "You mean those fool women went and— Well, I ask you, mister, who the hell knows what a woman's going to get up to next minute?"

They had to call a wagon to take them all in, and by the time it came the women were protesting volubly that there wasn't anybody to look after the kids— washing left in the machine—roast in the oven—and couldn't they take any clothes? Eichenhorn stood on the sidewalk and watched the wagon off, shaking his head slowly, and Mendoza had another fit of laughter, leaning on the Ferrari.

"I know I've got a perverted sense of humor. But talk about neighborliness and practical self-help— We haven't found out who owns the gun." He pulled himself together and took the evidence bag over to Eichenhorn, who looked at it in a puzzled way and said that was Mike Deasy's gun he thought, why Mike had wanted a gun he didn't know but Mike had showed it to him once and he thought that that was it, just a little gun like that anyway.

They went back downtown; Mendoza applied for an arrest warrant and talked to the D.A.'s office. It would be Murder One, and no bail; they'd have to talk to them again, find out which one had actually shot him, but with three talkative females that should emerge. Mendoza called Juvenile and explained. The Juvenile officer said briskly that someone would see the children were brought to Juvenile Hall, pending the location of any relatives.

Nobody else was in but Hackett and Higgins, both on the phone. The coroner's office in San Francisco had passed on the news to the Homicide office there, and a lieutenant had called in, said Hackett, to say they'd be out looking for any possible witnesses in the most recent deaths there, but after all this time— "George has got the police chief in Tulare. And Ferguson called. He's letting Mrs. Beebe go home with her daughter, but the old man's still not so good. Occurred to me, if he dies, there'd be more evidence for the murder charge."

"You're getting as ghoulish as Bainbridge," said Mendoza.

About then an autopsy report came in which proved another little surprise. Lenny Fritch, the longtime fag and addict, hadn't died of an overdose. He'd succumbed to a heart attack, and it could be assumed that if a pal had been with him at the time, he'd taken fright and run; or Lenny could have died alone in an alley, an appropriate end.

There was always the paperwork coming along. The warrant came up on William Scully. Conway was out looking for Scully's pal Lee Livesey, to get a statement about the Bradley car; they wouldn't be charging him with complicity, but they had to tie up the loose ends where they could.

Mendoza had had a guard on Leonard Wescott up to this morning, when he'd been transferred to the prison wing at the General. He now had a long talk with the D.A. on the phone about what might be done about Wescott. Obviously, nobody was going to call it Murder One. "If you ask me," said Mendoza acidly, "it ought to get written off as involuntary homicide, but I suppose you don't see it that way."

"Now, Luis, I see the point but I'm afraid we can't go quite that far." The D.A. settled on Murder Second. The warrant had been applied for this morning and ought to come in before end of shift. Mendoza contemplated possible schedules. Danny Morton would be arraigned tomorrow; Wescott probably Thursday: also probably Thursday, Scully.

There was nothing in from the pawnbrokers to tie to

the muggers, those of Rassky or Olga Anton. Mendoza reflected absently that she'd probably been buried to-day.

Nothing further had been heard of the stammering heist-man.

The three self-help females would come up for ar-raignment Thursday or Friday, always supposing they knew by then who had held the gun. He trusted Gale-ano had applied for the warrants.

Higgins, waiting for the phone to ring again, had found a paperback and was absorbed in it.

Mendoza suddenly remembered there'd been a new body last night, and went out to find the report on it.

Jason Grace, though as cynical as any cop, had a kind heart, and he felt sorry for the Widgeons. "Just like Hermione says, bread on the waters," he told Virginia, and he took some of his day off to attend the unofficial meeting in Juvenile with Mrs. Widgeon. She was pathetically grateful for support; Officer King said she could see Tommy, and took her off to Juvenile Hall.

Grace sauntered down toward the elevators, debat-ing whether he might drop into the office, now he was here, and see what new had turned up on Hermione. Ahead of him a wrathful voice rose in majestic com-plaint.

"—Come to a pretty pass when a man has to set the police on his own children! Running away from home! Causing all this upset and muddle! I don't in general believe in corporal punishment for children, but believe me— Well, where are they? You said you found them in the *railroad* depot? Where—"

Grace pushed. "Hello, Mr. Buller. Having a little more trouble?"

The square stocky man barely glanced at him. "Right here, sir," said the uniformed man escorting him. "Juvenile Officer Blakeley's been looking after them, they're all right, sir. I think they had some idea of hiding away on a train, you know kids." He opened a door on the other side of the corridor and Buller pushed ahead of him through it. Grace raised his eyebrows and punched the bell for the elevator.

"Just what do you mean by causing all this trouble?" Buller's voice was the carrying kind. "I've a good mind to give you both a whipping, running off just when your mother needs you—"

"I won't go back—I won't go back—nobody can make me go back—" A passionate young voice raised over his, and a flying figure came bolting out the door and up the corridor to collide with Grace. He caught the girl's arm to stop her falling and she wrenched away. A female uniformed officer, Buller and the Traffic man came out with a boy younger than the girl, and as the elevator landed with a thud, the door rolling open, she made for it in one leap. The rather portly Captain Goodis, in the act of stepping out, knocked her flat and said in dismay, "What the hell? What goes on?"

Grace set the girl on her feet and she tried to pull away again. "I won't I won't I won't!" she screamed, her face red with anger and panic. "You're a liar, she doesn't want me—and I stabbed her with the knife, you didn't know that, did you? I wish I'd killed her— I'll kill both of you if I ever get the chance—"

There was uproar, and Grace held on to the girl. Buller let out a bellow and made for her with fist raised, Goodis grabbed him, and the boy began to cry. The female officer, looking startled, came up and said, "Linda, you don't mean that—"

"Just a minute," said Grace.

"I do I do I do! I'll kill him—I wish I'd killed her, I ought to have killed her, there was enough blood—"

"Now what's this all about?" asked Goodis.

Buller suddenly started to curse; he hadn't a large vocabulary but went on monotonously repeating a string of obscenities directed at the girl. "You shut up!" said Goodis sharply, and Buller aimed a flailing blow at him. That was a mistake; Goodis was an excellent Juvenile officer with real understanding of children, but insolence from any man he didn't take, and he struck Buller backhanded with a hamlike hand and knocked him against the wall. The girl squealed in delight. "Now let's have some sense out of all this," said Goodis.

"Just a minute, sir," said Grace.

"Who're you? I've seen you around—"

"Robbery-Homicide, Captain. We had a case involving these people a few days ago, but it looks now as if we might not have got all the facts."

"I don't care what you do to me," said Linda loudly. "Put me in jail—I'd rather be in jail!"

"Please don't hurt Linda!" wept the boy. "It's not her fault—really it's not Linda's fault, it's all his—and she—"

"Joe! You promised never to tell, never—"

"I got to!" he wailed. "I got to, or they'll think you're a murderer!"

"Now let's all calm down and try to make some sense out of this," said Goodis. He looked at Grace narrowly. "A homicide?"

"Attempted. Another officer handled it, I don't know whether he's in the office now."

"Well, suppose we go down and ask," said Goodis.

They ended up down in Robbery-Homicide, and Galeano was in, finishing a report. Wanda and the other policewoman took charge of Linda, and Grace, Galeano and Goodis took the boy into an interrogation room.

"So what did you promise not tell, Joe?" Goodis' voice was a soothing rumble, as usual with the kids.

The boy was undersized and weedy, a pale youngster with a pointed face, eyes too large as if he'd been on a starvation diet. "I don't want to say!" he cried in an agony of embarrassment and fright. "But I got to— I got to, because it isn't Linda's fault, you got to see it isn't Linda's fault! And Ma doesn't know—that's just *it* —Ma works at the church most nights, the choir and missionary society and all—and she doesn't know— about—about Dad—" He dropped his head lower and his voice fell too. "About—how Dad's—been doing *that* to Linda, all last year, when Ma's not there—and

Linda hates it—she hates him, but she couldn't get away or stop him doing it—"

"My God Almighty!" said Goodis.

"I don't guess there is one," said the boy, his head drooping lower. "All Ma talks about, God, but it didn't do any good to pray about it—and then—and then—I don't know how she found out, but Linda's—you know, going to have a baby—she's just a *kid*, she's only a year older 'n me!—and Ma went on and on at her, wicked sinful girl and who was it—she shook her and hit her with the broom and Linda couldn't stand it, she grabbed the knife and— But she wasn't dead, it was all worse than ever and we just wanted to get away—get away from both of them—"

"Jesus and Mary!" said Galeano involuntarily. And seasoned police officers, who saw every sin under heaven on the dirty job, supposedly didn't get emotionally involved; but sometimes that was asking the impossible.

Palliser had been starting to look around on the new body; after Conway had failed to locate Lee Livesey, they joined forces on that and got some of the preliminary facts together.

The dead girl was Peggy Conyers, and she'd been sixteen, in her first year of high school. The parents were calmer now, bewildered and grief-stricken, but sensible enough to answer questions; they seemed like solid citizens. Conyers drove a delivery truck for Sears; the house was on Whitehouse Street, an old bungalow. They said Peggy had been a good girl, not wild, always obedient. They'd been fairly strict with her, and she didn't mind. They knew all her friends, all other nice girls, knew some of the parents who went to the same church.

"She was just over at Cathy's!" said Mrs. Conyers. "Just to do homework together—we told her to be in by eight, and when she was late—"

"Cathy?"

"Cathy Springer, she and Peggy are best friends, the Springers live over on Council—"

"Would she have been walking, Mrs. Conyers?" asked Palliser.

"Oh, no! We never let her go out alone at night, on the street—you know how crime's up, and a young girl alone— No, Mr. Springer would bring her home in his car, just as Jack'd do when Cathy was here—they're both only children—we always tried to be so careful—" She began to cry again and her husband patted her arm helplessly.

Palliser and Conway went to see the Springers. He was a little man with a big wife, and he wore the pants in the family. "I heard about it last night, acourse," he said unemphatically. "Jack Conyers called—naturally thought the girl was here, I'd be bringing her home. Which I would have if she'd been here. But I knew you'd want to talk to Cathy—expected you here sometime today, so I kept her home from school."

"The Conyers girl wasn't here at all?" asked Palliser.

"Nope. Often enough she'd come home from school with Cathy, stay to supper, and they'd do their homework together, and I'd take her home. Or they'd go to the Conyers'."

"Yes, well, we'd better talk to Cathy," said Palliser.

She came into the room hesitantly, a pretty dark-haired girl, eyes red with weeping. "I don't know anything," she told them forlornly, looking at her tightly clasped hands. "I don't, really—just like I've told Mother and Dad. We were best friends since kindergarten, it's all so awful—but I don't know anything about it—"

"Did you see her yesterday?"

She nodded. She wouldn't look at them. "Sure, at school. She'd been going to come home with me, but she said—in last class—she didn't feel like it, she—she wanted to play some records alone—she might come tomorrow instead, I mean today."

"Had she ever asked you to cover up for her, let her parents think she was with you when she wasn't?" asked Conway.

She raised her neat dark head and gave them a

wide-eyed stare. "Oh, no, sir! Peggy wouldn't have done anything like that!"

"Should hope not," said Springer. "Or you, my girl."

In Palliser's Rambler Conway said, "Do any good to talk to teachers? Other kids? She had other friends."

"Kids," said Palliser, "have a way of sticking together, Rich. And these two girls seem to have been— um—well-raised girls, strict parents, church and so on. But did you have a little feeling that Cathy was just a bit too innocent and naive?"

"Oh, yes, indeedy," said Conway. "What do we do about it? Haul her in and lean on her we can't. A minor."

"I think," said Palliser thoughtfully, "our best bet is to tell Springer we think she knows something. He'll get it out of her."

"Chestnuts out of the fire for us. That's a brilliant inspiration, John," said Conway with a chuckle.

"Of course," said Mr. McNair, "the acreage in La Cañada offers you a nice level building site. Unless you're thinking of a tri-level, the site in Flintridge could pose some problems, but all the existing trees are a bonus."

"Yes," said Alison. "Where are we going now?"

"This place just above Burbank. It's only recently come on the market. It may not be quite what you're after, but I'd like you to see it. Four acres, and we're holding it for only a hundred and ten thousand be-cause—well, I must warn you there are some draw-backs."

"Such as what?"

"Well, it was a winery at one time, and some of the old buildings are still standing—they'd have to be torn down, which would cost something. But it's a beautiful location, some thick stands of oak. The property be-longed to the same family for several generations, and it's been derelict for years owing to the last owner having been senile and incompetent for some time. He's dead now, it came to a great-grandson or some relative, and he's naturally anxious to settle the estate."

"I see," said Alison uninterestedly. It was threatening rain again; it had been an off-and-on day, the sun out five minutes and then in. They were cruising up Scott Road in Burbank; Mr. McNair turned on Haven and they began to wind up into the hills. The few new houses fell away behind them and presently he made another turn into a narrow street; there was a sign. Adornos Way. Ornament Street, thought Alison, with faint curiosity; it was queer how Spanish words got used for street names, the namers having no idea what they meant. That was, come to think, why they'd built the house on Rayo Grande, Luis taking a fancy to live on Great Thunderbolt Avenue.

The hill got steeper and the paved street ended suddenly. It all looked wild, above: live oaks, underbrush, manzanita. There were the ruins of a pair of gates, only the gateposts left. "I'm afraid you'd have to think about blacktop from here on," said Mr. McNair. It was just a track, wandering up the hill.

As they came to the top of the hill the sun came out suddenly, and Alison said in surprise, "I thought you said it was a winery. That's a house—a—" Not a house; a hacienda, sprawling wings, balconies, a red tile roof.

"Oh, that's the old farmhouse. The winery building's on the other side of the hill. All quite derelict," said Mr. McNair, "but you can see it's a beautiful site. All the trees, and we're quite high up here—do you know The Castaway restaurant? Famous for its view—I should imagine you'd get just as good a one from here. You can see—"

Now Alison had spent her first impressionable years south of the border, mostly in rural Mexico, and her emotional reactions to architecture, as to a number of other things, were largely Latin rather than Anglo-European. And at her first glance at that house she was seized with unreasonable affection for it.

"I'd like to look over the house," she said. "Have you got the key?"

"The house? It's ready to fall down. Like all the other buildings."

Alison felt just as unreasonably annoyed with him. "It certainly doesn't look like it," she said. It was a house—an *estancia,* she thought—quite like all the grand *estancias* she remembered, the important houses where the *patrones* lived, the *terratenienetes,* the big landholders. The track came up to it and went beyond to a long low building that might have been a stable. The house was two-storied and L-shaped, with the remnants of a big square brick courtyard in the L in front, and balconies above. It was built of plain white adobe plaster, and there was a pair of massive double doors at one side of the courtyard.

"The key," said Mr. McNair. "Well, no. The house isn't—it never occurred to me—"

"Damn," said Alison. There were iron grilles on the windows, quite immovable. She walked around the side, deaf to his protests, and at the back they found a rear door boarded up. "You might have remembered to bring the key, after all," said Alison. "See if you can pry these boards loose."

He managed to get two boards out, and Alison sidled in. Disregarding dust and cobwebs, she made a beeline for those double doors, round at the other side. Her instinct had been quite right. They gave on two massively simple rooms, separated by a wide arch, each at least thirty feet square, and floored with red tile. Some of it was broken and cracked. There was a stone hearth in each room. Down the hall she'd come in by, off the second room, was what had been the kitchen, easily twenty feet square, with a hearth halfway up the wall; and another room behind that contained the door they'd broken in. A long hall at right angles, past a staircase, led down the other side of the L past four more big rooms to a bigger one across the front of the L. The hall had windows looking out on the courtyard.

"Mrs. Mendoza! Please be careful—this building may be dangerous—the stairs—" He was following her gingerly.

"Don't be ridiculous," said Alison. "It's as sound as the day it was built. Not a leak in the roof—" And all red tile floors here; and the staircase was solid oak, like the double doors. She ran up it feeling suddenly very excited, and came out on a landing that faced a balcony over the courtyard. A hall ran two ways: to the left was a door onto a wide L-shaped room. To the right the longer hall gave on four big square rooms; there were windows along the hall onto the balcony, and a pair of doors. All the inside walls were of rough unpainted plaster, and there was a hearth in the L-shaped room and another in the big corner room.

"Mrs. Mendoza! Are you all right?"

"Of course I'm all right. I'm fine," said Alison. She came down the staircase, which spiraled rather intriguingly, and went back to the first main room. The double doors were carved with crosses. The wood here, and in the staircase, was black and dry with time, but solid, she thought, as the day it had gone in here.

"Well, now you've seen the drawbacks—" He wasn't very hopeful, but experienced salesman that he was, he went on gamely pointing out the advantages. "The view would be superb, and of course you'd be out of the smog this high up—and all the trees mature. It shouldn't cost a great deal to clear the site, you could get estimates—"

"I don't want to clear it," said Alison. "I love this house, Mr. McNair—it's a beautiful house—it's just what I want. I'll buy it."

He stared at her. "But it's got no plumbing or electricity!" he said wildly.

"Oh, we can put all that in," said Alison casually. "Some of the walls need replastering anyway." All sorts of specific ideas were running through her mind already. All the rooms so large—knock out that one wall between the two smaller rooms downstairs, and section off a bathroom—a splendid self-contained suite for Mairí. The other little room at the end of the short hall on the first floor, another bathroom. The room down the hall right next to that, a fine guest room. There was scads of room upstairs. The big L-shaped room, plenty of space to put in an enormous bathroom, that would be the master suite, and—count them!—five big rooms down that hall, a playroom for the children, rooms for Terry and Johnny and the new one—of course for a while to come, they might use the downstairs guest room as a nursery, but if she should be nursing this one, easy enough to make a nursery upstairs in that big corner room—

"But—plumbing—heating—electricity," said Mr. McNair faintly. "You can't be serious—this—this white elephant—"

"Certainly I'm serious. It's a house," said Alison lovingly, "with a lot of character." That other building—once a stable?—would make a fine big garage, room for Mairí's car too. There were other buildings—a winery—the other side of the hill. A place, thought Alison vaguely, for the pony. Or ponies. They could build a corral, and find somebody to take care of the ponies.

"But it's nearly a hundred years old!" said Mr. McNair, nakedly incredulous.

"All the better," said Alison. She put her hand on the old oak doors, and felt suddenly that she had come home. And, she thought, I can't wait to tell Luis—

10

MENDOZA DIDN'T SHOW AT THE OFFICE UNTIL NOON on Wednesday, just in time to go out to lunch with Hackett and tell him about the house Alison had found. "I had to go and admire it this morning. It's going to cost a modest fortune to update—there's no plumbing or electricity—"

"For God's sake, what's she thinking of?"

"—But I have to admit her instinct's quite right, it's a gem. Built like Gibraltar, and God knows plenty of square footage for all the bathrooms and bedrooms and playrooms she's talking about. Well, vintage Californiana you can say—an old winery up past Burbank. Four acres. You'll have to come and see it. I'm informed we're turning the old stable into a garage, and possibly the winery building will emerge as stabling for the ponies—if we can find somebody to look after the ponies."

"Has she gone nuts? That old a house—"

"Don't overlook her Scots blood, Art. It's one hell of a buy, a lot for the money in that location, and it'll be quite a place when it's embellished with all the bathrooms and a modern kitchen and all the new furniture it'll need—you could set our present house down in it with a desert left round the edge. Alison says it's got character. I just hope it isn't haunted. Do you know The Castaway?'

"Of course I know The Castaway, why?"

"Well, if we cut down a few of those old oak trees, we'll have about the same spectacular view from the living and dining rooms and the master bedroom upstairs. It's going to be quite a place," said Mendoza thoughtfully.

"I'll have to go and see it. Some more background's been drifting in on Hermione, by the way. The coroner in Tulare is hot on getting some exhumations—I referred him to Bainbridge. And the coroner here wants to sic a head doctor on to her."

"I can hear what Bainbridge'll say to that."

There had been two more heists overnight, and nobody had talked to the three self-help females again; in the interests of determining exact charges they ought to find out who'd held the gun. Mendoza went over to the jail after lunch and spent an hour unraveling the story; the women were calmed down and readier to talk. Ann Deasy admitted drearily that she'd shot Mike, but the idea had been Elise Jernigan's. Let the D.A. untangle it, thought Mendoza cynically; there wasn't much to choose among them, Mike Deasy had been no great loss, and with the courts as lenient as they were none of them, probably, would serve much time in.

He said as much to Galeano, coming in at three o'clock, and Galeano said with a grin, "I thought I'd heard about all the various schemes to defraud the welfare service—this was something new."

"I don't think it'd make an additional charge, Nick."

"Peggy never said anything to you about a special boyfriend?" asked Palliser.

"Oh, no, sir. She didn't have any. She wasn't allowed to go steady yet, her parents are pretty strict." Jean Kramer looked down modestly, and the other three girls giggled softly like a little flock of sparrows.

"She'd been on double dates with me and Ron Keller and Biddy Marsh and Bob Wirtz," volunteered Betty Jo Brown. "To the movies," and her wide eyes were demure. "But I guess that's not what you mean."

Palliser looked at Conway, a shrug in his eyes. They'd been talking to these girls, all school friends of Peggy Conyers', here in the girls' vice-principal's office at the high school, and it was a highly inhibited atmosphere, with Miss Frances Villers sitting there listening, regal and white-haired. The girls made Palliser and Conway, thirty-five and thirty-one respectively, feel as old as Methusaleh; they were fresh-faced, innocent-eyed, limpid of expression, exaggeratedly polite. Palliser nodded at Miss Villers and she nodded at the girls, and they all got up to file out. Before the door shut a lot of whisperings and giggles broke out.

Miss Villers said, "Well, you didn't get much there, did you? Very secretive, the young. What do you think they might know?"

Conway sat back and regarded her with cynical gray eyes. "It's not so much what we think—maybe as mere males we don't know what girls talk about together."

"Oh, don't we," said Palliser. "Look here, Miss Villers—it could be that these girls, her closest friends in school besides Cathy Springer, don't know a thing. We think Cathy does. But if any of these girls do know, they might not feel quite the same—er—loyalty to keep the secret. Especially with Peggy murdered."

"The girl had been up to the usual fun, I suppose. She seemed like one of the nicest girls in this class, and strictly brought up, but that doesn't mean much these days, does it? But are you thinking that has anything to do with the murder? Who," asked Miss Villers distastefully, "would be so upset by a thing like that, these enlightened times?"

"It's the only handle we've got," said Palliser.

"Well, I don't know how I can help you. I'm a figurehead," she said tartly. "The idea used to be, the young people coming to us—counselors—for friendly advice. The so-called generation gap is a chasm as far as I'm concerned. They're like a race apart. I don't understand these youngsters most of the time and what I do understand I don't like. I suppose I'm just hopelessly old-fashioned, ready for the boneyard."

"Well, thanks anyway," said Palliser. Her curious gaze followed them out. "That was an exercise in futility."

"As we might have known it would be," said Conway. "But there's one thing I'm pretty sure of, the big romance wasn't any of the boys at school. Not even one of the senior boys."

"No, I don't think so either," said Palliser. "It didn't sound like that, somehow. But it's got to go back to that, hasn't it?"

"We don't know she wasn't walking home from somewhere, but that's a quiet street, not a haunt for muggers, and she had four dollars in her jeans pocket and a wristwatch. And she'd got Cathy to cover up for her," pointed out Conway.

"True. If we could just get Cathy to open up—"

Conway sighed. Neither he nor Palliser was very interested in how Peggy Conyers had got herself strangled, but the routine had to be done. They had seen the parents again this morning, asked permission to look over her room; and there, among all the teenage paraphernalia, hit records, faddy clothes, fashion magazines, junk jewelry, they had come across that other expectable adjunct of the teenager, a diary. A five-year diary with the key confidingly in it; Peggy had had a good relationship with her parents, confident they wouldn't pry. It was a waste of time to speculate on whys and wherefores—as Conway said, that old devil sex had been around a long time.

Up to about ten weeks ago, the diary was full of artless sixteen-year-old comments and emotions: clothes, fads, TV shows, classes, other girls. Then it turned into incoherent jottings which, as they read between the lines, pretty clearly recorded a hot love affair. *Oh hes just so romantic and it seems like a dreem hes interested in me . . . I know its suposed to be wrong but I feel its just meant for us to be together . . . Its all so dreemy but I wish it could be some other way, but I love him so much I cant say no when he wants me . . . some day he says well be together before all the world and we just have to be pachient.* Rather a silly girl, Peggy, but sixteen wasn't the wisest of ages.

"You don't tell me," said Conway, "she poured all that out to a diary and didn't pour out more to a best girl friend."

"I don't. We'll keep prodding at Cathy."

"We might get the Lieutenant to tackle her. With the females he's got a touch."

Higgins was off on Wednesday. He'd picked up a paperback in the office yesterday and started it desultorily to kill time, sitting on the phones. Then he'd got interested in it and brought it home with him. He picked it up again after breakfast, and was absorbed in it when Mary said she was going out if he didn't mind babysitting.

Higgins looked up to find her wrapped in a becoming blue plastic coat and hood; it was raining again. "If it's groceries, I could go—no day to be out."

"I don't mind. Angel Hackett called and we're going to see the Mendozas' new house. It sounds rather exciting."

"Oh, she's found something, has she?" said Higgins absently. "No, you trot along, I'll see to the baby." He went to check on her now and then, presently got some lunch down her, and lunch for himself. He'd just finished the book—quite a character that old fellow had been—when Steve and Laura got home from school.

"Where's Mother?"

"Out for a while."

"Oh, well, I'll do my homework after dinner, George—I've got to practice first." The piano always came first with Laura. It was a good thing he'd finished the book.

Steve went clattering by on his way to the back door and the garage darkroom. He'd grown another inch in the last month and looked more like Bert all the time. "Hey, George, I finished that film—the one with the shots of the basketball game last week—I'm going out to develop it, you tell Mother I'll do my homework after dinner."

Higgins yawned and wondered where Mary had got to. Gadding all over in the rain—

It was still raining on Thursday morning; this was being a wet year with a vengeance. There wasn't much

in the night report but another heist, another freeway
crash with one dead. By the time Mendoza got in
everybody else was out on something, and he was
sitting at his desk reading the night report, other recent
reports on the business through the office the last few
days, when the phone buzzed at him and he picked it
up. "Robbery-Homicide, Mendoza."

"I just thought I'd let you know," said Bainbridge,
"that we've got Robert dug up successfully."

"In all this rain?"

"Oh, the coroner's crew rigged up a tent. I've only
had a brief look, but he's quite well preserved and I
think I can say definitely that if there's anything to be
got out of him we'll get it. We should know by tomorrow. When it comes to weighing quantities and possibly isolating brands and so on, it'll take longer. I've
just heard that Tulare's decided to dig up at least one
of their bodies. It's a waste of time, of course."

"Ace in the hole," said Mendoza.

"Oh, I don't know," said Bainbridge. "Didn't San
Francisco pass on her birth certificate?"

Mendoza looked at his desk, which was uncharac-
teristically untidy with scattered reports and notes from
phone calls; he pushed papers aside, looking, and said,
"Should they have?"

"Well, it turned up. Hermione Eloise Smith. Reason
I say waste of time, I'm pretty certain we'll get enough
out of Robert for a Murder One charge, and what with
the charge of attempt on the Beebes and the court
probably ordering a psychiatric examination to drag
out the proceedings further, *and* the birth certificate—
do you know, she's eighty-four, Luis."

"Hermione? *No me tome el palo,*" said Mendoza. "I
see what you mean—with the leisurely way trials go, if
she gets even a three-to-ten it might see her out."

"That's what I thought. She's happy as a jaybird
right now—I had another session with her yesterday.
She confided that she's never liked housework and
cooking, and it's so nice to have all her meals fixed for
her. Also told me about Roger Senior. She really had
to get rid of him, she said, because she was embar-

rassed to have a husband so much older, people were making remarks about it and it was a mistake to have married him. Now don't tell me that's evidence of insanity. These people aren't insane, they've just had something left out of them."

"Just a screw loose."

"No, it's a part missing," said Bainbridge seriously. "I'll be in touch as soon as we take Robert apart and see what shows."

Mendoza put the phone down and found the Xerox copy of the birth certificate. The mess on his desk annoyed him and he began to straighten it up, filing reports away in the tray and dropping the notes into the wastebasket.

He was thinking of going out for lunch when Galeano and Grace came in. Galeano sat down with a grunt and closed his eyes, stretching out his legs as if his feet hurt. Grace said he thought Mendoza had better be warned, Goodis wanted a session this afternoon to thrash out the Buller thing.

"Oh—that," said Mendoza with a grimace. "All I heard was the bare facts from Nick, I haven't seen a report. What have you been doing on it, just having cozy chats with Juvenile?"

"Are you kidding?" Galeano opened his eyes, sat up and brought out a cigarette. Mendoza handed him the flamethrower. "No, thanks, when I want to burn my nose off I'll tell you. That thing! My good God, these people! I thought you were writing a report, Jase—"

"I got waylaid by that doctor."

"Oh. Well, it's an all-round king-size mess, and it isn't going to be cleared up easy if at all. That woman went straight off her head when we got through to her what had been going on, Daddy having fun and games with the girl—God, she's only fourteen—I'd call it old-fashioned religious mania but I suppose the head doctors'll have a fancier name for it. And I do mean raving—we had to call an ambulance, and she's still in a straitjacket at the General."

"Mr. Buller," Grace took up the tale, "is officially charged with contributing to the delinquency of a minor, and in jail, but you know what kind of slap on the hand he'll get for that. I would hope he gets fired from his job with Social Security but I wouldn't even take a bet on that. The children are at Juvenile Hall—" He paused.

"And that is hardly a solution, is it?" asked Mendoza. "But what else do we do, how else do we handle it? It's still an imperfect world, *compadres.*"

"In spades," said Grace. He brushed his mustache back and forth. "The girl—it's too late for an abortion. There's one more unfortunate due to enter this vale of tears. Afterward, if they're lucky, there'll be foster homes—if they're damned lucky, good ones, but those are few and far between. At least we can see the parents don't get custody again. But what kind of scars those kids will carry all their lives—"

"Depressing," agreed Mendoza. "A lot of what we see is depressing, and no discharge in that war. Let's go out to lunch and try to forget it."

They'd all got soaked once that morning, on the way in, so it didn't make any difference, going out again. At Federico's they ran into Higgins, who was working his way through a steak. "And what have you been accomplishing?" asked Mendoza, pulling out a chair. The waiter hurried up with coffee.

"Dropping on a heister," said Higgins. "We got a pretty good description from that pharmacist, and he made two mug-shots. I just located one of them."

"He come apart and tell all?" asked Grace.

"I don't know if he will. I've had a busy morning, I wanted lunch, so I stashed him at the office. I'm just going back to hear what he has to say. Oh, by the way, Tom finally got hold of that Lee Livesey. Nothing much in it, he backs up what Scully said—just thought Scully'd picked up a heap for a joyride, and helped him ditch it. He never saw the blood inside."

"A little progress," said Mendoza.

Hackett was feeling bored and restless on his day off. He hadn't anything to do, anywhere to go, even if it hadn't been raining like hell. There wasn't anything on TV, he hadn't anything interesting to read, and Angel had gone out. Mark was at school, but that ordinarily good little girl Sheila was fretful and fussy.

It was four o'clock before Angel's car turned into the drive, and he complained loudly about being left to babysit all day. "I *am* sorry, darling," said Angel, "the time just got away from me. I was dying to see Alison's house again, you know I had that dental appointment yesterday and just got one hasty look. The owner lives out of town and they can't clinch the deal right away, but they will. I drove up there and she was there, she's already got some marvelous ideas for remodeling. A half bath on that big back porch, and one of those smaller bedrooms down the hall—I suppose they were meant for bedrooms—can be cut in half for two big bathrooms, one opening on the hall and one into the next bedroom. And this enormous room across the front, she's going to knock out the wall into the next room and build a big bath and walk-in closet to make a beautiful suite for Mairí—oh, Mairí was there too, she's delighted about it and has all sorts of ideas too—"

"Not having seen it, I can't follow you. But I understand there's no electricity, how did you see anything, a day like this?"

"Kerosene lamps," said Angel. "Mairí understands them." Her mountain-pool eyes were thoughtful, looking around the living room. "You know, Art, I've been thinking just lately, this house isn't really as big as we need. And this whole area's been running down, the rezoning and all the apartments going up—I think it'd be the sensible thing to do, sell before it goes down more in value, and look for something bigger in a better neighborhood."

"Oh, my God, females!" said Hackett in dismay. "Just because Alison's gone and found a damned mansion that'll cost a mint to fix up, not to speak of heating and taxes afterward—"

"Well, you do have to look ahead," said Angel reasonably.

"Going to uproot me now! Going to have everything upset for the next six months—and if you ask me," said Hackett, "Alison's not acting very sensible, trotting all over in this damned weather, with the baby due in July. Be lucky if she doesn't fall down the stairs, wandering around that place in the dark—"

"Oh, she's feeling fine now," said Angel.

Thursday night, and Shogart was off. Piggott and Schenke didn't miss him. The day watch hadn't left anything for them to do, and they sat talking desultorily for a while. They had to keep up with the reports, of course; and they kicked that Buller case around, and Lila Wescott. Piggott was sometimes ambivalent, if that was the word, thought Schenke; on the one hand he was an earnest fundamentalist Christian with a few rather narrow ideas, and on the other an experienced cop who had seen more of the dirt at the bottom than most ministers or timid sinners ever see, and was aware that there really weren't any pat answers. He shook his head over Lila and talked about the devil, but rather more doubtfully than usual.

Schenke said, "That's a comforting idea, Matt, the devil. Somebody else responsible—oh, I know the idea is you have to give in to temptation, but put like that it's all the devil's notion. Some of the things we see— the way I look at it, it's people's own responsibility, their own decisions."

"Well—the devil operating in every man," said Piggott.

"Maybe so." It wasn't worth arguing over.

At nine-twenty they got a call from Traffic. "Another heist," said Zimmerman.

"So what's the address?" Schenke poised his pen.

"You can get it all down in the report." Zimmerman sounded amused. "We've got 'em—we're bringing 'em in. The victims nabbed 'em and held 'em for us."

"Be damned," said Schenke. "Little twist." Zimmerman said there was more to it than that, they'd be in. He and his partner brought four men into the office ten minutes later, and Schenke and Piggott saw what he meant."

"Mr. Aloysius O'Leary and Mr. James Kent," said Zimmerman. "And this is Dave Williams and Andrew Porter. Mr. O'Leary runs a service station on Rampart and Mr. Kent works for him."

"Say," said O'Leary anxiously, "I didn't hurt you when I grabbed the gun, did I? You feel all right? You better sit down. Listen, you let them sit down, you guys, hah?"

"I wouldn't've hit him if I'd looked first," said Kent. "I heard Al yell holdup, I come running out of the garage and just grabbed him from behind, but when I seen him—"

The two heisters, Williams and Porter, stood looking a little sheepish and oddly shy in the middle of the room. Williams was a tall thin man with a long hooked nose and a pair of wrinkled jowls like an old hound dog. Porter was a chunky little man with a red face; his hands were crooked and crippled, and he walked bent over slightly, with a limp. Both of them looked past eighty.

"Now you sit down, take it easy," urged O'Leary. "Say, I bet you two don't have a dime, do you? Old and can't work and flat broke, you're maybe too proud to take charity, hah? Not that I'm gonna say it was right you should hold me up—"

"And not just you," said Schenke, shutting his mouth after the one look. "This'll be the pair we've been looking for on a couple of other jobs. What about it?"

"Guess I will sit down," said Porter. "This rain plays hell with my arthritis." He limped over to Higgins' desk and subsided into the chair thankfully. "I guess we got to tell them, Dave."

"I think you'd better," said Schenke. He took the gun from Zimmerman; it was an old thirty-ought rifle, quite empty of any load.

"Two poor old guys like this," said O'Leary.

Williams gave a rueful chuckle and came to sit down

at Grace's desk. "Well, you got it a little wrong, we aren't as poor as that. We got enough to eat, if nothing fancy, and we got a place to live—"

"If nothing fancy," said Porter. "Place to end up in, only we didn't feel like it. Single rooms in a nice enough boardinghouse over on Benton, you want to know. The woman sets a good enough table, but kind of plain. I got the Social Security and a little pension from the railroad, and Dave's got the Social Security and a little pension from the bus company, and there we were. Wives both dead, and never had any families. I got to admit we were comfortable enough—but there wasn't any—any excitement left to anything. You get me?"

"One day like another," said Williams. "And who knows how much longer we got to look forward to? I'm eighty-three and Andrew's eighty-four. And one day I looked at him over that damn fool checkerboard and I said, Andy, I said, let's go out and raise a little hell, and he said, let's."

"Maybe the doctors'd say we're senile, hey, Dave? Never even had a parking ticket all my life," said Porter with a grin that showed even store teeth. "But what's the odds, we said, neither of us got any families to disgrace if we get caught, and meanwhile we'd have some fun, go on a real spree—"

"And if we did get caught," said Williams, "there ought to be some more interesting people in jail than these doddering old idiots at the boardinghouse, sitting around waiting to die."

"Did you go on a spree, with the money?" asked Schenke gravely.

They both cackled, "Oh, my!" said Porter. "We've had a real dandy time, haven't we, Dave? You know, we always wanted to see that Disneyland place—not just a place for kids, a lot of interesting things to see there. We took the bus and stayed at the hotel two days, it was just fine. And not that we're either of us hard drinking men, we both like a nip of Scotch now and then, and on the little left after the rent and all, there just wasn't enough to buy it—awful price it's gone to now—and we had that too. Bought myself a new suit, and so did Dave, and we went out to dinner at all the fancy restaurants, cocktails and cigars and I don't know what all—"

"I see," said Schenke, not daring to look at Piggott. "Where'd you get the gun?"

"Oh, I had the gun," said Williams cheerfully. "I used to like to go hunting, took two, three weeks every fall—not so much for shooting anything, just the country and the fall weather and colors, getting out of the city. Been I dunno how many years since I had any ammunition for it, but we thought—and it worked just fine." They looked at each other and chuckled.

"Well, I'm afraid," said Schenke, "that we'll have to arrest you and take you over to jail."

"I suppose so," said Williams. He looked at Porter and they both brightened. "Be a new experience, won't it?"

On Friday morning, with Galeano and Conway off, scheduled arraignments made them even more short-handed. Mendoza had no more than come in than he was hailed off to a meeting about Hermione with the D.A., the coroner and Bainbridge.

Palliser came back at eleven o'clock from seeing Scully arraigned and found Conway reading a report. "There you are, brother—read it and weep," he said succinctly, handing it to Palliser. "Nothing new under the sun." It was the autopsy report on the Conyers girl; she'd been pregnant. And these days, with a lot of girls, that wouldn't have been anything to cover up or even get excited about; but with these people—moral, rigidly respectable people—it would be. It was a tired old story.

"And we are going to get Cathy to open her mouth or know the reason why," said Palliser. "Come on."

At the house on Council Street Springer didn't waste words. "I'd have known something was wrong with her, way she's been acting, even if you hadn't said you figure she knows something about Peggy. Can't get at her any way"—he gave his taller wife a faint smile—

"stubborn old chip off the block, eh? She lies in bed crying all day—make herself sick—and if you ask me it's not crying over Peggy, but mostly because she knows she did something sinful and foolish, if she was covering up for Peggy doing something wrong."

"That's what it looks like, Mr. Springer."

"Well," said Cathy's mother calmly, "if you can get her to tell about it, it's more than we can."

"Let's have a try," said Palliser. "Where is she?"

They pointed out the bedroom, and the detectives knocked and went in. Cathy was lying huddled on the bed, not crying, just staring at the wall. "Go away," she said in a muffled voice.

"I'd like to show you something, Cathy," said Palliser harshly. "The autopsy report on Peggy. Your best friend Peggy. Did you know she was pregnant? It was probably the boy who got her in trouble who killed her—here, look at what it says—she was strangled by a pair of big hands, and then thrown out of a car into her own front yard. You know, it hurts to get strangled, Cathy, and she thought he loved her, didn't she? She thought he might marry her, didn't she? Who was it, Cathy? You know, because you covered for her—all the time she was with him, her parents thought she was with you. Who is he?"

"You think I haven't thought of all that?" she screamed suddenly. She pulled herself up in bed, and the tears were streaming down her face. "You think I don't hate him like poison? If anybody'd *believe* me—only nobody would, you all side together and you'd say it couldn't—you *wouldn't* believe it—"

"Try and see."

"Oh—oh—oh!" she sobbed, and gulped down sobs and told it in breathless little gasps. "She had just an awful crush on him, a lot of the girls did—and she couldn't believe it—when he had her stay—and told her he'd noticed her and how pretty she was—and then he asked her out, and she said I had to say she was here, she'd just die if she couldn't go out with him—and then she'd meet him after school and he took her to his apartment—"

"Who, Cathy?"

She gulped a last sob and looked up at them through tear-studded lashes. "Our Eng-English teacher—Mr. Underwood."

Hackett had found a paperback book on Wanda's desk and started to read it over a solitary lunch. It was interesting; he wished he'd had it on his day off. He was a little annoyed when he got back to the office and found Higgins had brought in another suspected heistman.

Galeano was feeling a little more cheerful. He'd got Marta to go out to dinner with him last night. She had to be at the restaurant at seven, and she wouldn't drink a glass of wine with him, but she had on a new dress, a nice shade of blue, and she looked fine.

"How does the job go, Nick? You have some interesting cases?"

"A couple," said Galeano. He nearly started to tell her about the self-help females, and then didn't; she might not think that was so funny, having been suspected of murdering a husband herself. He told her about Olga Anton instead. "That's a lesson for you. Don't go holding a decent man at arm's length, he might have honorable intentions."

"I think I would always be wary of a cunning Italian."

"And I don't know why I'm trying to butter up a stiffnecked German." They laughed together, and he felt comfortable about it. Everything would be all right.

On Saturday morning, with the weather temporarily clear, Mendoza and Alison drove down to the Red Carpet Realty Company in Hollywood to arrange for the official purchase of the property. Mr. McNair greeted them effusively, hand out. "Very punctual—so happy to meet you, sir. This is Mr. Valdez."

"So pleased," said Valdez formally. He was a stocky dark man about fifty, very correct in a conservative dark suit. He looked faintly surprised and interested, looking from Alison to Mendoza. "I hope you'll be very happy with the—land."

"It's a beautiful house, Mr. Valdez," said Alison warmly.

Mr. McNair wiped his brow. He had handled many real estate transactions, but he had never had such peculiar clients in all his professional life. This Mrs. Mendoza had made no counteroffers at all, and he felt that Valdez might have taken five or six thousand less. I'll buy it, she said, just like that, that monstrosity of a white elephant.

"It's going to be such fun," she said, "making it all new."

Valdez started. "You're not going to tear it down?" he asked. "We took it for granted—"

"Certainly not—it's going to come to life again," she said. "Electricity, I thought maybe this new cable heating, and bathrooms, and new tile, and all that lovely oak restored, and two rooms downstairs made into a playroom for the children—"

"But that would be a miracle!" said Valdez emotionally. "Oh, I'd like to see that, Mrs. Mendoza. You see, the house—that place—it was my great-great-grandfather who built it—started the winery. The business was long gone when I first knew it—my great-uncles had gone into cattle and land farther north, the family mostly lives up the coast now. But that was the old family place, where we all used to gather for holidays. It was always a family house. The old people lived there until they both died, and it came to my grandfather—poor old man, senile for years and we've been sorry to think of the house standing there empty. The old man liked to call it the house of happy people."

"La Casa del Gente Feliz," said Alison. "I like that. We'll call it that again, Luis. We'll have iron gates with the name on them."

Mendoza was sitting smoking, watching them with a little smile. "Well, now, I think we'd better get to business," said Mr. McNair gaily. "I'm sure there'll be no difficulty about the loan, of course you understand, Mr. Mendoza, that all our facilities will see to the details on that. It's just the little details we have to get down on paper—shall we say, for instance, a down payment of ten thousand and a first trust deed—"

"Oh, I'll give you cash," said Mendoza, and lit another cigarette. "The full amount."

Mr. McNair's jaw dropped. "C-cash? You want to pay—the full purchase price—in cash—right now?"

"If you'll take my check. You'll want to call the bank."

Mr. McNair goggled at them. Alison and Valdez were now chatting volubly in Spanish. Mendoza had a checkbook out. Wordlessly Mr. McNair took it and took down the name of the bank in shaky ballpoint. He had known Alison was crazy; he hadn't reckoned on a lunatic husband as well. His faith in immutable law was shattered; he was a broken man.

"Well, *mi corazón,* there's your house. Just don't kill yourself working on it—there's plenty of time."

"I won't, *amado.* Now I know where we'll be—all settled—we can take our time to get it all just right. It's going to be a lovely, lovely house," said Alison dreamily. "The house of happy people. Mr. Valdez is nice—I'd like to know more about the family. I promised to invite him and his wife to see it when it's all finished."

"Just don't wear yourself out."

"Oh, it's going to be fun. And I never thanked you, *amante*—"

On Monday, Hackett got in early and was looking over the night report when Mendoza came in. "Oh," he said, "that's where it came from."

"What?"

"Piggott left a note—he's missing a book. This one." Hackett picked it up where he'd left it yesterday in Wanda's desk tray. "Very good book too, Luis—you'd enjoy it."

Mendoza took it. *"The Man Who Was Sherlock*

Holmes, a life of A. Conan Doyle—John Dickson Carr. I'll look at it when I have time," and absently he dropped it into a drawer of the desk. The phone buzzed at him, and it was Bainbridge.

"Just as I expected, there's enough arsenic in Robert for a dozen murder charges. Tulare has another autopsy for us, more arsenic. The coroner has a meeting set with the D.A. for ten o'clock, if you can make it."

"Así, así," said Mendoza. "I'll be there."

On Tuesday afternoon a pawnbroker by the name of Kravitz called in, and Hackett went to talk to him. "Well, I been sick," said Kravitz defensively, "the store's been closed. I just came back in this morning and saw the new hot list." He had that signet ring with the HXA initials, and Olga Anton's jade jewelry along with it. He hunted out the scrawled receipt for Hackett: it said J. Hoyt, an address on Malabar in Boyle Heights. Just on the very outside chance that it wasn't a made-up address, Hackett went looking, and there large as life in a dingy old apartment was an unshaven lout about twenty who said he was Jackie Hoyt, what about it?

Hackett felt inexpressibly tired of all this stupidity. He took him in, and he and Mendoza talked to him. Hoyt didn't know what they were talking about at first, and when it was spelled out to him he said, "Oh. Yeah. How'd you drop on me for that? There wasn't much on that dame—ten bucks in her purse and some fake hardware. I only got three for the hardware." He was more surprised than scared when they told him the woman was dead. "Dead?" he said. "I only hit her a little tap with the hammer—how could she be dead?"

Mendoza drove home on Wednesday night through the pouring rain. His mind turned over idly on the various business on hand at the office. That damned English teacher hadn't showed up yet—there was an A.P.B. out on him and his car, and doubtless they'd drop on him sometime. All the coroners' offices concerned with Hermione's past were in a frenzy of activity; more reports on exhumations and autopsies were drifting in every day. A couple of new bodies had turned up, but not to make much paperwork, probably. There was always a new heist to make for the routine legwork, and the victim on the one last night said the heist-man stammered, so they'd be looking for that one harder, and nowhere much to look.

The garage door was open. He dodged through rain and went into the back porch to find Cedric slurping at his water bowl. Mairí was inspecting something in the oven.

"At least," she told him, "she's settled down some, planning out all the work. Och, it's going to be a grand place—just fine for the bairns, space to run about, and all the animals too."

Mendoza went down to the living room, treading cautiously past Terry's room where the twins were having an acrimonious discussion about ponies, and found Alison engaged in sketching remodeling ideas. The cats were draped around her on the sectional.

"You see, we'll have a new wall here to make a full bath off the end of the ground-floor hall. And *what* a room we're going to have," said Alison. "A fireplace, and an enormous bath—I do like a tub I can stretch out in—and a walk-in closet eight by twelve. And you know, *amante*—that great big room at the front upstairs—it would make a marvelous studio. I haven't been really working at painting lately—"

"You're having fun," said Mendoza, bending to kiss her. "Can you have a drink before dinner?"

"Just a little one—creme de menthe."

Mendoza went back to the kitchen for the drinks, and El Señor arrived before him. "That cat!" said Mairí. Mendoza poured him a little rye and carried the drinks back to the living room. He could, listening to Alison's plans, shelve all the blood and dirt and mess, the debris that human nature left behind it in its wayward progress, until tomorrow. Tomorrow was also a day.

ABOUT THE AUTHOR

DELL SHANNON is the author of over thirty books including *Felony File*, *Streets of Death*, *Appearances of Death* and *Felony at Random*. Meticulous in her research of the Los Angeles Police Department, she has a firsthand knowledge of police procedures and criminal laboratory techniques. This accounts in large part for the vivid realism and strong characterizations in the Lieutenant Mendoza mystery series. Dell Shannon lives in Southern California with a menagerie that includes several cats, two sheep and a dog.

MEET THREE TOP-NOTCH MISTRESSES OF MYSTERY

They all write under pseudonyms. They all have created favorite detective characters. They all are highly praised for their spellbinding novels of murder and detection. Catherine Aird (British, born Kinn Hamilton McIntosh); Dell Shannon (American, born Elizabeth Linington, also writing as Lesley Egan and Anne Blaisdell); and Patricia Wentworth (British, known as Dora Amy Elles Dillon Turnbull).

CATHERINE AIRD

Ms. Aird, whose novels are now being introduced in paperback for the first time, began writing in 1966 with THE RELIGIOUS BODY (to be published in July). Other books include THE STATELY HOME MURDER (July), and HIS BURIAL TOO (Oct.). All feature CID Inspector Sloan. *The New Yorker* calls Ms. Aird, "a shining new star . . . a most ingenious lady."

DELL SHANNON

Under the Dell Shannon name her more than forty books feature Detective Lieutenant Luis Mendoza of the Los Angeles Police Department, who himself has gained thousands of fans interested in his fictional private life. He appears in STREETS OF DEATH (July), FELONY AT RANDOM (July), and APPEARANCES OF DEATH (Nov.). Ms. Shannon-Linington-Egan-Blaisdell has been called the "Queen of Procedurals."

PATRICIA WENTWORTH

The late Ms. Wentworth is best known for her series of thirty-two novels featuring private enquiry agent Maud Silver, a stubborn spinster who has great English common sense and an iron will to succeed. Ms. Wentworth has received critical acclaim for THE FINGERPRINT (July), THE LISTENING EYE (July) and POISON IN THE PEN (Sept.).

WHODUNIT?

Bantam did! By bringing you these masterful tales of murder, suspense and mystery!

☐	10706	**SLEEPING MURDER** by Agatha Christie	$2.25
☐	13774	**THE MYSTERIOUS AFFAIR** **AT STYLES** by Agatha Christie	$2.25
☐	13777	**THE SECRET ADVERSARY** by Agatha Christie	$2.25
☐	13407	**A QUESTION OF IDENTITY** by June Thomson	$1.95
☐	13651	**IN THE BEST OF FAMILIES** by Rex Stout	$1.95
☐	13145	**TROUBLE IN TRIPLICATE** by Rex Stout	$1.95
☐	12408	**LONG TIME NO SEE** by Ed McBain	$1.95
☐	13314	**DEATH CAP** by June Thomson	$1.95
☐	13234	**MEET ME AT THE MORGUE** by Ross MacDonald	$2.25
☐	12115	**SLEEPING BEAUTY** by Ross MacDonald	$2.25
☐	13471	**THE ROSARY MURDERS** by William Kienzle	$2.50
☐	13784	**NO MORE DYING** by Ruth Rendell	$1.95
☐	13789	**THE BLUE HAMMER** by Ross MacDonald	$2.25

Buy them at your local bookstore or use this handy coupon for ordering:

Bantam Books, Inc., Dept. BD, 414 East Golf Road, Des Plines, Ill. 60016

Please send me the books I have checked above. I am enclosing $_____ (please add $1.00 to cover postage and handling). Send check or money order —no cash or C.O.D.'s please.

Mr/Mrs/Miss_____

Address_____

City_____State/Zip_____

BD—9/80

Please allow four to six weeks for delivery. This offer expires 3/81.